H

A shuffle of soft slippers on the floor of the cargo hold . . . soft rustling of Bedouin robes. Hunter waited . . . lunged out and pushed the unconscious soldier into the Arab. The surprise of his rush and the weight of the inert body caught Ali Djinn off guard. His knife thrust powerfully upward in an almost instantaneous reaction. The sedated man was disemboweled, but in that moment Hunter moved quickly behind the Arab and snapped the garrote wire around his neck, drawing it tight.

The usual reaction to the garrote was for the victim to attempt to tear it away. Ali Djinn, however, swung his knife backwards at Hunter. It ripped along Hunter's side, tearing flesh and scraping bone along his rib cage. He could feel blood flow—then a searing pain.

HUNTER

JERE MAUDSLEY

JOVE BOOKS, NEW YORK

This Jove book contains the complete
text of the original hardcover edition.
It has been completely reset in a typeface
designed for easy reading and was printed
from new film.

HUNTER

A Jove Book / published by arrangement with
The Permanent Press

PRINTING HISTORY
The Permanent Press edition published 1985
Jove edition / September 1987

ISBN: 0-515-09166-9

Jove Books are published by The Berkley Publishing Group,
200 Madison Avenue, New York, New York 10016.
The name "JOVE" and the "J" logo
are trademarks belonging to Jove Publications, Inc.

PRINTED IN THE UNITED STATES OF AMERICA

10 9 8 7 6 5 4 3 2 1

To be poised against fatality, to meet adverse conditions gracefully, is more than simple endurance; it is an act of aggression, a positive triumph.

—Thomas Mann

We are capable at the same time of taking risks and of estimating them beforehand. Others are brave out of ignorance. When they stop to think, they begin to fear. But the man who can be most accounted brave is he who best knows the meaning of what is sweet in life and of what is terrible, then goes out to meet what is to come.

—Pericles

PROLOGUE

Libya: April, 1982

Muammar Khaddafi's eyes glittered snakelike in a nascent combination of genius and Napoleonic psychosis. In his presence, Pehzad Hasebe felt torn by many emotions, chief of which was the extraordinary exhilaration at being close to a man whom he was certain was in the grip of destiny. Yet behind the smooth, handsome, benevolent facade of the Libyan dictator, one could sense madness. One could smell the stench of death.

Hasebe's eyes moved constantly, fitfully. He was a short, swarthy man. Gold rings encrusted with diamonds dug deeply into his fleshy hands which moved involuntarily, a physical manifestation of his deep fear . . . a fear that very nearly immobilized him. Hasebe, more than anything, was a coward.

They had just finished eating—a Spartan repast of couscous and mint tea taken in virtual silence.

"And now, Mr. Hasebe, you may begin."

"Thank you, your Eminence." Hasebe shivered. "Israel must be destroyed," he stated, then glanced briefly at Khaddafi for any reaction. There was none. "We are now in a position to place in motion a sequence of events that will accomplish this end. And, at the same time, put you and your Soviet ally into a position of pre-eminence."

Again Hasebe sought a reaction.

"Please continue." A smile curled at the edge of Khaddafi's mouth, but his eyes were icy. The result was a cruel grimace.

Hasebe began again, quickly, hurrying to set the hook. Thoughts of wealth and power beyond his fondest dreams ran through his consciousness.

"I am sure, Eminence, that you will be pleased with what has been accomplished. For the past year we have been transshipping and installing wing tank modifications for the Saudi Air Force's F-15 fighter bomber wing. This is commanded by one of our allies in Saudi Arabia. The planes now have the operational range to attack Israel—a capability that has been continually denied them by the U.S. Government. It has created a sore point in the relations between them.

"Israel is massing her armed forces on the border of Lebanon. She will almost certainly attack . . . and soon. When she does, she will be vulnerable. Then we will strike." The emphasis was on *we*. "The key is Saudi Arabia. Although the Saudis are close allies of the Americans, there are certain elements within the ruling family who are in favor of closer ties to Moscow. Interestingly, the most prominent is the current heir to the throne. He is in favor of a permanent solution to the Palestine problem and has very little sympathy for the Zionist state. All we need is to manipulate the players correctly, and we will emerge as the victors. The Americans and the Israelis—losers."

"A most interesting premise, Hasebe. And how do you propose that we proceed?"

"In order to succeed, we must have power in Saudi Arabia. King Khalid must meet with a fatal accident."

He did not have to wait for a reaction this time. Khaddafi began to laugh, to clap his hands like a child. Hasebe sat frozen. The sudden outburst suddenly stopped.

"The old fool has lived too long. He has grown soft on American dollars. His death will be welcomed. Continue, Hasebe." Again it was a command.

Hasebe wanted to remove himself as quickly as he could, but he was trapped by his greed and cowardice. He trembled, as he realized that his fear of the Libyan leader was capable of totally unnerving him. He continued in a high, keening voice.

"When the Israelis launch their attack, when their military capabilities are concentrated on the PLO in Lebanon, they will be counting on Arab disunity. That is when the new king will be persuaded to attack Israel. It will be considered somewhat of a token gesture, a warning to Israel that the new regime will not tolerate a Jewish warrior state. It will also put the U.S. on notice: if they want oil, they must discontinue supplying Israel with more materials. But there is something further. What no one but you and I know is that the Saudi planes will be specially equipped. I have arranged for the delivery from Canada of some Shrike class air-to-ground missiles. In a matter of days, the man who will arrange all this for us will be appointed to a high post in the Ottawa government. The warheads he will procure for us have been modified slightly . . ." Hasebe paused for effect, his confidence returning slowly. "The missiles will contain neutron warheads. They will annihilate the population of Israel. The Jewish state will cease to exist."

Khaddafi laughed—a tangled, guttural sound. It lasted longer this time and seemed more irrational to Hasebe. He waited, hoping desperately that a clear thread of sanity would prevail . . . that the skein would not snap. He looked around, seeking an exit from the tent. The shadow of a tall man guarded the entrance. Hasebe wiped his sweat-beaded forehead. His shirt was drenched.

"It's an ingenious plan," Khaddafi said, "but how will the F-15's penetrate Israel air space? The Israeli Air Force is well equipped. Their pilots are the best in the world."

Relaxed now, smiling again, Hasebe said, "Oh, they will be picked up on radar. That cannot be avoided. But the Israeli Defense Forces know that the F-15's do not have the range to fly from Saudi Arabia to Israel and return. Their takeoff and approach will be ignored . . . until it is too late."

Khaddafi nodded in satisfaction. "How many warheads?"

"Ten. But we are delivering only eight. The remaining two will be maintained here—for you to use as you see fit." Hasebe's tone was fawning. "The ultimate weapon will then be in your hands."

Khaddafi's eyes became hooded, like a snake about to strike. "Tell me this, Hasebe. You alone have dealt with the Canadians? There is no chance of a break in secrecy?"

"I trust no other man but you, Eminence."

"What is the name of your contact in Canada, Hasebe?"

Hasebe hesitated. Khaddafi's eyes glittered slightly, menacingly. I must trust him, Hasebe thought. We fight for the same cause, for the same God.

"His name is Regis Bennett," Hasebe replied.

"And the final shipment has been scheduled?"

"Yes."

"Has anyone other than you dealt with the Saudis?"

"No, only I." Hasebe was smiling, finally sure that he had been successful, finally sure that Khaddafi was satisfied. In his euphoria, he did not detect Khaddafi's slight nod nor did he sense the presence behind him.

Not until the wire of the garrote bit deeply into his fleshy neck did he realize that he was about to die. Khaddafi's laughter rang in his ears; his attacker's hands pulled powerfully. Hasebe's legs raised from the ground, jerking spasmodically as his head was almost severed by the final wrench of the wire. His toupee flopped forward obscenely. In one final insult his bladder and sphincter released. It took only that long for him to die.

Khaddafi spoke. "Well done, brother."

The executioner was a tall Bedouin named Ali Djinn. His black, pock-marked face was dominated by a nose that hooked like a sickle.

Ali Djinn nodded, picking up the body of Hasebe as if it were a rag doll. "I will dispose of this garbage."

=PART 1=

1

PALM FRONDS WAVED gently in the ocean tradewinds, their outlines etched as if by an artist's hands, silhouetted in stark contrast against the growing twilight. With the April rains, vegetation had exploded in brilliant greens. To the east, the deep purple blue ocean reflected high flying cumulus clouds, lit by the dying sun's rays. To the west, the emerald Everglades were overflowing with the spring's early rains.

In his office, high above Palmetto Park Square in Boca Raton—on the same day that the Bedouin, Ali Djinn, slipped his garrote round the neck of Hasebe—Owen Hunter was finishing up a day which had begun twelve hours earlier at 6:30 a.m. His office was one of the two on the fifteenth floor of the headquarters building of Caldwell-MacGregor Corporation. The building dominated a large shopping center complex, including a mall, restaurants and a peripheral area of smaller office buildings. It had been designed to showcase the construction capabilities of the company run by Owen Hunter.

The headquarters building of bronzed glass had been built diagonally on its lot—diamond-on-square effect. Those who thought such an arrangement had anything to do with aesthetics were mistaken; it had to do with the function of the two offices located on the top floor. Both were L-shaped, one with a southeast and southwest exposure, the other northeast and northwest. From Hunter's office on the south side, he could view most of the original properties that had been developed by Caldwell-MacGregor. Many considered this to be Hunter's private domain, his own creations, while Paul Caldwell MacGregor, with his northern view, could see some of the newer Caldwell-MacGregor developments, most particularly Indian Trace.

Paul MacGregor was a visionary. He had studied the historical developments of cities in the USA. Unless there was some natural impediment, development and growth always took place to the north and west. It was in this direction—the one in which he looked every day—that Boca Raton would grow. Where others only saw swampland, he had the ability to see homes with families, parks and shopping centers; in short, living space.

Owen Hunter was the chief executive officer of Caldwell-MacGregor Corporation. He was responsible for the day to day operations of the more than 25 separate companies under the corporate banner of Caldwell-MacGregor. What had started as a land development company in the early 1920's by Paul MacGregor's mother, Teresa MacGregor, had burgeoned into a consortium of companies.

In the late 1950's, a mass migration to the Sun Belt had begun. Veterans of World War II and Korea, trained in Florida, seduced by its climate and sunny lifestyle, began to return en masse with their families to settle. Fueled by this influx, Caldwell-MacGregor—under Owen Hunter's direction during the last eight years—had expanded from land development and real estate sales into the construction of hotels, condominiums, shopping centers and even into the ownership of banks and insurance companies. The company had become one of the largest and most profitable in Florida.

Just last year, Hunter had been successful in arranging for a joint venture with Comtec International, a multinational giant. Comtec's backing ensured the success of the company's most ambitious project to date, Indian Trace. It was no secret that an agreement in principal had been signed for the acquisition of Caldwell-MacGregor. Most of Owen

Hunter's time currently was devoted to finalizing the tax free exchange which would eliminate all of Paul Mac-Gregor's IRS problems.

Indian Trace was a resort community planned to house over 25,000 people. It was MacGregor's vision, his biggest dream come true.

In addition to his duties with Caldwell-MacGregor, Hunter was also a full partner with MacGregor and his assistant, Hallie Norton, who was in fact Mac's alter ego. The company was simply known as TC Industries. When Hunter had negotiated the Comtec deal, MacGregor had specifically requested that certain properties in the Caldwell-MacGregor portfolio be withheld from the joint venture. These were some of the original holdings of the company dating back to the days of Teresa MacGregor. But sentimentality hadn't been all that was in MacGregor's mind; TC Industries owned the largest of three banks that MacGregor had formed, a substantial savings and loan, and several acres of prime land on the beach that just happened to contain high-rise condominiums on lucrative 99-year leases. The TC Industries' portfolio was rounded out by some high-income producing shopping centers, office buildings and a hotel marina complex on the intracoastal waterway.

Hunter's holdings in TC Industries alone made him a wealthy man; his duties with Caldwell-MacGregor and Comtec made him a powerful one. This classic combination of wealth and power was not one he had consciously sought. It had come to him unbidden—but hardly undeserved.

Hunter stood silently at the L corner in the center of his office. Over on the beach he could see Sunrise West. The second tower of the 35-floor condominium complex had been topped out that day. Hunter spotted the traditional evergreen tree which had been hoisted by the crew. By now they would be well into their "topping out" party.

That should be a hell of a celebration, Hunter thought, smiling—in his earlier days he had been no stranger to such celebrations. As he moved away from the window, he stopped, surveying his domain.

The work area in his office measured 50' × 20'. It was dominated at one end by a large circular table ringed by twelve swivel rockers. On the end wall he had hung a Matisse portrait, ornately framed. Like a benevolent sun, the colors radiated brilliance. A large drafting table and stool provided Hunter a work area in the center of the room, while at the other end, a modest library was stocked with both fiction and technical books. A couch and two comfortable loungers were placed in the library facing a working fireplace. The fireplace and massive bar were both MacGregor's idea. "I like a good fire and good bourbon wherever I go," Mac had told Hunter. The bars here and in MacGregor's office were both well-stocked with Jim Beam.

The other side of the room housed a large display arch. Here three-dimensional mock-ups of the first phases of Indian Trace were set up. The success of this development had placed him at the top of his profession, and Indian Trace appeared to be a continuing home run. Even Hunter's competitors, many of whom feared him as a business antagonist, referred to the new city in superlatives.

The remainder of the office contained a good-sized home gym, including a sauna and steam room. There was also a full kitchen.

The center core of the building housed the elevators and reception area. At either corner, private offices had been set aside for Hunter's assistant, Ginny Williams, and Hallie Norton, MacGregor's right hand.

At thirty-five, Hunter looked and felt five years younger. He was six feet tall and consistently weighed in at one hundred seventy pounds. His lithe build belied his strength. More than once his quiet manner had been taken for granted—a mistake that once made was never repeated. He had fought for everything in life. Admired by his competitors and given a wide berth by his enemies, he was capable of a cold, deliberate and uncontrolled fury.

Hunter glanced at his tanned image in the mirror behind

the bar. His hair, once coal black, was now slightly salt and pepper, graying prematurely at the temples. His nose had been broken twice. Close scrutiny revealed scar tissue on the right side of his face and across his nose, souvenirs of his tours in Vietnam. His eyes were a steel-and-ice blue. Like the man, they rarely displayed emotion.

Hunter poured himself a shot of Chivas over ice, then added a splash of water and a lemon twist. As he turned toward the couch at the other side of the room, he loosened his tie and kicked off his shoes. He sat down, propping his feet on the coffee table, sipping his first drink of the day. He pressed the switch on the intercom. "Ginny, do you have a few minutes? I need to get caught up on what's happening in the world outside Caldwell-MacGregor."

He relaxed, sipping his Chivas. It was Friday night. I'll finish up here, he thought. Maybe I'll give Leo Birch a call.

Judge Leo Birch was Hunter's closest friend. Hunter had received a call from him earlier in the week—a typical Birch conversation. There was some new talent in town, and therefore a party at his home Friday night. Hunter was invited. A smile crossed his lips. To Birch, God bless his soul, the definition of a party was somewhere between a Busby Berkeley movie and a Roman debauch. To him, every night was Saturday night; and Saturday night, of course, was New Year's Eve. Judge or not, Leo loved a party.

Hunter's thoughts were interrupted by Ginny Williams' entrance. A tall, slender woman of thirty-two, she had been with Caldwell-MacGregor since graduating from the business school at the University of Florida in Gainesville. It took almost an hour to go over his schedule. There was a board meeting on Monday with Commerce Bank; then, on Tuesday, the monthly hotel meetings—reservations for conventions, occupancy percentages, union problems, bar and restaurant costs. Wednesday, another bank meeting; Thursday and Friday, management planning sessions at Comtec. Another week with no breathing room. That was fine with Hunter; he thrived on commitment.

"That's about it," Ginny concluded, "but I've got a suggestion . . ."

"Go ahead."

"You've got that awards banquet for Mr. MacGregor in two weeks."

"Damn, I forgot about that. What kind of award are they giving the old bastard anyway? Something for torture?" Hunter smiled; he was proud that MacGregor was being honored by his peers. It was only sad that his health had prevented him from accepting in person.

"Why don't you take a week off, Owen, and go up to your place on the ocean? Hallie and I can handle things here. You really need the rest. The Comtec deal is nearly wrapped up. I can trouble-shoot it for you."

Hunter was grateful. "I'll let you know Monday. By the way, where are my newspapers?"

Ginny had a habit of holding back Hunter's daily diet of papers, especially when she thought he had worked long enough. It had become a game between the two of them. She capitulated grudgingly, extracting *The New York Times, Wall Street Journal, Miami Herald* and *The Washington Post* from the stack of materials she had brought.

They both laughed as Ginny turned at the door. "Have a good weekend, boss."

Hunter poured himself another scotch, then began leafing through the *Post*. His glance was caught by a small item at the bottom of page five, and his feeling of well-being instantly faded.

"REGIS BENNETT II, INTERNATIONAL BUSINESSMAN, APPOINTED CANADIAN MINISTER OF EXTERNAL AFFAIRS."

Hunter read on, slowly, picking out sentences.

"Following the recent Conservative Party victory over the Liberals in Canada's general election . . . at 39, Mr. Bennett, heir to Commonwealth International, Ltd., a multimillion dollar corporation with offices around the world, is the youngest person ever appointed to the post of External Affairs Minister . . . He is expected to make immediate appointments of Assistant Ministers, and some names most often mentioned are those of Dr. Dale Sommerville, Chief Executive Officer of Commonwealth International, and Mr. Robert Villard, a vice-president of that corporation . . ."

Hunter folded the paper and walked to the window overlooking the ocean. All of his earlier elation had evaporated. He felt weary and frustrated. The old wounds still festered. The power that was now in the hands of Regis Bennett, Dale Sommerville and Robert Villard filled Hunter with dread.

2

PAN AM'S FLIGHT 703 rose quickly from the wet tarmac of Miami International Airport, and the 747 rolled and bounced on its way to its cruise altitude of 35,000 feet en route to Los Angeles. Dirty brown clouds, from a late afternoon thunderstorm over the Everglades, enveloped the plane streaking the windows of the jet.

Owen Hunter sat comfortably in the first class cabin staring out of the window. The company jet was just not cost-efficient for a cross country trip; besides it was out on short-term lease, making money for Caldwell-MacGregor. Hunter's thoughts were interrupted by the captain's cabin announcement.

"Ladies and gentlemen, this is your captain speaking. Welcome to Pan Am's flight—" The announcement droned on. Hunter adjusted the gold Rolex on his wrist, to account for the coming three-hour difference.

As the plane finally broke clear of the clouds and storm, Hunter reached for his briefcase—an expensive alligator bag, a present from Hallie and Mac. In material matters, life had been good to him. He released the goldplated clasp; the combination had been set to his age. Lack of imagination? He wondered.

He pulled out a legal folder and began to run through the speech which had been typed double-spaced with an extra

17

large font. It was an acceptance speech for the honorary award being presented to Paul MacGregor.

The International Association of Land Use and Development was meeting at the Bonaventure Center in Los Angeles. They were a group of the largest and most successful real estate, land development and construction firms on the North American continent. They had named Mac "Developer of the Decade." The Indian Trace development had been what triggered it, but Mac's reputation had spread throughout the country, and the overall developments of Caldwell-MacGregor in Florida, Arizona and Southern California were considered models of the industry.

Mac had been selected by his peers as their best. It was a tribute to the entire organization, and Hunter was proud of the role he had played in building Caldwell-MacGregor. Also, he was more than a little proud of the role he had played in finalizing the Comtec deal.

He was looking forward to a quiet convention, with the exception of the speech at the Awards dinner. Then he was to take off for a weekend in San Francisco, a few days in the wine country and a hopefully well-deserved rest at a small motel that he owned north of Point Arena on Highway 1.

The jet had just cleared the west coast of Florida. The flight attendants had done their job well: Hunter had a Chivas on the rocks on the tray beside him, his shoes were off and his feet were resting on the convertible stool that came out of the base of his seat. He liked the 747 cabin configuration; the circular stairs at the back of the first class cabin formed a line of demarcation between first and clipper class. A large center podium just in front of the staircase acted as a serving area for the flight attendants.

He was making some notes on Indian Trace in the speech when he felt a tap on his shoulder. He was in the aisle seat—the window seat next to him was empty.

"Mr. Owen Hunter?"

She was a honey-blond: blue-eyed, very pretty and very serious, wearing the uniform of a senior Pan Am stewardess.

"Yes, I'm Owen Hunter. Can I help you?"

"We have an urgent message for you coming through on our radio-phone upstairs. Would you please follow me?" Her tone continued to be one of quiet urgency.

Hunter slipped the file back into the briefcase. As he followed her up the circular stairs he could not help noting that her legs were long and shapely.

The bubble of a 747 was split into two parts directly behind the cockpit. "Mr. Hunter, would you please take a seat in there?" She motioned toward a door through which the right-hand section of the cabin was visible. "I'll get the message from the navigator and bring it to you."

Hunter entered the private cabin. It was about seven feet wide by twelve feet long, tall enough to stand in comfortably. A wide couch filled one end and a circular table was set on a chrome base bolted to the cabin floor center. Four swivel chairs surrounded it.

She was only a few minutes. She entered the cabin closing the door behind her. Her hand held what looked to be a telex. She said, "I hope this isn't bad news."

Hunter opened the envelope. He turned his back on the girl and read quickly: *To Owen Hunter from Leopold Quinn Birch III; Subject: Mile High Club à la Pan Am.*

A smile began on Hunter's face; he read on.

"As a mentor constantly concerned about the quantity and quality of your social awareness, I have taken it upon myself to nominate you for membership in this most exclusive social club. As you will find out, the club has a rather unusual initiation rite. The cabin in which you now stand has been reserved for your private use all the way to Los Angeles. The young lady who delivered this message is Paula. She is at this moment icing a bottle of Dom Perignon champagne. The champagne is not part of the ritual, but it will no doubt heighten the pleasure. Enjoy."

Hunter shook his head. Crazy son-of-a-bitch, he thought. He turned—but nothing could have prepared him for what was waiting. Paula stood next to the round table dressed in nothing but an open silk robe with a champagne bucket in her hand. It was obvious to Hunter that blond was, in fact, her true color. "I'll be damned," he said. He sat back on the couch and began to laugh.

It took nearly the full bottle of champagne for Hunter to get into the mood. But Paula was more than a match for his temporary reluctance. The couch at the end of the cabin provided the altar for the mile-high ritual. Paula, it turned out, was herself an initiate. She made love with an expertise reserved to those women who enjoyed sex for the sake of its unadulterated pleasure.

It was getting dark as the huge jet made its way across the sky above the California desert. The fading light cast a strange color on Paula's face. Her expression was soft, almost loving.

Through his dreamlike reverie, Hunter heard the end of a public address announcement.

". . . cabin service will be interrupted at this time. We hope you've enjoyed the flight."

Never had the words meant quite so much to Owen Hunter.

By the time the tires of the big 747 touched runway 45 at Los Angeles International, Hunter had returned to his seat. One hell of a flight, he thought.

3

TWO DAYS LATER, the lights of the Grand Ballroom of the Bonaventure Hotel glittered on the grand finale of the developers' convention. Hunter sat at the dais flanked by the mayor and the junior senator from California; on the senator's left was an ageless veteran entertainer who was to be the evening's master of ceremonies.

It was an affluent gathering: the most successful in the real estate business. It made sense for the politicians—where there was money and power, there was the opportunity for contributions of both.

The comedian was finishing up his act with ancient scatological humor, but was being received by the audience with polite responses and occasional applause.

Hunter was uneasy as he looked out at the assemblage. Tuxedoed men, most exhibiting the corpulent effects of the good life. Their complexions were ruddied by too much alcohol. Their wives, some aging and diamond-encrusted; others young, hanging on tightly to their passports to prosperity.

The comedian's voice droned through. "And now, folks," he said, looking at the man next to Hunter—"they say it takes a thief to catch a thief. If that's true, the man I'm about to introduce has done it all from cop to politician . . ." He hesitated, letting the line hang. ". . . and you can draw your own conclusions." The audience responded with laughter and applause. The comedian grinned and, with a flourish of hands, said: "His Honor, the Mayor."

Hunter paid scant attention to the mayor's banal comments. His attention was drawn to a press table to the right of the dais. A girl sat there who looked familiar. Her dark hair was cut very close to her head and her green eyes sparkled. She was conservatively well-dressed. Everything she wore was carefully understated. And yet, he could not place her. His musings were interrupted by the mayor's words.

". . . your Association's award—the most coveted award that can be offered by developers and communities alike—to Mr. Paul MacGregor, your Developer of the Decade. Accepting this evening for Mr. MacGregor is his close friend and partner, Mr. Owen Hunter."

Hunter moved toward the podium. Flashbulbs popped as he accepted the statuette: solid gold on a marble base, a figurine holding a small globe in upraised arms. Hunter stood waiting for the applause to die down. He looked at the base and began to read: "To Paul Caldwell-MacGregor, for his lifelong contributions to our industry and for his never-ending pursuit of excellence. The International Association of Land Use and Development—Developer of the Decade." The applause began again. Hunter raised his hand.

"Only those of you who know Paul MacGregor as I do, can understand what a sincere pleasure it is for me to be here this evening, accepting your applause and congratulations . . ." He paused briefly for effect. ". . . Because, as most of you know, we rarely get it at home."

Laughter rippled through the group. MacGregor's reputation as a hard taskmaster was well-known, as was his frugal nature when it came to plaudits.

"As I said," Hunter continued, "it's a great honor for me to be here with you tonight. Paul MacGregor would have enjoyed immensely accepting this honor for himself, but his health prevented him from making the trip. In fact, this is the first time I've spoken to a group of MacGregor's peers when he has not been in the audience. I just realized, standing here, that I can finally tell you the real truth about him."

The audience accepted his comments with a little light humor, with innuendos suggesting that some rumors of MacGregor's tyrannical capabilities might just possibly be true.

But Hunter had something else in mind.

"I've worked closely with Mac since 1971," he said, "in over ten years of partnership. And here's the real truth." He paused, smiling. "Mac is a man who looks at swampy ground or arid deserts or raw foothills, but his mind is full of the sights of homes to live in, of landscaped lawns, of shopping centers full of commerce, and of parks with slopes leading to lakes full of sailboats. He takes raw land, and with the creative instinct of a Picasso, he converts it into something that other people can only fantasize about. He does it with style and with grace. He loves the land. His first concerns are how to control water pollution, industrial growth and noise pollution. He wants to have low density population per acre, and plenty of recreation areas for golf, tennis and other sports. He has made extinct the Quonset hut developments that spewed forth after World War II and scarred our country with future slums. His style has always been to save the trees, the rivers, the streams—nature's natural contours. He set an example and dared us all to follow."

He had been speaking for about twelve minutes when he closed. ". . . A wiser man than I has said that 'the best investment on earth is earth.' I agree. But the challenge to all of us is to use that earth wisely. If we can meet that challenge, we can all hold our heads up with the special pride that comes with a job well done. Like Paul Mac-Gregor. On his behalf, tonight—thank you."

He had meant every word of it.

Once again, as he sat down to the sound of applause, he caught the eye of the young woman at the press table. Then he remembered her name. Maggie Mayes. A reporter from . . . San Francisco? Anyway, somewhere in the Bay Area . . .

She smiled at him with her cool green eyes, and clearly, across the room, mouthed the word, "Bullshit."

Hunter glared across the room. But in a moment he was staring at an empty chair. Maggie Mayes had disappeared.

4

A HEAVY LATE afternoon fog had already settled over San Francisco when Hunter's flight arrived from Los Angeles. The fog suited him . . . another one of the city's garbs. He was pleased with himself. Except for the comment from that one damned reporter, his speech had gone well. The Comtec deal was behind him and he had a few days on his own to enjoy life.

An hour later he seated himself comfortably at the bar of the Raphael on Geary Street. It was an intimate hotel just down the street from the more famous and garish St. Francis. At a smaller hotel people seemed to treat you better; service always improved when you were known. He had been coming here for five years and now most of the staff knew him.

The hotel, in a miniature sort of way, reminded him of the Caldwell Arms, his company's first beachfront hotel in Florida. The location was prime, just a short ride to Ernie's. And, across the street was Lefty O'Doole's, a favorite hangout for local personalities. If he wanted color of a local nature, it was a good place to go. The bar in which he sat was semicircular, with heavy dark wood beams, used brick and stained glass, giving the place a stolid warmth. Framed posters hung announcing happenings from colorful yesterdays, adding to the sense of the city's continuity and history. A variety of glasses hung attractively from parallel teak

25

racks over the bar. In the corner, a fireplace flickered warmly.

Hunter looked up from his drink and surveyed the bar. There were two other patrons at his end. One, a man who seemed as if he had had too much to drink, and the other, a well-dressed young woman who reminded him, unfortunately, of Maggie Mayes, the upstart journalist. But even in the dimmed light, the woman at the bar was attractive.

He returned to his Chivas, allowing the scotch to do its soothing work. He could feel his body tension unwind. Success certainly had its drawbacks. One of them was incessant pressure. On top of that, one Paul MacGregor. If anything bothered him, it was the thought of all the projects Mac would have ready for him to start when he returned to Florida. But he had some vacation time, and the rugged northern coastline fascinated him. He enjoyed the area so much that four years ago he had bought a small cottage hotel just north of Point Arena. If he was lucky, he made it there twice a year, but lately he hadn't had any luck at all.

The widow from whom he had purchased it had agreed to stay on and run it for him; she looked after it as if the place was still her own. She reminded him of the ship's captain, Wilhelm Gotz, who befriended him so long ago, and who was now dead. Her husband, too, was dead, of lingering cancer. The medical bills had been staggering but she had vowed to pay them off even if it meant liquidating everything she owned. Hunter had not heard the story from Eva Schmidt; he had picked it up at the general store in Point Arena. It seemed that she had made plans to move into a local rooming house, arranging for room and board in exchange for some domestic work. To him this was carrying pride too far. Instead he had offered her the job as caretaker at the cottage motel she loved so much, with a modest salary and a piece of the profits. It was an arrangement that worked out well; she was a frugal manager and each year the motel turned a modest profit.

Smitty, as she had become known, had practically adopted him and they both looked forward to his infrequent visits. His West Coast mother, she called herself. For a man without a family, he was doing pretty damn well—Hallie Norton on one coast, Smitty on the other.

His mental meanderings were interrupted by a commotion at the end of the bar. The drunk that he had observed earlier had decided that he wanted company. He had accosted the woman sitting near him. The bartender was either oblivious to what was going on or chose to ignore the commotion, hoping it would just go away.

The pink-faced man was a sloppy drunk, a left-over conventioneer. His clothes looked as though they had been slept in. His voice rose coarsely. Apparently he didn't accept feminine rejection. He stood threateningly over her. "All you broads are alike. You wear all that makeup, you stick your tits out at us—and then you're too damn good to have a drink. Fucking hypocrites, all of you."

Hunter had moved away from the bar, suddenly angered by the verbal assault on the woman, whose back was toward him. Even so, she seemed vulnerable. No one, he thought, deserves to be talked to that way. He moved behind the drunk and grabbed his left wrist, snapping the hand high into the shoulder in an armlock. Hunter tightened the grip, applying pressure and forced the drunk against the bar.

"What the hell . . ." The drunk's voice dropped to a whisper, as pain cut through his alcoholic haze. Hunter steadily increased the pressure on the arm.

"Bartender," he asked, "how much is this man's tab?"

"Seven-fifty," the bartender said. "But I don't want any trouble here."

Hunter snapped, "If you'd looked after this idiot when he got started, you wouldn't have any trouble." He redirected his attention to the drunk. "Now, my friend, reach into your pocket with your free hand and pay the man seven-fifty. When you do, I'm going to let your arm down, very slowly. And I have another suggestion for you. Are you listening?"

The drunk nodded.

"Get the hell out of here."

Cursing, the man drew a handful of loose bills from his

right pocket and threw down two fives. Hunter loosened his grip and drew back slowly, realizing at the same time that the drunk wouldn't be smart enough to walk away. He was one of those inherently nasty types who defied any outside effort at reason, authority or kindness.

He began to shuffle toward the door, rubbing his strained shoulder; abreast of Hunter, he suddenly whirled and threw his right fist clumsily at Hunter's head. "Fucking bastard!" he yelled.

But Hunter was prepared, and the man's hand flailed harmlessly by. Hunter jammed the stiffened fingers of his left hand hard into his stomach just below the sternum. The man doubled over, gasping for breath. Hunter didn't wait. Grabbing him by the hair and collar, he half-dragged him through the door into the street and shoved him hard in the direction of the St. Francis Hotel.

Hunter returned to the bar, straightened his jacket and tie. *That drink will taste damned good,* he thought.

He had just pulled the stool out to sit down when a hand grasped his right wrist firmly. Hunter could not have been more surprised. Standing in front of him, feet planted firmly, stood Maggie Mayes—the woman the drunk had been bothering. *My God,* he thought, *it* was *her. My nemesis!*

She was livid. Her chin jutted forward, her flushed face only inches from his, her hands on her hips.

"Go ahead, macho man. You want to hit me, too?"

Hunter stood speechless, shocked.

"Just who the hell do you think you are?" she demanded. "Just because you're some hotshot Eastern businessman, do you think that gives you the right to push people around?"

He was unprepared for the venom of her attack and the attention they were attracting. "I'm free and over twenty-one," she continued. "I can take care of myself!"

"Miss Mayes, if you'll just calm down . . ."

"Calm down?" she snapped. "Leave me alone. If we ever meet again, and I hope that occasion never arises, do

me a favor. Just keep your mouth shut and your hands in
your pockets!"

Hunter had suppressed his anger, but now he had had
enough.

"You know," he said, raising his voice, "it's been my
misfortune to meet you twice and both times you made an
ass of yourself. Your vocabulary would do a mule skinner
justice, but it doesn't hold a candle to your bad manners."
He reached in his pocket, throwing several singles on the
bar to cover the cost of his drink. "Let me assure you that if
you were on fire, I wouldn't throw water on you."

He turned and stalked from the bar to the accompaniment
of cheers and loud applause from several of the male
patrons. His last glance at Maggie Mayes caught her jaw
slack, surprised and more than a little embarrassed. She had
had her wings clipped.

"Serves her goddam right," he said, muttering to
himself.

He jaywalked off the curb in the middle of the block,
barely avoiding being hit by a cab, and quickly hoofed for
Lefty O'Doole's.

"What'll it be?" said the bartender.

"A shot of Chivas. Neat. With a beer chaser."

He threw the Scotch back and took a large mouthful of
beer. Looking up, he caught his reflection in the mirror. He
raised the glass of beer. "To Miss Maggie Mayes," he said
softly to himself. "Bitch of the month."

Hunter had reservations for dinner at Ernie's. He finished
another Scotch and paid the bartender. He returned to his
room at the Raphael to change his clothes, taking special
pains to avoid the bar area. Although he was sure that his
antagonist would no longer be there, he was taking no
chances.

With his dinner he enjoyed a bottle of Mondavi Cabernet
Sauvignon Special Reserve 1974. Hunter had thought about
stocking the Mondavi collection for the gourmet dining
room at the Caldwell Arms. On his trip he was carrying a
special introduction for a tasting tour at the winery.

But on the cab ride back to the Raphael, Hunter couldn't get Maggie Mayes out of his mind. What had he done to deserve such malice? What bothered him most was why the hell it bothered him at all.

He awoke the next morning to one of those San Francisco days that the natives brag about and the Chamber of Commerce lies about. The temperature was in the mid-50's and the sky was clear as glass. Hunter found the temptation of an early morning walk too difficult to resist. The thought of ten days to himself was hard to believe.

Returning to his room at 7 a.m., he showered, then dressed in flannel slacks, a sports shirt and a dark blue blazer. His car was waiting and already packed when he arrived curbside. He tipped the bellman and valet and slipped behind the wheel.

It was almost noon by the time he reached the Napa Valley. His drive had skirted San Pablo Bay. He had stopped off in Sonoma, the old mission town, and filled his cooler with cold cuts, dill pickles, sourdough rolls and Michelob Lite. He was a traveling picnic.

The Mondavi Winery was the first vineyard entering Napa Valley from the south. Although a relatively new winery, the owner and architect had combined to make it resemble a mission. It had soft brown adobe walls with a barrel tile roof. Vineyards covered the open area in front of the building and ringed the parking lot.

Hunter approached the building slowly, greeted by the scent of flowers in beds lining the winery entrance. A large arch joined two individual buildings. Off to the right appeared to be the winery itself; to the left a retail area, tasting rooms and the administrative offices. The back of a lawn area met a vineyard, which rode a long slope back and upward to the crest of the hills that rimmed the valley. There was no wind and only the occasional muted call of a bird. Even the voices of tourists were subdued. It was as if he were in some giant open-air cathedral.

He entered the retail area and approached a young woman

behind the counter. He handed her his letter of introduction.
"I was instructed to deliver this to your resident sommelier,
or the person in charge of tastings."

"That's Melissa Hill," the girl replied.

Hunter was not left waiting long. He was approached by
a tall, young woman about thirty. Her hair fell loosely over
her shoulders; she wore sandals and a brightly flowered
dress.

"Mr. Hunter. Welcome to Mondavi. I'm Melissa
Hill . . . Melissa, please." Her smile, captivating and
friendly, put him at ease immediately.

"Please call me Owen. I know that you must be terribly
busy, but if you have someone who could take a few
moments, I'd like to sample the wines. We've made a
decision to stock some California vintages at our hotels in
Florida. I hope it will be Mondavi."

"Don't worry about my being busy," she said. "I intend
to look after you myself. But I do have a favor to ask. We
have a newspaper reporter here today. Good press, as you
can imagine, is very important to us. Would you mind if I
take her along with us?"

"Not at all."

"Give me ten minutes."

He wandered through the shop and out toward the
vineyard behind the winery. He saw her staring up at the
roof of a chalet on top of the hill. Christ! *He couldn't escape
her!* It was Maggie Mayes! Obviously she was the reporter
that Melissa had spoken of. Three times in 48 hours . . .
it was hard to believe. But, Hunter thought, anything is possible. He had another uncomfortable thought: there was no
such thing as coincidence.

He, at least, had the advantage of surprise.

Approaching quietly from behind, he tapped her lightly
on the shoulder. She whirled around, recognizing him, and
was speechless. He was going to enjoy this.

"We're really going to have to stop meeting this way," he
murmured. "People will begin to talk."

"Are you following me?" she sputtered, still nonplussed.

"No, Miss Mayes. I'd just as soon follow a school of piranha in ten feet of water. If I'd known you were heading north this morning, I would have been in San Diego by now. It seems we're both victims of bad timing. For Melissa Hill's sake, why don't we try to make the best of it?"

"What's Melissa got to do with it?" she snapped. She had regained her composure.

"She's arranging for a private tasting. She asked if I'd mind sharing the tour."

"Sharing with *me?*"

"I thought it was rather gracious of me to go along with it. If I had known it was you, I might have chartered a jet for Mexico City."

He stopped, not mentioning the fact that he would be placing a rather large order with Mondavi. "If you'd give me a chance," he added, surprising himself, "you might find out that I'm not half the monster you think I am."

"Half a monster is still a monster." Her voice was even. Suddenly her reporter's demeanor had returned. Whatever advantage he had enjoyed up to now disappeared. Hunter sensed that they were antagonists on even terms again.

"Mr. Hunter. Look up there," she said, pointing to the slope and the vineyards beyond. "Tell me what you see."

Hunter considered for a moment, then spoke slowly. "A mature and beautiful land," he said. "When land is being used for a purpose suited to it, you have a remarkable marriage. This land used to be barren, unyielding—almost hostile. Then in the late 1800's, some Europeans saw how closely the soil and temperatures resembled those in the wine country of France and Germany, and they transported the vines and planted them with love and care. As a result they transformed this valley. The land became blessed. I was thinking earlier that being here is like standing in a place of worship where all the negative emotions, all the noise and all the clamor cease to exist. And there's more. Do you know what I *don't* see? I don't see bulldozers. I don't see Burger Kings or McDonalds or Safeways. There's no better purpose for this land than the purpose it serves now." He stopped, eyeing her warily. "You think that's also bullshit, Miss Mayes?"

They both stood quietly for a few seconds. She broke the silence. "No," she said. Her voice was no longer strident. "But it was the last thing I would have expected from you. You were right, I really expected bulldozers leveling the land, and ticky-tacky houses." She hesitated. "You really believe what you said in Los Angeles, don't you?"

"Yes, I do. We've all got a responsibility. The trouble is that some of us let greed get in the way. Don't you think so?"

"I didn't think you and Paul MacGregor did. I thought you were convincing, sincere . . . but hypocritical."

"And now?"

"I'm not sure." Her tone was quizzical, as if she were really trying to decide.

"I'll tell you what. Why don't we have lunch together— after the tour. Then you can have time to make up your mind."

"I'd like to, but I'm with a bus tour. If I'm not there, I'll be stuck."

"Compromise then. We'll have lunch and I'll drive you. You can catch up with them a little later. I'll make sure that you don't miss the bus."

"All right, but just tell me one thing." Hunter missed the mischief in her voice. "I come from a big family with older brothers," she said, frowning. "The expression at home was that 'if you were on fire, I wouldn't piss on you.' Wouldn't you at least do *that?*"

Hell, thought Hunter, she still hasn't given up. It didn't matter. All that he could think of was that she was one hell of a woman.

"And there's my tour now," she said, pointing to a group of people just emerging from the winery.

Hunter watched as she moved toward them. She was quintessentially a California girl: long-legged, full-breasted, tanned the color of eighteen-karat gold. Although she wore a loose-fitting sweater and floppy designer slacks, there was no disguising her abundant curves. She moved gracefully, like a Persian cat.

This trip, he thought, is improving every minute.

They sat at a tiny Fench restaurant recommended by Melissa Hill. A Frenchman had immigrated to California at the end of World War II to make his fortune in wine. Broke and without work, he met and married a socialite widow. According to local legend, her sexual appetite was unquenchable and, as a substitute for her persistent sexual demands, he took to cooking for many of the charity parties she hosted. He spent more and more time in the kitchen, honing his cooking talents. His growing reputation for superb cuisine spread throughout the valley. At the urging of friends he opened a small restaurant. What had eventually become of him, Hunter was yet to discover. Part of the charm of the story was that it had no end, and they were laughing about it over their second carafe of Chablis.

"That poor man," said Maggie. "Hunter, do you always dig into local color?"

"Doesn't everybody?"

"You'd have made a damn good reporter."

"You want the story, you got it." He looked at her. Her green eyes were heightened by the reflected sunlight of the late afternoon.

"You're a beautiful woman." His voice was full of warmth; she had triggered a response mechanism deep inside him—something that had been suppressed. Emotions that he had never experienced were welling to the surface like oil from a long abandoned well; it was as disconcerting to him as it was pleasurable. Somehow, sitting across from her, he began to feel more alive than he had ever felt before.

Maggie touched his hand lightly. "Coming from you, that's quite a compliment. You know, you're a different person than I had expected. I have a confession to make. I did some research on you when I found out that you were going to be a speaker at the convention. A reporter's privilege, I guess. It's odd. Everything I was able to read about you is almost diametrically opposed to the way that you really are."

"I'm a victim of bad press," he said, smiling.

"Don't get me wrong. I don't think there's anything wrong with it. It's just that the picture is one of a hard-driving businessman, a real loner. According to what I read, your only interest is work. Only . . . well, there's only sketchy information on your background . . . Anyway, if there's any chink in that moral armor of yours, it has to do with some of the exploits of you and that friend of yours . . . what's his name . . . ?"

"Leo Birch," said Hunter. He frowned. "What else did you discover?"

"That you're the architect of Caldwell-MacGregor's success, and that you were the driving force behind your company's recent acquisition by Comtec. The *Journal* said it was quite a profitable coup."

"No wonder you walked out on my speech."

"That's the contradiction. It's not what I've seen today, it's what I saw at the hotel last night when the drunk took a swing at you. I saw something dangerous in your character. Today, you're warm, understanding and sensitive. It's almost as if you're two people. Do you know what I mean?" She looked at him quizzically, waiting for his response.

"Do you always read people that carefully?"

"It's a reporter's job," she said.

"Don't believe everything you read. Maybe your research did pick up the real Owen Hunter. I don't know. Frankly, I don't quite understand *this* Owen Hunter. I've never enjoyed a day or someone as much as this. It's more than a little frightening sitting here with you and . . . telling you how beautiful I think you are."

"Don't worry about it."

"When we say goodbye a few minutes from now, I'll revert to type. I'll grow my horns back."

"I'd like to do a story on you—an in-depth look at a

successful executive. The man behind the man—the man who talks to people, who discovers old legends . . ."

"If Mac ever reads something like that, he'll send me to a shrink. Besides, wouldn't your boyfriend get upset about your spending a week with a notorious bachelor from Florida?"

"There isn't a boyfriend."

"I've got a week to spare. So do you." He spoke as simply as he could. "Let's spend it together. No strings attached. Separate rooms, but on my tab. If or when either of us gets bored, he or she splits. No questions asked, no hard feelings. You can get to know me . . . and if you let me, I'll get to know you. After that, we'll see what happens."

"You mean it, don't you?" she said slowly.

"I do. Surprisingly, I do."

She thought for a minute, lowering her eyes. He was grateful. He found it difficult to look directly into their cool but tingling green light.

"Yes," she said. "I'll go with you."

He filled their glasses, emptying the last chablis from the carafe. "A toast. To seven days and nights. To discoveries."

5

STRETCHING IN A stainless arc from horizon to horizon, the
copper sky was broken only by the motionless date palms of
the Agheila Oasis. The temperature of the Libyan Sahara
hovered just over one hundred degrees, yet the water in the
deep wells was as cold as that of the Atlantic Ocean in June.

Sipping a silver mug of the precious liquid, in a Bedouin
tent made of white cotton-and-silk lined with goatskin,
Muammar Khaddafi sat cross-legged on a rich burgundy
Bokhara rug like the desert chieftains of old. At his side,
silent and attentive, was his faithful servant and bodyguard,
the hawklike Ali Djinn.

Across from him, squatting somewhat uncomfortably on
yet another Bokhara, were two visitors. One was an Arab,
but not a Libyan. He wore a lightweight gray summer suit
that had been tailored for him on Savile Row in London; his
shoes were benchmade in Rome; his tie had been a gift from
a young socialite who lived on the East Side of Manhattan,
and she had purchased it at Brooks Brothers. The only thing
Arab about this man, whose name was Abdullah al Saud,
was his slightly ochre skin, his deep liquid dark eyes, and
his mind. He was a young cousin of the current King Khalid
of Saudi Arabia . . . but not a favorite cousin. He was the
son of the heir-apparent to the throne.

The other visitor was a pale, slightly pockmarked
Canadian in his middle thirties. His name was Terrence

Giles. He wore a white golf shirt, dacron slacks and new Nike running shoes. He and the young Saudi had been flown by Lear jet from Tripoli to Benghazi, and then by helicopter to the oasis. They also gratefully sipped the cool well water.

"There will be a sea of blood," Khaddafi said quietly. "It will be greater than Vietnam, Cambodia and Pearl Harbor. It was rival Hiroshima. And at the end, my friend"—he nodded at al Saud—"out of this chaos and pillage will emerge the inevitable: a pan-Islamic empire stretching from the Atlantic Ocean to the Red Sea. An empire that includes the remains of the parasite Zionist State of Israel. An empire ruled jointly from Riyadh and Tripoli."

"*Inshallah*," al Saud murmured. "God willing."

"*Inshallah*," Khaddafi repeated, and then continued in Arabic. "And also with the willingness of our greedy friends from Canada." He turned his clear gaze on Terrence Giles and smiled with perfect white teeth. Now he spoke in English.

"You have brought the list of prices and the delivery dates, Mr. Giles?"

Giles nodded solemnly. "Mr. Bennett is a man of his word, Your Eminence."

Khaddafi kept smiling. He knew the Canadians believed him to be a madman; believed that they were using and manipulating him as a pawn. Money was their god. They understood nothing else.

"My friend Ali Djinn will accompany you on your return to Toronto, Mr. Giles," he said pleasantly. "He speaks excellent English. I trust him totally. He will remain there with you in Canada until the deliveries have been arranged . . . just in case there are any mishaps."

Behind him the blankly stern expression of the Bedouin's knifelife face never changed.

Giles nodded. "Mr. Bennett will take good care of him," he said sincerely.

6

THEY SPENT THEIR first night together at a country inn a few miles north from where they had eaten lunch. Maggie had insisted on paying for her room. They had dined together, the host good-naturedly showering attention on them. They were enjoying themselves and each other. For Hunter, each moment with her was filled with a new sense of discovery.

It was noon of the second day. After a late breakfast, they had started up the valley, progressing slowly. They'd stopped at wineries along the way—Sterling, Inglenook, Krug and Barringer. They had just reached the car. Both were flushed with the excitement of their adventure as well as with the aftereffects of their morning tastings.

"Maggie, if I were to spend any more time here, I'll end up a wino. We've got to stop for a while."

"I know what you're up to," she said with a cockeyed giggle. "You're going to get me drunk and try to take advantage of me."

"How about some lunch?"

She looked around. "Any place special in mind?" There was nothing in sight.

"Up there," he said, pointing to the top of the hill overlooking the road.

"I'm with you," she said, opening the door and bouncing into the car. "Floor it!"

Hunter spun the car off into a side road leading up the

hill. A sign a few hundred yards back had announced Vista Point, Roadside Park.

They reached the crest of the hill. Lush green vineyards carpeted the valley below. They sat, suddenly quiet, beside each other. Their hands touched and held.

She looked up at him. "I've never met anyone quite like you. Most men are afraid to be what you are." She turned to him, her arms suddenly around his neck. He kissed her softly and tenderly. The gentle swelling of her breasts warmed him. Her breath became ragged.

"Owen, I want you. Now. Here."

The thick green grass made a soft blanket. He undressed her, his hands exploring her slowly. Everything seemed in slow motion. She traced his side and her hand slid over his stomach. She stroked him. He was strong and erect. She guided him into her, looking at him as he entered.

"I've never wanted anything more than I want you," she said.

They lay locked together, neither wishing to break the spell. Maggie spoke first, jokingly. "Do you realize that we've been fornicating in public? Can you see the headlines? 'San Francisco Reporter and Florida Land Baron Guilty of Fornication in a Public Place.' Let's get dressed before we get arrested."

They had barely finished dressing when a camper full of kids came into view. "Trouble in paradise," he said.

"Another five minutes," she said, "and we could have made history. Like the Frenchman in the restaurant. Imagine the stories they could've told about us. By the way, it seems to me somebody offered to buy lunch. I'm ravenous."

"In there." Hunter pointed to the trunk of the car. He had restocked the cooler that morning with cold beer, cheese, cooked sausage, and deviled eggs. He flipped the trunk keys to her.

Maggie murmured with delight as she inventoried their larder. "My favorite beer," she said, tossing a can to him.

"Not only are you a great lover, but a great provider. My white knight in shining beer cans!" His lips met hers again as she leaped into his arms. Legs raised off the ground, she swung on his neck. "God, I'm happy. How about you?"

"I don't know if I've ever been *as* happy."

They stopped in the early afternoon at a hotel just outside Nice, on the north shore of a clear lake. The motel at the top of the hill was framed by pine trees edging the redwood forest. Grass carpeted the hill down to the water's edge. Maggie had taken a nap and Hunter took advantage of the time by returning to town. As they had passed through the center of town, he noticed a sign announcing Italian pastries in a bakery. There must have been a dozen varieties, and he picked out one of each. As he entered the motel room, balancing the two boxes carefully, he heard the sound of running water. He opened the boxes on the bed and began to place the pastries side by side, buffet style, from the pillow to the foot of the bed.

He had just finished when the shower stopped. Maggie walked into the room, naked except for a white towel wrapped around her head. She moved to him, unable to see the pastries on the bed. He had stood in her line of vision. She gently pushed him backwards. He remembered, but too late. The pastries slid in every direction. She screamed in surprise, and then their passion dissolved into laughter as he turned over quickly, rolling her in the thick Italian cream.

Her body was covered with lemon yellow, white and chocolate. He kissed her again, tasting the Italian cream, licking lemon from the side of her breast, then chocolate from her nipples. As he rolled her onto her stomach, she crushed custard onto his bare chest. Her hands sought him, undressing him quickly. His tongue explored her body. Her back and buttocks were a rainbow of colors. Each became alternately the aggressor, rolling and touching. They locked together. Sex and confection mingled with heat and release. They held back nothing.

• • •

They arrived at Point Arena at the end of the week and drove five miles northward to Owen's property. He hadn't told Maggie, but had managed to call Smitty to let her know they were on their way.

The road from Point Arena wound dangerously around the edge of the ocean, sometimes rising three or four hundred feet above the sea, at other times falling almost to the water's edge. The tall pines and redwoods climbed the cliffs to the sea.

As they made the final bend in the road, Hunter's property came into view. The nine cottages rode the hill upward from the road. They were set sufficiently far apart so that each one commanded a separate view of the ocean.

Maggie turned to Hunter. "We don't have to go any further tonight, do we? Let's stay here," she said, pointing to the cottages. "It's so beautiful."

Hunter, suppressing a grin, pulled off the road and up the hill. Smitty had done her work well. The driveway was a cacophony of colors with flowers of every description already in bloom or blooming. Hunter parked the car.

Smitty burst out of the door. "You're here!" she yelled. "Owen, it's so good to see you!" She was a boisterous woman, big-boned and heavy, and she embraced him tightly.

"Smitty, you look great. You've done wonders with the place." He hugged her, genuinely pleased, then disengaged. Maggie had been standing in her tracks, confused.

Hunter chuckled. "This is the surprise I promised you. Finally, I've got you at a loss for words." He gestured with his arms sweeping toward the horizon. "Welcome to Hunter's Hotel."

Eva Schmidt moved quickly over to embrace Maggie. "He didn't tell you?" She shook her fist at Hunter. "You ought to be ashamed of yourself." She turned to Maggie. "I'll take good care of you. Mr. Hunter may be the owner of this establishment, but what I say goes. Oh, by the way, Owen, I have a surprise for you. All the things you sent are set in Number Two, just like you asked. It's never rented. I sent the boy down to the point to pick up some food for dinner tonight. Maybe we can fix up something special."

He motioned toward Maggie. "Treat her with tender loving care."

Smitty winked. "You must be something special," she said. "It's the first time he's ever brought anyone up here."

They were resting together on the beach at sunset on their last day. Hunter lit a small fire of driftwood. Shadows danced behind them on the sheer bank that rose fifty feet into the dense pine.

Maggie's head rested on his shoulder. "I hate the thought of going back tomorrow. I've never had a week pass so quickly. It's not going to be goodbye . . . is it?"

"Hard-bitten female reporters aren't supposed to show their emotions," he said.

"Stop teasing. I don't think of this as just a week-long fling."

Hunter became quiet. He rose, extending his arms. "Let's walk. It's time I told you some things. But it can't go any further than you and me."

"Strictly 'off the record'?"

"It's private and personal."

"No story," she agreed.

They walked several hundred feet before words began coming slowly from Hunter. "I don't know where to begin—maybe the end, maybe the middle. First let me tell you, I'm not Owen Hunter. Owen Hunter is a creation of Paul MacGregor. All that I am now, I owe to Mac. He brought me into this business—he gave me an identity and a new life. If it weren't for him, I'd probably be out there somewhere." Hunter pointed to the sea.

She dug her fist into his side. "Owen, be specific. I don't understand."

"I'm trying, Maggie . . . but it's awfully hard. What I'm trying to say is that I'm not really what I seem to be. Owen Hunter was really born in 1971. Prior to being with Mac, I was wandering. I spent three years in the Merchant

Marines, sailing over half the world. I never cared for anyone. I had no family, no home. It was a pretty senseless existence. The only constructive thing I ever did was to educate myself, and when you're at sea, that's pretty easy. You have nothing but time."

"I still don't . . ."

"I'm coming to it," he interrupted. He began slowly, reluctantly. "When I was a kid, I was involved in some trouble . . . not of my own making. But I had to run away. I was a scared kid with no place to go, with no past and very little future. I changed my identity and enlisted in the Army. When Vietnam came along, I was there, and that's where I met Mac. After Nam I went into the Merchant Marine. Then I went to see Mac in Florida. That's when Owen Hunter was conceived. It was Mac's idea. So there are really three people: the kid I was when I grew up, whose name was Eddie Villard . . . Josh Williams, the hard case in between . . . and Owen Hunter, the man I am now."

"Owen, it sounds horrible. My family and my home town are just around the corner. Old friends, relatives—I take it all for granted. It's no wonder that you don't let anybody get near you."

Hunter thought for a moment. "I guess it's true. But there's something that bothers me. To me it's far more sinister than just a different identity and the outward trappings. You got a glimpse of it in the bar at Raphael. I suppose it started because of the way I had to leave home. Because of the hatred I feel for the people who caused me to leave, I decided never to back away from danger, never to be afraid physically—never to run. The Army gave me my chance. I learned to kill and not to care. It was kill or be killed, the old cliché. It became senseless. I don't know how to explain it. I hate violence, but the world is full of it.

"But not only just over there. That drunk the other night, and other times, too. Even in business, someone is always trying to beat you, con you. That's another kind of bloodless violence. Making a deal, taking one away from my competitors."

He stopped. It was beginning to emerge; he felt a giant catharsis. He had to blink back tears. He turned to Maggie. The sensation of sharing his secret with the woman he had come to love was a new emotion. His life seemed to shatter apart, the past and present no longer joined . . .

7

"YOUR LINE, VILLARD."

Late in the game, with the teams changing on the fly, the hockey coach's voice rang out. Eddie Villard reacted instinctively, hurdling the boards. He skated effortlessly into his end of the rink. His movements were graceful, catlike; he seemed to have been born for this game. Lean, compact and apparently fearless, Eddie moved swiftly behind the net. He picked up the puck and moved toward center ice, gaining momentum, his mind working. The score was tied at four-four.

It was, to some, a meaningless practice game, but to Eddie, a freshman on scholarship at St. Mary's prep school, it was his chance to establish himself. He had already scored two goals; one more and he had a hat trick, and the Junior Varsity team would win over the Varsity. This was something that just didn't happen. But Eddie was always challenging the accepted rules.

The players seemed to be moving in slow motion. He sensed an opening for an end-to-end sweep. It was just his style of play, pitting himself against the entire opposition. Moving across center ice, he quickly outdistanced the opposing line. He had caught the Varsity team off guard.

He had only one defenseman to beat. He shifted slightly to the right, crossing the blue line just left of the right point. Dipping his right shoulder, he feinted right, drawing the defenseman toward the boards. Once the defenseman committed himself, Eddie flipped the puck against the boards, angling it deep into the opposing zone and, shifting left without breaking stride, moved around the surprised defender. With one smooth movement, his stick found the puck that caromed off the boards, and he let loose with a wrist shot that climbed high over the left shoulder of the goaltender, finding the net. The red light flashed. He raised his stick high, victoriously. The crowd roared its approval. He eased his stride and moved past the net, accepting the reluctant praise of the goalie.

"Villard, behind you!"

The goaltender shouted too late. A pain shot through his calf. His right leg collapsed under him. He slid heavily into the boards behind the net. He turned, getting up slowly, favoring his leg.

"I'll teach you, you son of a bitch—"

He heard the words and looked up from a kneeling position. Regis Bennett stood over him, glaring angrily.

"Next time it'll be your fucking head . . ."

Bennett had slashed Eddie viciously after the goal, repayment for Eddie's having beaten him on the play. A senior being made a fool of by a freshman. Bennett, the Big Man on Campus, with family, money and tradition. Whistles blew.

Eddie rose slowly, anger rising. His instinct demanded that he retaliate, but he fought for control. He took a deep breath, turned and skated back toward the bench, favoring his injured leg.

As he resumed his place on the bench, Greg Eshelman, his right wing, congratulated him. "Great move, Eddie. We sure showed those pricks a thing or two, didn't we?"

His congratulations were interrupted by the announcer's voice. "Goal, St. Mary's JV. Penalty Bennett, at 18:52. Two minutes slashing."

A second cheer rose from the crowd.

Moments after the final buzzer sounded, Eddie was in the dressing room. He removed his skates, shin pads and garters, and rolled down his right sock. He rubbed the large red welt on the back of his right leg. It had already begun to swell.

His teammates stopped, one by one, slapping him on the back and congratulating him on his performance. But the hat trick and the victory were hollow consolation to him now. He was angry with himself. The type of treatment that Bennett had meted out required retaliation. In this game, if you didn't, you became an easy mark.

If it weren't for the scholarship, he thought, or Bennett's father . . . or the alumni . . . his thoughts were jumbled. He shook his head wearily. It wasn't worth it. He needed the education more than the revenge.

He sat for a long time waiting for the dressing room to clear out, then showered and dressed slowly. Everyone else had gone. This was his favorite time, a chance to be alone and to think. St. Mary's Academy was the dream of every young Canadian, the most prestigious prep school in Canada, with an alumni that read like Who's Who in society. It was the prep school of the future movers and shakers of the country: lawyers, doctors, executives and politicians, all developed around academic excellence.

It was, however, an Eden with more than its share of snakes. The problem was that of tradition, for St. Mary's was the perennial prep school hockey power in Canada, a Notre Dame on ice. Simply stated, in this world of specialization, there was a distinct lack of hockey talent in the world of academia. The alumni had soon learned that in order to assure St. Mary's winning ways, a scholarship program was necessary. That these grants were made by and large to boys who were somewhat less than academic heavyweights, and who just happened to be world class hockey players, was overlooked. At St. Mary's, winning wasn't important; it was everything. The privileged few, like Eddie Villard, had to learn to walk the line. But a St. Mary's education was a plus. Playing hockey at St. Mary's was a steppingstone to the pros.

So, he thought, I'll put up with whatever I have to.

They came to the games in Cadillacs and limousines to win their JV and Varsity letters as members of another St. Mary's championship squad. They needed to create future memories: plaques, trophies and other memorabilia would be placed on walls of dens, and the glory of the memories would grow greater with each passing year. Eddie Villard felt like a hired gun—hired to assure that these championships would continue, that *their* future memories would be bought and paid for.

His father was only a shadow of memory and his mother, whom he loved dearly, had died nearly five years ago. That experience had taught him to hide his grief. It wasn't until after the funeral services, after all the mourners had left his aunt's house, that he walked alone, down by the river's edge and let his grief rush out of him. He was too proud to let anybody see him that way. Never reveal your feelings to anyone—it was a trait that would last throughout his lifetime. "Brave" is what the mourners had said.

"Ice Man" was what his teammates called him.

But as cruel as life had been, living with an aunt who did not want to be responsible for him and growing up with an older brother who barely tolerated him, nature had been kind. At nearly sixteen, he would easily pass for three or even four years older than that. He was nearly six feet tall, a handsome youth with blue eyes and unruly dark curly hair. He had a slender, muscular build; hockey in the winter and baseball in the summer kept him in shape. The thought of his future kept him going. Three years at St. Mary's—then, with any luck, a transfer to St. Michael's in Toronto; then, if he was good enough, the NHL. The scouts had already been to see him. "Keep at it, kid," they said. It was the next three years that worried him the most.

What was ironic was that it was his brother Bobbie's academic excellence that had brought attention to Eddie. His brother received one of the few academic scholarships awarded by St. Mary's. Regis Bennett's friend and secret tutor, he was being groomed by Bennett's father for law school and, eventually, a place in the Bennett business empire. But Eddie's relationship with his brother was tenuous at best. His brother hated him because he was stronger, faster, quicker with his hands. And yet—he was told constantly—his brother had the brains . . .

Eddie hurried along the sidewalk at the top of the breakwater. The river ran through the campus of St. Mary's. In the summer or fall it was picturesque, but now it was cold and forbidding. The river was off to his left, half frozen with ice. It was 14 degrees, and a cruelly cold north wind whipped up from the river. The snow that had begun to fall an hour earlier was beginning to drift as Eddie made his way warily between the patches of light cast by bare bulbs riding loosely beneath metal stanchions. The bulbs rattled in the night wind. It was an old part of town and the streetlights were made even dimmer by the falling snow.

He was hoping to avoid any encounters not only with the winos who frequented this stretch of the river, but also with the gangs who hung around waiting for the opportunity to roll the winos. He crossed the streets, leaving the campus and the river behind. He paused momentarily, looking up at the Bennett Textile Mills building, which loomed in front of him. The mill had seen better days. The dowager queen of the Twenties Era, at one time it was considered a local landmark. Now, after years of neglect, it could only be considered a sweat shop. The black building stretched back from the street for a block and a half. The windows, which had not had the benefit of soap and water for seventy years, were covered with filth and soot. Most of the windows had been barred by the Bennett family when they had taken over the building and converted it into a mill.

He turned and started to move away, when something caught his eye. A light burned at the back of the building. He had been here many times before and had never seen any lights at this time of night. He stood watching it for a moment . . . then moved toward the back of the building.

I wonder who the hell's in there. Maybe somebody's broken in . . . maybe they're vandalizing the place. Despite himself, he smiled, realizing that the thought didn't make him unhappy.

The first-floor windows were high off the ground. A packing case stood close by and he pulled it toward the brick wall of the building. Climbing up, he saw that frost and grime had smeared the windows. With his gloved hand he rubbed away some of the dirt.

The scene that unfolded before him numbed his senses.

A bulb shone dimly from a partially opened office door, spilling onto the floor of the mill. A girl, her dress partially ripped off, was being held, spread-eagled, by two men. A third man had mounted her, was stabbing himself at her. The girl's legs were bruised and bleeding. She was writhing with such force that the two men were having difficulty holding her down. As her head rolled from side to side, Eddie could see that her right eye had been blackened and was partially closed. Her face was tear-stained. On a nearby cutting table an almost empty bottle of rye stood as mute testimony to the party.

Eddie's numbed senses slowly cleared. He knew her—he knew them, too. Her name was Ruth, a Jewish girl who had arrived in Toronto only a few months ago from Czechoslovakia. She worked as a scrubwoman for several families on Eddie's block. He had tried twice to talk with her, but she spoke hardly any English. Her parents had been victims of the Holocaust, gassed with a million others at Auschwitz, and she had been brought up as an orphan in post-war Europe. She had never had a home, but had passed from one poor refugee family to another, living the first five years of her life in camps for displaced persons.

Somehow she had managed to produce a tourist visa for Canada, and now she was working here illegally. He had heard from a friend who spoke some Yiddish that she was unhappy and hoped to emigrate to Israel.

Regis Bennett held her on one side; Dale Sommerville, the other.

"For Christ sake get it over with, will you?" Sommerville's voice was a whine. "This bitch is getting hard to hold!"

Bennett's attention wavered, and her mouth found the back of his hands. Her teeth bit hard and deep.

"Son of a bitch!" he screamed. Blood spurted from the raw wound. Her free hand groped for the tool rack at the base of the cutting table, and found a curved knife. She arched the knife toward the third man who was still thrusting into her, bringing it down across his ear and into his neck. Blood sprayed her breasts and face.

His reaction was immediate; he smashed his fist into her face. Her head snapped back, striking the floor with the sound of a melon bursting. She was suddenly very still. It had taken less than fifteen seconds, but time had no meaning for Eddie. He slumped against the windows, rattling the casement. Both of the men who had been holding the girl down looked up at the window, realizing that someone was watching them.

Two of the men moved toward the door. Eddie stumbled and fell off the packing case, but fear brought him back on his feet. He raced quickly back toward the bridge spanning the river—he could hear his pursuers pounding after him.

He had one advantage: he had grown up around the river. He slipped quickly under the bridge onto a beam supported by a cement abutment. Only seconds passed before the first man reached the edge of the abutment. Eddie held his breath so its condensation in the cold night air would not betray his hiding place.

The second man came up quickly, standing next to the first, and spoke. "I looked for him along the river at the back of the mill . . . couldn't find anything. Any luck here?"

It was Dale Sommerville. Eddie recognized his voice. Unused to any exertion, Sommerville was panting heavily.

"It was Eddie Villard at the window, wasn't it?"

"That meddling little bastard," Bennett replied, his voice slurred by alcohol.

Sommerville said, "We've got a problem. The girl is dead."

"Who gives a shit? . . . just another fucking yid . . . probably would have gotten knocked up anyway. Now we don't have to take care of her."

That drunken son of a bitch, Eddie thought, doesn't care about *anything*. As far as Regis Bennett was concerned, the girl was just an object for his use.

"Let's get back in there and clean things up," Bennett said. "If we don't panic, we can get out of this. Maybe we can put the blame on Villard at the same time."

The two men moved quickly away from the bridge, heading back to the mill. Eddie came out of his hiding place, quickly crossing the concrete abutment, moving to the other side of the river. He was climbing up onto the bridge when he heard an explosion. He turned back to look at the mill—flames leaped from the first floor windows and began to climb upwards. In the distance he could hear the wail of fire engine sirens, but it didn't really make any difference to him. They would pin the fire on him and when they discovered that Ruth had been murdered, he would no doubt be charged with that, too. He had to get out of there. No one in the world would believe his story. There was no way he could convince the police that the sons of two of the wealthiest families in Canada were responsible for the murder of an illegal Jewish immigrant. The statement that Regis Bennett had burned down his father's mill would be dismissed as preposterous. There was only one way out for Eddie. He had to run, with no way of knowing how far or for how long.

The freight switching yards of the Canadian Pacific Railroad were just a short distance from the Bennett mill. Eddie headed straight for them in panic.

The yard spread out before him. The new snow was already slushy and blackened. The condensation from the two coupled engines hung in the cold air; cold metal rails gleamed with a thin layer of ice. He was in luck. As he approached, the diesel engines throbbed, drive wheels skidding on the icy tracks, then grabbing as the engineer sanded under them. The block signals flashed green as the engines moved toward the main line, cars strung out, snaking behind the engines. It was a westbound freight.

Eddie moved quickly over the tracks toward the train, careful not to lose his footing on the treacherous path of ice and snow on frozen crossties. He could see, as he approached the train, that there were several open boxcars. Hopefully, he would find an empty one.

The train was rapidly gaining speed as he approached, staying just out of the glare of the spotlights ringing the yards. He paced himself carefully, running parallel to an open car. He braced his hands and wrists on the floor of a car, pushed up, and came to rest on his hands and knees on the floor of an empty car. Quickly getting to his feet, he pulled up on the door lever, closing the door as far as he could, giving him some protection from the biting cold wind.

Until now he had been reacting on instinct, on fear. In the space of a few minutes his life had been changed forever. He was to be hunted like an animal, forced to survive by his own devices. The future he had planned was gone, wiped away by one violent stroke of fate. "Poor Ruth," he whispered to no one. He held his knees to his chest trying in vain to hold back the tears. He should have helped her, he thought. He was a coward.

He lay back against the boxcar wall, staring into the darkness. A long night lay ahead. . . .

He was awakened by the jerking motion of the cars; the freight was grinding to a halt. For him it was a rude awakening. The early morning light came through the partially open car door. He rose slowly, the pain in his right leg a reminder of the events of the previous night. It was time to move out.

He opened the door cautiously, looking for railroad police. It was early. The train had stopped temporarily on a shunt, off the main line. A large factory to his left caught his eye. Its large sign read: "Chrysler Corporation of Canada—Assembly Plant No. 2, Windsor, Ontario." He had made it this far. All he had to do now was to get across the Detroit River. There he would have a measure of safety.

The temperature had warmed up slightly. The weather was always less severe near the lakes. He jumped down from the car and began making his way toward the auto plant, hoping to find a main road and some form of transportation.

At 4:30 p.m. Eddie was sitting in a small diner on Woodward Avenue in Detroit, reading the Windsor afternoon paper. On page two, a large headline read: YOUNG WOMAN FOUND DEAD IN TEXTILE MILL FIRE. The smaller print below read: Prep School Athlete Sought. He closed the paper quickly and felt his face flushing.

He stared into his coffee. He realized he could never return to Canada.

8

JOSH WILLIAMS MOVED at a steady trot just inside a tree line of the dense growth paralleling a dirt and macadam road. The shell holes and destruction along the road made it difficult to tell whether it was more dirt than macadam. The road ran west toward Khe Sanh and east toward Hue. There had been steady traffic on the road; yellow-brown men and equipment continued unabated. The Tet Offensive was in high gear.

Some goddam way to bring in the New Year, Williams thought bitterly. He had been trapped for six days, surrounded by Charlies, and moving east during the night to avoid detection.

The first sign of day glowed in the eastern sky. A heavy morning fog steamed out from the Vietnam jungle, giving the landscape around him an ethereal look. The jungle provided very little safe cover, and he would soon have to seek shelter for the day.

Up ahead, no more than two hundred yards away, he spotted the twisted wreckage of a Russian PT-76 tank, victim of a well-aimed artillery shell. At that point, the jungle closed narrowly against the ditches flanking the road. The tank sat upended in the ditch, a discarded relic of the North Vietnamese offensive against the south.

Williams had been on the move for almost nine hours. Living with the Montagnards on and off for nearly two years had left him more native than military. He hadn't had a bath in more than a week. His clothes, which bore little resemblance to anything military, were sweat-stained and putrid. It's a good thing there's no breeze, he thought, or the VC could find me just by the stink.

The war was supposed to be nearly over, but the Tet Offensive had caught them all offguard. North Vietnamese regular units were everywhere and they were well-equipped. It wasn't guerrilla warfare anymore.

He would never forget the sound of those tanks, just like the one he was sheltered in now . . . the eerie squeaking of their metal treads approaching Lang Vei. It had been his first real taste of facing North Vietnamese regulars. The Montagnards had fought well, but they had been outgunned and outmanned by the North Vietnamese. They had radioed for support. None came. Khe Sanh, to the west, was under siege. The fighting was at close quarters, hand-to-hand, the type Williams had been trained for and at which he was skilled. His M-16, its barrel overheated, had accounted for more dead than he could remember. At close quarters, the knife—now resting in his boot, still caked with patches of dried blood—had found its mark more than once. But he had seen the fiercely gentle people he had lived with for almost two years crushed and mutilated, and there was nothing he or anyone else could do about it.

They had been overrun and survivors such as he had scattered in all directions. When he had returned at dawn, no one was left alive. Nearly a thousand people were killed or gone.

Then he saw her. He had called her Tameo. It was as close as he could come to pronouncing her Montagnard name. Her small, delicate body had been split apart from her chest to her pubic arch. A tiny, partially formed fetus lay with the contorted remains of Tameo's intestines. The sight was grotesque. She had been his woman. She hadn't told him that she was pregnant. He didn't love her, or she him; they had sought each other as an outlet for the other's primitive needs; they had cared for each other, providing comfort and escape. It was as lasting a relationship as he had ever known in his young and disrupted life.

He remembered being on his hands and knees, tears flowing from his eyes as he gouged out a shallow grave for the wreckage of her body and the fetus.

He erected a makeshift cross of sticks and covered the shallow grave with an improvised cairn of small stones— some protection, at least, from roving animals, human or otherwise. It was only when he had finished a silent prayer that he realized he was not alone. A black pajama-clad VC stood silently, no more than eight feet away from him, watching intently. His fascination with what Williams was doing proved to be fatal.

The Cong soldier had no chance to raise his rifle barrel more than a few inches before Williams crashed into him, his hands reaching for the VC's throat, crushing his esophagus in one swift motion. He could hardly remember the rest, how long it had taken or why he had done it. What lay before him was the result. Bones, flesh . . . raw meat. Twisted and contorted, they hardly resembled anything human. And then a strange animal cry erupted from inside him—a primal scream. His hands and arms were covered with blood. He was an apparition, black-bearded, wild-eyed and crazed.

The next two days were a jumble; he had vague recollections of moving through scrubland and elephant grass. It was the leeches, the green bloodsucking leeches that had brought him back to reality. He glanced at his arms. The blood he saw was his own. He scraped the leeches off, full of loathing for himself. He had fought for control, the control he knew he needed if he were to survive. And he had survived.

It had started long before Nam. And he was now farther away from Canada than he ever could have imagined. His situation had not improved appreciably. Wanted in Canada by the RCMP for a crime he didn't commit, he had escaped to, of all places on earth, Vietnam.

Somebody up there must have it in for me!

He thought back to the time when he had wandered aimlessly through the streets of Detroit for almost two weeks, avoiding all human contact, his isolation complete. Nights he slept in the flophouse hotels that dotted Detroit's inner city like festering sores; he ate sparingly at cheap diners and fast-food hamburger stands, carefully protecting the little money he had left. He needed a job, but in order to get work, he needed a new identity and a plausible story on his background. He had to avoid any suspicion, any investigation.

His assumed identity came to him while sitting on a park bench across the street from a cemetery. What better identity than that of someone already dead and buried? He could make up his own story; no one would check it out.

It had taken two days of searching through the cemeteries near Detroit. Finally, he stumbled acorss a pauper's grave, just a brass plaque in the ground. No headstone.

"Joshua Williams, born March 30, 1944—Died December 12, 1948."

Adjoining Joshua's grave were plots holding the remains of Joshua's parents. They had died within months of each other in 1951. So, on a raw, gray day in a cemetery just outside of Detroit, Eddie Villard had creased to exist and Joshua Williams was reborn.

Eddie stood staring down at the grave for a long time. The more he thought about it, the more it seemed proper that he would find his identity in a graveyard.

That had been in 1963, almost exactly five years ago. He had taken basic training and transferred to Special Forces, the Green Berets. It had been a good time for him and for the United States, led by a President with charisma. Patriotism was still a virtue, and so was national pride. Josh Williams had developed a tense jingoism and, like all Americans, felt an almost unutterable sense of loss that November day in 1963 when an assassin's bullet found its mark.

Perhaps it was out of the sense of emptiness following Kennedy's death that Josh applied for duty in Vietnam. By

January 1964 he was in Saigon. Then came Johnson's Gulf of Tonkin episode and Westmoreland's escalation which began the excess of carnage and death that came to be known as the Vietnam War. Search and Destroy—a euphemism for burn and kill . . . and the VC were like ghosts; here and there, and gone again.

Williams' first tour ended in 1966. He had requested special duty at Lang Vei to train the Montagnards. That was his kind of war, unstructured and unfettered by the stream of untried officers coming in from West Point. His transition from spit-and-polish to a paid, cunning killer had been complete.

Now, sequestered in an abandoned tank, he wondered what would happen if Charlie did get him. The Army, he thought, would have a complicated time trying to dispel these thoughts. He was a long way from being dead.

Josh Williams—he thought of himself that way now—had paid dearly for a false certificate and Social Security card. He had used the last of his money to buy a new wardrobe from the Salvation Army Thrift Shop. His intermediate needs were a job and money. The kindly uncle in red, white and blue, depicted in pictures plastered all over the United States, seemed to be pointing directly at Josh, making an offer he couldn't resist. The Army recruiter was delighted to see him.

He glanced at his watch. Only fifteen minutes had passed, but night had vanished. He slid further down, half in and half out of the tank. He covered the rest of his body with grass and leaves. He would have to get some sleep.

It was late afternoon; he had slept fitfully. There had been sporadic traffic nearby his hiding place all day—all eastbound, all the enemy. It would soon be dark enough for him to travel again.

It wasn't the approaching vehicle that had caught his attention, but the direction from which it was coming, the east. He peered through the firing slits of the tank. An American jeep flying colonel's colors was barreling along heading straight into the advancing enemy. He may be brass, thought Josh, but his driver's got his head up his ass. Dumb son of a bitch! . . .

Just then two incoming mortar rounds lifted the jeep's front end skyward, blowing off the wheels and dropping it half in the ditch on the opposite side of the road from where Josh huddled. The top half of the driver's body hung out of what remained of the window screen, with most of his head blown across the hood.

Josh waited, stunned. Several VC advanced cautiously down the hill toward the jeep. Shots rang out from the side of the jeep, kicking up grass around the feet of the VC, causing them to retreat quickly. He realized that whoever was beside that jeep couldn't shoot straight, and judging from the sound of the shots, he was probably firing a small caliber pistol. It had the same effect as shooting a popgun at a herd of elephants.

He assessed the situation. From his position, he could crawl into the ditch and cross under the road through a culvert and reach the other side without being seen. He judged the culvert to be about fifty yards from the jeep. The ditch on the other side of the road was deeper. As long as the enemy was occupied, Josh was fairly certain they wouldn't notice him. With a little luck, he might be able to help the idiot in the jeep.

It took about five minutes to reach the culvert, which was about four feet wide and was laid in two sections, each at about a thirty degree angle toward the other. The culvert had been built that way to divert the water flow and reduce the amount of erosion in the ditches when there was a heavy rain. He hesitated at the bend, his caution rewarded. Two VC were silhouetted at the end of the culvert, their backs to him. They were eating, oblivious of his presence.

He unloaded half a clip from his M-16, practically guillotining them at their beltlines.

Josh stepped backwards so that he could see in both directions. He waited, silently, to see if his shots had alerted the other VC, but apparently they were still occupied by the action at the jeep. When he reached the end of the culvert, he pulled the bodies of the two VC into the culvert, out of sight of the others shooting at the colonel. He wanted to come back this way and there was no sense in leaving them where they might attract attention.

It took him about ten minutes to make the last fifty feet during the split-second lulls of the small arms fire and occasional mortar shell. They must be using the jeep for target practice, he decided. And judging from their lack of accuracy, Hanoi must be recruiting latrine diggers.

He finally reached the jeep, which hung crazily on the lip of the ditch. Two shots ricocheted off the vehicle, whining dangerously past his head.

"Hey, you!" he shouted. "The Marines have landed! Get your ass out of there and slide down into the ditch!"

"Who the hell do you think you are?" was the reply.

"I'll be damned," Josh said, incredulously. "Look, you got about five minutes before the whole fucking Vietnamese Army gets here, and a hell of a lot less than that if the gook who's been playing games with the mortar gets lucky."

There was no reply.

"If you think I'm going to hang around here while you make up your mind, you're crazy." I've got to get through to him, Josh thought, in order to save us both.

The colonel finally moved, sliding out from under the jeep and dropping heavily into the ditch. He was portly, over fifty, mostly gray, and mad as hell. "You damned insubordinate . . ."

But that was as far as he got. Josh clapped a hand over his mouth and pushed his head as deeply as it would go into the wet grass at the side of the ditch.

"You listen and get it right. I've killed so many people in the last two days that one more isn't going to make any difference to me. I've crawled half a mile to save your ass. If you want to get out of this alive, shut up and listen to me. Understood?"

The colonel nodded, but his dark eyes sparked with anger.

"Start crawling toward that culvert over there. You'll find

two dead VC. They both carried automatic weapons. Get rid of that popgun of yours—grab those guns and as much ammo as you can carry. Wait for me inside the culvert. Keep your ass down . . . sir."

The colonel scrambled down into the ditch and crawled away. He kept low and out of sight just as he had been ordered to do. As the colonel reached the culvert, Josh pulled the pin of a fragmentation grenade, counted to three, then rolled it up under the rear of the overturned jeep.

The force of the concussion knocked Josh to his knees. He started scrambling toward the culvert, and the secondary explosion from the half-filled gas tank whipped searing heat along his back and neck, singeing his hair. But the diversion worked. He had reached cover without drawing enemy fire and caught up with the colonel. It only took a few moments to retrace his steps.

They stopped briefly in the cover of the tank. The enemy would not be fooled for much longer. Josh looked at the man he had just rescued. His chest heaved—he gasped for air and wheezed—sweat covered his face and discolored his uniform. The exertion and closeness to death were taking their toll on the colonel. Josh knew he would have to give the man a chance to recover his composure, but not too long. Time had become an enemy. Josh extended his hand.

"Josh Williams . . ."

The colonel gasped, "Colonel Paul Caldwell Mac-Gregor . . . you insubordinate son of a bitch."

Christ, thought Josh . . . the RCMP, Viet Cong and now some armchair colonel. What's coming next?

"I should have let them off you," he said, "but instead I saved your ass. What the hell is wrong with you?" He regretted the words before they were out of his mouth.

But the words must have struck home. The colonel hesitantly extended his hand. Josh's arm remained rigid at his side for a spiteful moment. Then shrugging, he said, "Okay . . . the hell with it . . ." He clasped the colonel's hand and they grinned foolishly at each other.

"Colonel, we've got to move. First, get rid of the eagles.

They make you an easy mark for the Cong. Second, the North Vietnamese would like nothing better than to shoot the balls off a staff officer—if they hear me call you 'sir', they'll figure it out. So let's dispense with the formalities. Agreed?''

"Agreed."

"We'll travel east. Nighttime only. Any questions?"

MacGregor shook his head. He was satisfied to let Williams take control . . . a man who seemed to know the art of survival.

"Call me Mac."

"Okay, Mac. One more thing . . . we avoid contact with the enemy whenever possible. I hope you're not one of those gung-ho types that has to shoot at every gook he sees."

"Patton I ain't."

MacGregor discarded his eagles.

"Let's move out." Williams headed toward the trees. "I'll take the point." The colonel followed obediently.

Josh and Mac sat in a glen that had been carved out of the jungle by a stream of clear, bubbling, unpolluted water. They were about 300 yards from the road, and hidden. The brush growing on the stream's banks provided enough cover from the road, even though a defoliant had been used and the area was almost entirely nude of vegetation. They were traveling due east. Josh hoped to arrive in Hue before the Viet Cong. A trip that would normally be an hour's ride by helicopter had turned into a three-day nightmare. ARVN troops were retreating in disarray. There were no front lines. The fighting was sporadic and occurred whenever groups of fleeing allied forces encountered the advancing North Vietnamese regulars. The situation had forced Williams and MacGregor to travel in the jungles by night; they holed up from daybreak to nightfall, near the river, avoiding the VC whenever possible. They split watches in the daytime, Josh in the morning, Mac in the afternoon.

A grudging mutual respect had developed between the two men. Mac had placed his trust in Josh because of his

superior field experience. Twice on the first night, and once
the following day, they had narrowly avoided capture by the
VC. Shots were exchanged, but Josh and Mac had broken
contact with any troops, friend or foe.

They were now closer to the road in order to get their
bearings so they could direct themselves east toward Hue.
Josh had sustained a minor flesh wound, but he was more
concerned about Mac's condition than his own.

Mac, he had learned, had had his World War II
commission reactivated; he had been Army liaison with the
OSS. He had no battle experience during his three years in
Europe and was certainly in no shape, physically, to
undergo the ordeal in which they were now involved. He
had been sent to Vietnam only to assist in the transfer of
power from a military to civilian government at the end of
the fighting or during pacification. Further, he was also to
assist the South Vietnamese Government in establishing an
intelligence operation. Translated: a short tour of duty in a
combat area to get a star.

In 72 hours they had moved east, near the outskirts of
Hue. En route Josh had worked out a plan to steal a boat and
sail out to the Gulf of Tonkin. If the U.S. Navy had not
given up their claim to the Gulf, there was the possibility of
an open sea rescue. They had only to reach the bay, north of
the city.

It was almost dark when Mac awakened Josh. "I think
we have company. I've been watching over there. There's a
squad of VC and about twenty of our guys prisoners."

"Let's get a closer look." As Josh got to his feet, he
noticed that Mac stiffened. Josh mouthed the question:
"Charlie?" Mac nodded briefly. Josh reached for the top of
his boot, extracting his knife. He whirled around quickly,
spotting the Charlie at the same instant the man's slanted
eyes detected their presence. The Charlie had stopped to
relieve himself. Their eyes met. One hand on his fly, the
man reached frantically with his free hand for his gun.

Josh's knife caught him in the throat, penetrating his
neck, impaling him onto the urine and blood splattered tree.

He made no noise other than the involuntary death rattle as life left his body.

Josh dropped to his hands and knees, coiled like a spring, ready to attack. Mac squatted on his haunches, aghast. Josh crept quickly over to the corpse and wrenched his knife free. He wiped the knife blade clean on the dead man's tunic, flipped the body over with his boot and rolled it into a small ravine behind the tree.

Mac watched Josh, fascinated by his lack of emotion. "You just killed a man . . . but you act like nothing happened. You're some cold son of a bitch."

Josh's expression became impassive, his mouth a thin line. What the hell does he know about killing? he thought. All he's ever done is push buttons.

He pointed to the ravine where the dead man lay. "Whether you like it or not, this is what the war's all about. You sit on your ass in Washington and read memos. Here it's winner take all."

Visibly shaken by the killing, Mac seemed even more so by the grim visage of his companion. The two stared at each other in grim silence.

His anger spent, Josh turned as if nothing had happened. "Keep your fingers crossed that his friends don't start hunting for him."

By following the creek, they were able to angle nearer to the edge of the road, apparently without being observed.

A North Vietnamese regular was speaking to a Marine Sergeant. His English was fluent and crisp.

"Sergeant, your men will be required to assist us in unloading some barges. We will march immediately to the dock area, about an hour's walk from here. Your men will follow my orders or be shot dead. Do you understand?"

The Marine muttered something that was unintelligible to Josh's ears, but it was obvious that he intended to cooperate, because the Charlie smiled.

Josh rejoined Mac. "We may be in luck. We're within an hour of the bay . . . it should lead into the Gulf. If we can get there and steal a boat, we may be home free."

Following the Cong and their captives was easy and allowed them to travel over easier terrain. An hour later they arrived at the dock. The pier extended about a hundred feet out into the narrow bay. Green slime covered the water close to shore. Sailboats, junks and barges crammed the dock on both sides. At the back, to one side, reaching to the edge of the clearing, were discarded ammunition boxes and empty barrels that provided an ideal vantage point for Josh and Mac. They could see without being seen. Josh left Mac to scout the area. There were about a half dozen large stakebody trucks waiting along with half-ton pickups. Most of it appeared to be captured American equipment. Undoubtedly, the barges were too. Josh counted four guards on the two barges, added to the dozen or so men guarding the American prisoners and personnel in the vehicles. Josh guessed there were about 20 unfriendlies, give or take one or two. The personnel in the vehicles did not appear to be heavily armed. Josh finished his reconnaissance and returned to Mac.

"Mac, cover me. We need another diversion."

"What are you going to do?"

"Steal a boat. I don't know about you, but I'm tired of the countryside. The sea air will be good for our health. I'm going to blow up those goddam barges."

"You're crazy!"

"Have you ever seen a limpet mine?"

"No."

Josh pulled a burlap sack and a black saucer shaped device from the front of his jacket. "This is one. I've got three more in there." He pointed to the sack.

"Where'd you get those?" Mac said, astounded.

"I sneaked into the shed and helped myself." Josh pointed to a boat, its sails furled. It was downstream of the dock, not far from the barges. "I'm going to untie the lines and let it float downstream. You stay here and cover me."

The edge of the river was about fifteen yards from where he and Mac were hidden. His greatest exposure would be in those fifteen yards. He sprinted over the open area, body low, dove over the bank, sliding on his stomach along the muddy bank to the water below.

He stopped to listen. Nothing. He had not been seen. He was on the upstream side of the river. He worked his way under the dock. Kerosene torches mounted on the shed above cast long shadows on the polluted water, giving him a perfect cover. Grabbing a hollow reed, he submerged himself in the water, breathing through the reed, moving noiselessly, slowly. Through the water's surface he could see that the pilings rose about eight feet from the surface to the dock. The filthy water burned his eyes. He reached the first boat, hoisted himself onto the craft, placing the sack of mines inside. He crept from boat to boat, taking only a few minutes to get to the one he was going to cut loose from the dock.

It was about eighteen feet long; mast, sails and center board were in the cockpit. It had a small cutty cabin and a small kicker. There were two other boats beyond this one that would provide cover in case one of the guards on the barges happened to glance in his direction. Josh swiftly unfastened the lines to the pier and carefully moved the boat out of the slip, turning it so that it was stern to stern with the skiff next to it. Then, he quickly resecured it, realizing that if he released the boat now the current might carry it too far downstream. He would have to wait until he had finished setting the mines. He figured it would take about ten minutes for the boat to drift to the spot he had pointed out to MacGregor earlier.

Josh was not fully prepared for the deep water. He had been scuttling submerged on the bay bottom before. He almost cried out in panic as he went over the side, the weight of the mines dragging him down. Struggling to reach the surface, groping for a hold, he finally managed to grasp the stern of a small rowboat, barely pulling his head above the water. He fought to regain his calm.

Darkness was his ally. His head hit something solid. It was the first barge. He submerged, kicking hard for the final lunge to the other side. His lungs seemed to be bursting; his body ached from the effort. Suddenly he was on the other side, clear of the water, gulping for air. He set the first mine to explode in fifteen minutes. He moved to the second barge, using up a minute, setting the timer for fourteen minutes. This time it wasn't necessary to go underwater. He skirted the front edge where there was a three-foot overhang that provided him with cover. He moved down the other side, using up another two minutes to set the third limpet mine, this one set to go off in twelve minutes. He moved sluggishly to the back barge, checked his watch, and set the last mine for eleven minutes.

It was all he could do to pull himself up and over the side, falling into the boat. He forced himself to the stern of the skiff. His hands and arms felt like hundred pound weights. His agility impeded, he fumbled with the lines, securing the two boats. Reaching over, he jammed the rudder of the sailboat into position so that the boat would drift into a right turn and toward shore. His hands shook; his muscles felt weak. Finally, he pulled the ropes free of the dock. He watched momentarily as his and Mac's ticket to freedom drifted off slowly into the night. Teeth chattering, lungs nearly bursting, he sprinted back across the fifteen foot clearing, and flopped down next to where Mac was waiting.

"Are you okay?" Mac asked nervously.

Josh glanced at his watch. "Three minutes to zero . . ."

"Our North Vietnamese friend has ordered the American prisoners to unload the barges in a couple of minutes."

Josh was back on his feet. "Our luck is holding, so far. Stay here . . . I'll be back in a couple of minutes."

He scooted around the edge of the shed. He was within fifteen feet of the Marine sergeant. The only source of light, the two kerosene torches, dropped shadows over the compound. The guards were not paying much attention.

Josh picked up some small stones and tossed them at the Marine's feet. He threw some more and the sergeant peered at Josh, mouth dropping open in surprise. Josh quickly brought his finger to his lips. The sergeant remained silent, sauntered in Josh's direction and unzipped his pants.

"Listen carefully," Josh whispered. "In about two minutes those barges are going to blow. When they do, we'll take care of as many VC as we can. You guys will have to help. There're plenty of guns and ammo in the shed."

The sergeant nodded, zipped his pants, turned silently and headed back to his fellow prisoners. Josh scurried back to MacGregor and their hiding place.

"When the first barge blows, you take the guard on the left . . . then run like hell down to the boat. If I'm not there in three minutes, take off."

Mac opened his mouth to protest.

"Just do what I say," Josh snapped. "Get to the open sea . . ."

The first two mines attached to the barges blew simultaneously, raising the barges almost out of the water. Several VC rushed down toward the end of the pier just as the other two mines went off and blew the pier away. Secondary explosions from the ordinance began immediately and the concussions rolled deafeningly, one over the other, blowing out the walls of the supply hut.

Mac jumped up, aiming, taking out the first guard with a burst from his automatic rifle. Josh hit the other two immediately and moved off toward the land end of the pier where the remainder of the VC squad were fleeing in disarray. He was grateful to hear the Marines' covering fire coming from behind him. He and Mac had bought enough time; the Marines could take care of the rest.

Josh sprinted to where MacGregor was readying the boat, hoisting the mast. The shoreline was lit by the blazing fires eating up the barges and the pier. He could still hear sporadic small arms fire from the drivers who had fled at the first explosion.

Suddenly the world turned upside down. An explosion seemed to come from afar. Floating, Josh felt sharp searing pain in his head and legs . . . then blackness.

• • •

Consciousness came to Josh in waves. He was aware of pain, hot and consuming. A voice penetrated his brain. He struggled to move, making the pain worse. Someone was talking to him, but he couldn't understand the words. He was tied down. There was no clarity or reality. He felt a tiny pinprick in his arm . . . and again, blackness.

9

CONSCIOUSNESS CAME IN throbbing, sealed bursts. Tubes, white-masked faces, pain, muted voices, all merged together in a fog of unreality. He opened his eyes, but they rebelled at the light streaming through the window next to his bed. Pain flooded his body. A good sign, he thought. At least I'm alive.

An IV bottle hung from a metal stand beside the bed, one of several GI issue cots that lined both sides of the white, monastic, linoleum-floored ward. His right hand was immobilized, bandaged to a board. The tubes inserted into his veins dripped nutrients into his body.

He began a silent inventory. His right leg was elevated above him in a cast, suspended by pulleys and weights. Bandages were wrapped tightly around his chest, constricting his movement and breathing. His reward for one try at a deep breath was hot knifing chest pains that spread down his entire right side. His head throbbed and his face and nose felt swollen. He could only breathe through his mouth. He gingerly touched his face to explore the bandages that wrapped his forehead. His nose was covered with gauze and tape. The bandages reached from ear to ear. But everything seemed to be in place. All in all, he decided—remembering what he had been through—he was lucky.

His throat was parched; he needed a drink badly. He

looked around for some sort of signaling device. It wasn't necessary, a nurse was approaching the bed.

To anyone else, the nurse might have seemed ordinary—medium height, stocky build, brown hair, even a little plain—but to Josh she was Florence Nightingale, Marilyn Monroe and Joan of Arc rolled into one package.

Her wide smile was beautiful; she had white, even teeth. "Just stop right there," Josh ordered.

She obeyed, a quizzical look on her face.

"Now, do a 360 for me . . . slowly."

She pirouetted gracefully, then faced him. "What was all that about?"

"I was checking for wings."

The nurse chuckled. "You seem pretty sure that you were headed up instead of down . . . but if God heard what I've been hearing out of your mouth these last few days, you'd be on the down escalator." She pulled the bed curtain, suspended overhead from a U-shaped track, around Josh's bed.

To Josh, her playful mood was medicine of the best kind. "How long have I been here? Where's Mac? How did . . . ?"

The nurse raised a finger to her lips. "One question at a time. You've been here for three days. Before that, three days in intensive care. You're the guest of Tokyo General Hospital."

"Can I have some water?" he whispered.

She poured water from a pitcher on a nightstand next to the bed. She held a large paper cup with a flexible straw for him to sip through. It brought cool relief to his dry throat. He finished quickly and slumped backwards, resting his head back on the feather pillow. Just the exertion of raising his head to drink had worn him out.

"You're a hero around here, Mr. Williams. A regular Audie Murphy."

"And what about Mac?"

"If Mac is Colonel Paul Caldwell MacGregor . . . he's been driving us up the wall."

A doctor entered the room—tall, big-boned, his red hair thinning. His brows were deeply furrowed. He introduced himself, his voice a reassuring baritone. "Bert Spira, and welcome back to the living."

Josh felt uneasy about his celebrity status. "I'm glad to be alive." He gestured for Dr. Spira to come closer, and whispered in his ear. "Could you . . . take that tube out?" As he pointed to the catheter, he could feel his face redden.

Spira grinned, turning to the nurse. "Get me some surgical scissors and a tray."

As soon as the nurse left, Spira pulled back the sheets and swiftly removed the catheter. The relief was enormous.

"Thanks, doc."

The nurse returned. "On your side, hotshot." She rolled a surgical tray up to the bed. The removal of the catheter had not escaped her keen medical eye. "A little shy, are we?" Josh rolled over. The alcohol soaked swab was cold on his buttocks, and a minute pricking sensation was the only sign that the hypodermic had been inserted.

Spira began the ritual of cutting away the dressing.

"How bad is it, and when can I get out of here?"

"Hold on, sport. Let me do some checking here first. I'll give you a complete rundown."

He continued to cut away the dressing from the wounds, swabbing them with alcohol, poking and prodding for almost twenty minutes. He removed some stitches. Josh felt no pain.

"You're healing faster than I thought you would, but the war is over for you. Infected flesh wounds, one on the scalp, two on your right arm." His voice droned the litany of injuries.

"The next time you decide to blow something up, get the hell out of the way. Apparently, during all the fireworks, a case of high explosives blew off the barge and landed behind you, hot. From what we hear, the explosion sent you flying through the air like Peter Pan. We took enough shrapnel from your right side to build a jeep." The doctor paused. "That's the good news. Here's the bad. Your right leg was pretty badly messed up. Broken, and a lot of muscle in your right calf was mangled pretty badly. The pin we put in will stay with you. A souvenir."

He waited for a reaction. None was forthcoming, so he continued. "Now, this may frighten you a little, but hang on. The face you see in the mirror the next time you shave is going to be a surprise. We had the best plastic surgeon in Tokyo working on you. He says you'll be prettier than ever, but he doubts your mother will recognize you. There'll be minimal scarring, but a good suntan will cover it up almost completely. Any questions?"

"Not about me."

Spira looked at him, puzzled. What he didn't know was that it didn't matter to Josh what he looked like.

"What about Colonel MacGregor?" Josh asked.

"He's fine. He hauled you into an eighteen foot skiff and sailed the damned thing all the way to the Gulf of Tonkin. Good thing you picked an Army Colonel who's also been a sailor all his life. By the way, most of those Marine prisoners got through, too. There's a sergeant who's been insisting that he see you as soon as you can have visitors."

Josh smiled, remembering the cool behavior of the Marine.

Spira rose, turning to the nurse. "No restrictions on diet . . . no visitors until tomorrow." To Josh: "I'll see you tonight when I make my rounds."

Josh contemplated what the doctor had told him. A mixed bag. On one hand, he wouldn't play hockey again; on the other hand, he had been provided with a new face, a new identity. The RCMP would never identify him. He felt isolated and alone. His dog tags read Josh Williams, soldier. But inside, always, he felt like Eddie Villard.

Monday dawned bright and sunny at Tokyo General. He began refusing the morphine-based shots that had been prescribed for him. He felt that as long as the pain wasn't unbearable, he could work through the healing process faster without pain killers. Karen, the nurse, kept a special watch on him.

"A lot of the men who come through here suffer from extreme alienation," she told Josh. "I suppose it comes from seeing your buddies killed or wounded—the people that have become your whole world, taken away suddenly, lost forever. The scars on the inside can be far worse than the ones on the outside. I'd like to be your friend . . . if you need one."

"I'd like that—seems a long time since I've had one."

"Okay, then, friend, I've got a surprise for you."

Josh's eyes lit up, and for a moment he felt like the youth he had been before the war.

Karen went out into the hallway, and returned rolling a wheelchair up to Josh's bed.

He grabbed it, rose shakily, easing his weight onto his left leg, then dropped into the wheelchair, heaving a sigh of pleasure and relief. He was on his way back to self-sufficiency.

Karen wheeled Josh out into the hallway. They rounded a corner, into a hall that opened on to a large sunroom. Josh spotted Mac in conversation with a small group of people. He stopped talking as soon as Josh appeared.

"Josh, it's good to see you!" There was genuine warmth in his greeting. "Are they treating you all right? Do you have everything you need?"

Josh nodded and glanced over Mac's shoulder, the question in his eyes unspoken. The people he had been talking to were journalists.

"I'm sorry about that. They're the Pentagon's idea. Josh, the war isn't popular at home. The brass needs a hero. You've been elected." He paused. "Just a few questions. Okay?"

"Shit," he said. "But all right. For you."

Mac was obviously at ease, an old hand with the press, but Josh felt stripped. He was without the trappings of war, the facade he had come to wear most comfortably.

Fortunately it didn't last long. Mac had prepped them well. But still, afterwards, Josh felt drained, and Mac sensed his unease.

"What's troubling you, son?"

"For my own reasons, I don't want . . . I can't have any publicity stateside. No citations. I don't mean to be ungrateful, but I have to have privacy. I'd like to see this publicity thing die where it is."

Mac paused slowly, puzzled. He stopped, turning to Josh.

"Why don't you tell me what it's all about? Maybe I can help you."

"Mac . . ." Josh sighed sadly. "I wish you could, but let's just leave it where it is. If my being a hero is good for anybody's morale, so be it. I'll do what I can to live up to your billing. What did you say I was? A genuine, one hundred percent all-American hero? Sounds like an advertisement for a breakfast cereal."

They both laughed, and Mac glanced at his watch. "I've got to go. I understand you're being shipped to Pearl for rehab in a couple of days. My tour is up. I'll be stateside within a week."

Josh tried to joke away his sense of sadness. "Got your star, eh?"

Mac grinned foolishly. "You made me work hard for it." More seriously, he said, "I know you've got problems. Here's some advice—free. Let someone help you to look at things from a different perspective. You did that for me. In that jeep I knew I was a dead man, going out in a blaze of cowardly glory. You may have been angry enough to forget about death, but not angry enough to quit. I owe you for that."

He embraced Josh awkwardly, leaning down to the wheelchair. He had made the offer. There was nothing more he could do for Josh other than wait.

Mac headed for the door. "I have a little real estate business in Florida. Caldwell-MacGregor is the company name. Look me up when you're stateside . . . the door is always open to you."

Josh was moved, his cool blue eyes warming slightly. "Thanks. I'll think about it."

Mac started down the hallway. Josh called after him, "When you get the war bug again, remember what I told you."

"I know . . ." In unison they said, "Keep your ass down." Mac's laughter disappeared around the corner.

It was Wednesday afternoon. Josh's recovery was proceeding rapidly. The dressings on his right arm had been removed. The permanent scarring would be minimal. The only remaining bandages were the new dressings that had just been placed over the plastic surgery on his face and the bindings around his ribs. They hadn't yet let him see his face, but judging from the touch of it, it was still badly swollen. That didn't bother Josh. No one could visualize the changes in his appearance. He hoped that identification would be nearly impossible. His only other concern was that he get into the rehabilitation hospital, learn to hop on crutches. He wanted mobility.

He said his goodbyes to Karen in the ward at Tokyo General.

"Promise me you'll stay in touch," she said. They had become very close in a very short time. He agreed, knowing full well that he couldn't. It was something he truly regretted. The file that he and the recruiter had doctored up would fall apart as soon as the news stories hit the stands. People would begin to ask tough questions. If it wasn't so serious, the situation might just appeal to his bizarre sense of humor. He wondered how they would explain away a hero one week, and in the following week, further explain how he could be dead for more than twenty years. Knowing the military, they'd think of something.

Finally, Josh was underway. As one of the more seriously wounded and a VIP, which he was now considered, he was transported by air, hopping from Tokyo to Guam and on to the Island of Oahu. Destination: Tripler Military Rehabilitation Hospital in the hills of Honolulu, rising to the back of Pearl Harbor. It was a long and tiring trip, but he was stirred by his first glimpse of Hawaii.

The sun had just risen, and he couldn't remember seeing water so blue. High white cumulus clouds rolled out over the ocean. As the plane banked on its final approach, Josh could see the clouds touching the peaks of the mountains of Oahu. He identified the beautiful proud face of Diamond Head.

Josh's first week went well; he progressed from a wheelchair to a walker. The new cast was braced and had a steel reinforcement under the foot. He was healing well, and his intensity in the regimen he followed allowed him to keep his mind off much of what was around him. He realized how lucky he had been. Here at Tripler, the horror of war was visible everywhere. In this island paradise, the refuse of war was visible: the amputees, burn victims, the legless, armless and faceless; and, the most pitiful of all, the mindless, standing out in stark contrast to the beauty and tranquility of the place. Almost ashamed, Josh avoided them as they shuffled through the halls.

The sights and sounds of the hospital compelled him to work harder each day toward recovery. He knew that time was running out for him. He was so preoccupied he didn't realize it was close to Easter. Decorations had been strung in the hallways and in the nurses' stations. Josh felt alienated from all the festivities. Other patients in his ward had been receiving parcels of food and clothing. Cards from home decorated hospital bedframes.

On Easter morning, Josh ate breakfast, then spent two hours in the weight room, as he did every day, working on his chest, arms and stomach. He had returned to top condition with the exception of his leg cast and bandaged face. He had even regained some of the weight he had lost in the two tours in Nam.

A new face, he thought. A new life. Why not?

10

TWO DAYS BEFORE Easter, Josh went to the Bank of Hawaii in downtown Honolulu. He was arranging for a transfer of funds from his bank in Detroit to the Islands. He had saved much of his GI pay, close to $3,000, in just a little more than four years. The personnel at the bank seemed pleased to help this young veteran. He was told it would take about two days to complete the transfer.

Leaving the bank, he headed to a shopping district. He knew exactly what he wanted and chose a store specializing in work clothes. He bought light denims, shorts, T-shirts, underwear and a poplin jacket, two pairs of rubber-soled walking shoes, a heavy knit sweater and a Greek fisherman's cap. While the sales clerk was removing price tags from Josh's purchases, he went next door and picked up a sturdy denim zippered bag with a broad shoulder strap. From a showcase of assorted knives, he picked up a well-balanced, eight inch steel hunting knife. Good for throwing—long enough to do damage from close range. He added a matching leather scabbard. His final purchases included a waterproof plastic pouch for his passport, personal identification and money, a shoulder variety leather holster and a small but very complete first-aid kit. He packed everything into his denim bag but the pouch; that he carried with him.

He hailed a cab and instructed the driver to take him to

the Honolulu bus depot. It took him only a few minutes to
find and pay for an empty rental locker.

Next, Josh visited the Honolulu docks. He secured from
the dockmaster a list of the boats in port and their sailing
schedules. Culling the list, he found two freighters of
Panamanian registry. One sailed next Tuesday, the other on
Sunday. Today was Thursday. He couldn't wait much
longer.

He returned to the bus depot on Friday and changed into
his newly purchased civvies in the men's room of the
terminal. Then he headed for the docks.

A Panamanian freighter, the *North Star,* was bound for
Hong Kong via the Society Islands and Japan. The trip
would take seventy days. There were quarters available for
a few passengers.

The *North Star* had seen better days. It was obvious that
it had been a long time since anyone had ventured aboard as
a passenger. This made her ideal for Josh's purposes: not
much chance of running into other passengers.

The ship's captain was a salty German, Wilhelm Gotz,
who spoke heavily accented English. He seemed delighted
at the prospect of a passenger for at least a portion of the
voyage. He didn't find it unusual that his passenger was on
crutches and that his face was bandaged.

Josh assumed correctly that Captain Gotz would pocket
his fare and that his name would never make the ship's
manifest. The open sea had its own underground economy.
The cost of the trip was negotiated. The final terms: $400 in
cash, to be paid on boarding; he would have a separate
cabin, and take his meals with the captain and the first mate.
He was told to stay out of the way of the crew. The captain
described them as a "mixed bag." The bargain was struck.

"You board at three p.m. on Sunday," Gotz said,
grinning. "We sail an hour later."

More than four thousand miles away, at Maury's Restaurant on Yonge Street, in Toronto, three men sat in a private
room in the rear of the restaurant.

Maury's was a favorite haunt of politicians and businessmen, wheelers and dealers, and contained a number of private rooms in addition to its popular public dining room. Most of the business of the city and the province was conducted in those rooms. The restaurant was known for privacy and discretion. Nothing said in clandestine meetings was ever repeated.

A lunch had been served. Beer bottles and mugs littered the table. The diners were dressed conservatively. A copy of *Time* magazine lay open on the table—next to it, a yearbook from St. Mary's Academy. It was also open to a full-page photo of Eddie Villard as a young hockey player in a posed action shot, skates kicking up sprays of ice. The player was full face to the camera. It was evident to them that the face of Josh Williams' picture in *Time* was the same as the face of the young hockey player pictured in the yearbook. Josh Williams, Green Beret, was Eddie Villard, from St. Mary's Academy.

Dale Sommerville, tallest of the three men, spoke first. "There's no doubt about it. That's Eddie, but we don't know when this picture"—pointing at the magazine—"was taken. It says it's an enlistment photo. I had one of our people in Windsor check the records in Michigan. Now, get this. Josh Williams died as a child in Detroit. He was an only child. His parents died not long after the kid. Train accident. So Josh Williams reappears in 1963, three weeks after our little . . . let's say, accident, and he enlists in the Army. What's your conclusion?"

Robert Villard was shorter than Sommerville, although over six feet. He had a head of thick, unruly hair, prematurely graying at the sides. He nervously fingered a thin scar running from the top of his right ear down his neck, disappearing into the collar of his shirt.

"That's him. That's the little son of a bitch."

The third man, Regis Bennett, was obviously the leader of the group. Heavyset and shorter than the other two, he spoke with confidence and authority. "So, we agree that Eddie is alive and in a military hospital somewhere."

"We've been able to trace his duty assignments," Sommerville said. "Right now he's recuperating at a military rehabilitation center in Honolulu."

"Good. I don't have to remind either of you of what threat he poses to all three of us. *Time*'s made him a hero, but the charade won't stand up. No doubt our friends in the RCMP have seen this, and Washington's probably checked out his background and come up with the same information that we have. Now he's a war hero, not some punk kid on a scholarship. He can finger all of us, and even if they doubt his story they'll be obliged to check it out. If that happens, we're finished—our deals go down the drain. So do we. We've got to get him . . . and fast."

Cigarette ashes littered Sommerville's vest. The dim light overhead gleamed dully on his prematurely balding head. "I figured that would be your reaction. I've already contacted some of our business associates who are experts in eliminating such problems."

"How much?"

"$10,000, plus expenses."

"For that punk?"

"He used to be a punk. Now he's a hero—the stakes are higher. He'll be difficult to get at, and anything that happens to him will attract attention."

Bennett relented. "All right. Arrange it." He slammed his fist against the table. "I want that bastard dead. I want his police records destroyed . . . and I want everything destroyed. I want to forget that Eddie Villard ever existed."

It was Saturday and Josh was sitting in the sunroom at the end of the corridor to his ward. He threw down the copy of *Time*. It had been published earlier in the week, but had just now been delivered to Tripler; it was already well-circulated on the mainland.

The caption read: "Vietnam War Hero and Rescued General." The photo spread, however, was worse. Because Josh's face was bandaged, some enterprising reporter had ferreted out his enlistment photo. He felt ill. He guessed that it had already begun—in Detroit, in Washington, D.C. and worse, in Canada. He only hoped that tomorrow he would be safely aboard the *North Star*.

He spent the rest of the day prowling the corridors. Frankie D'Angelo noticed Josh's unease. "What's the matter? Something on your mind?"

Josh, feigning casualness, said, "Just thinking about tomorrow." He and Frankie had planned a small celebration together to mark D'Angelo's first one-day pass.

"Worried about being seen with a monster like me?"

D'Angelo had developed a self-deprecating sense of humor; hours of reconstructive surgery had left his face badly scarred.

"Yeah . . . I'm afraid you'll scare all the broads away."

The banter helped Josh, relieving the anxiety he felt.

"Shit . . . we'll knock them dead. Two to one I get laid before you do."

"You're on, dago. Put your money where your mouth is."

"I would if I could find it. After every operation it's in a different place."

Josh and Frankie left the hospital at ten o'clock the next morning. The plastic pouch containing Josh's money and precious ID were safe in the shoulder holster he had purchased earlier in the week. As they got out of the cab at Waikiki, Josh asked, "Just in case we get separated, you got enough cash to get back to Tripler?"

"This dago can take care of himself. Let's get a beer and see if there's some action on the beach . . ."

By one o'clock they had done Waikiki and opted for the Surf, one of the popular smaller bars off the beach. Frankie, to his credit, had not reacted, but Josh had been openly hostile to the waitresses at two hotel bars. They seemed repulsed by Frankie's scarred face. But something else was bothering Josh. A strange sixth sense was warning that he was being followed. He scanned the faces of the people around him, but found no one who looked suspicious. He tried to put this feeling aside. Paranoid, he decided. Par for the course.

The Surf was a friendlier place for him and Frankie. It catered to servicemen, and Josh recognized several rehab patients. Waitresses went out of their way to provide special services to the men with the worst disabilities. Disfigurements, like Frankie's, were considered a badge of honor.

Josh was standing at the bar nursing his last beer. He calculated his time: one hour to the bus depot and change to his civvies. Another thirty minutes to get to the docks and the *North Star*. There was no time to waste.

Josh did not see the man approach and was not aware of his presence until he spoke. "You're Josh Williams, right? I recognized you from your picture . . ."

It didn't ring true. Because of the bandages, no one could have recognized him from the pictures in *Time,* and he wasn't wearing ID.

"Nice to meet a genuine hero." The man's speech was slurred, as if he had been drinking too much.

"I don't really feel like talking." Throwing some money on the bar, Josh grabbed his crutches.

"Move another step, hero, and you're in trouble." The voice was threatening, crisp—coldly sober. The barrel of a small caliber weapon pressed hard against Josh's ribs, so that pain stabbed into his right side.

"We're going to take a little walk," the gunman whispered. "Past the bar and the restrooms, out into the alley. Slow but sure. You're having a good time. Now move."

As they edged slowly toward the back exit, Josh remembered that he had left his cap on the bar. He twisted on his crutches, slightly, just as they reached the exit. He saw the bartender pick it up. As they slipped out the door, Josh's only hope was that the bartender would try to catch up with him.

He hobbled only a few feet when a voice rang out behind him.

"Hey, soldier . . . forgot your hat! You don't want the Shore Patrol picking you up for being out of uniform."

Josh braced his right crutch under his arm; pivoting on his left leg, he swung his left crutch like a baseball bat. The crutch caught the gun and knocked it out of his escort's hand. Josh arched the crutch upward, slamming his assailant across the bridge of his nose. Josh could hear cartilage and bone breaking and tearing. Blood sprayed from the man's nostrils and mouth as the bone of his nose was shoved upward.

The bartender had frozen. Josh's hat fell to the pavement. "Call the cops. He was trying to rob me."

The bartender wheeled around, pushing his way back into the bar. Josh retrieved his fallen hat and scooped up the gun. Stuffing it into his pants at the waist and adjusting his uniform jacket so that it wouldn't show, he started down the alley, pumping on his crutches.

As he reached the street, he slowed his pace, melting into the crowd and the traffic moving back toward Waikiki.

At five p.m., dressed in denims and a T-shirt, he stood on the aft deck of the *North Star,* watching Oahu and Paradise disappear behind him. Below, in his cabin, was everything he owned: a few civilian clothes, over $2,000, a passport, a knife and a gun loaded with bullets that had been meant for him. He let his thoughts drift with the waves.

The throbbing of the ship's engines numbed him. He was running again.

They had cleared the Society Islands and had been at sea better than four weeks. Josh had not gone ashore at any point. He spent each day on deck, by himself, exercising. His skin was the color of burnished copper; his black hair was bleaching out at the temples.

Tonight was his coming-out party. He had borrowed some wire clippers from the captain. In his small cabin, he began to cut away at the plaster cast on his right leg. He cut carefully down the front of his leg, one to two inches at a

time, then the same on the back of his leg until he reached
the steel reinforcement at the bottom of his foot. With the
cast cut through to the foot, he grabbed both sides and
pulled them apart. The bottom gave way with a sharp crack.
His leg was freed.

It was not a pretty sight after two months in a cast, but it
had healed well. There was some muscle atrophy, and the
color of flesh was chalk white with angry red scars
crisscrossing his calf. I'll have to get used to it, he realized.

Hoisting himself up with his crutches, he hobbled over to
the mirror. The bandages covering his face, which he had
changed frequently, came off with one quick pull. He had
learned that this was the least painful way.

The swelling was almost gone. His once aquiline nose
was no more. His features looked heavier, more rugged,
mature. The lower portion of his face was covered with an
unruly heavy growth. The upper part was deeply tanned,
hairless. Where the bandages had been, the skin was dull
white and pale purple from the bruising of plastic surgery.
Time would take care of that. The doctor had been right.
The transformation was complete. If his mother still lived,
she wouldn't recognize him.

=PART 2=

11

THE HORIZON WAS at first a stark, thin white line separating sky and water. Then it brightened and enlarged. The sun painted the high clouds a burnt orange, then gold. As the sun rose further, it framed the freighter, the *San Miguel*.

Josh Williams, completing his night watch on the bridge, watched the day being born with new lights dancing across the water. The wake of the *San Miguel* glowed phosphorescently. He checked the instruments one last time and signed out on the ship's log at 0600. His replacement signed in.

The ship was directly off Fort Lauderdale beach and on course. Off to starboard, the markers leading to Port Everglades came into view. Josh closed the book he had been reading as his relief brought him a mug of coffee.

Rather than return to his berth immediately, he walked out on deck. The trade winds carried a breeze from the southeast. They also carried the rich smell of salt air. The *San Miguel* sailed just inside the gulf stream. The delineation between the ocean's green and the gulf's deep blue was startling. It looked like a river within an ocean. Fascinating. But then many things were fascinating to Josh. The sea had become his home for three years. He had sailed the world.

He smiled to himself. What was it he had said to Karen . . . the nurse at Tokyo General? "You have to take what life dishes out and make the most of it." He had

learned the true meaning of that flip remark. He would
never forget the pain of his voyage from Hawaii to Hong
Kong, where he learned to use his right leg again. He had to
teach himself to walk, and then run. He had discovered that
there had been adhesions brought on by his injuries and the
surgery. They still gave him occasional pain, but they were
a good barometer of weather changes. More than once his
injuries helped him to predict foul weather before the
meteorologists did.

He took a final sip of coffee and spilled the dregs
overboard. He went below to shower, shave and pack his
gear for shore leave.

It was nine o'clock by the time the port tug snugged the
San Miguel safely against the pier. Josh was below, packing
the last of his gear. He had enough clothes for at least three
days. He picked up the loaded .38 caliber Smith & Wesson
and the hunting knife and packed them so they would be
easily accessible. His money and passport were secured in
the waterproof pouch, carried in the now worn, sweat-
stained shoulder holster he had used for so long. Where his
money and ID were concerned, he had become a creature of
habit.

Swinging his seabag over his shoulder, he climbed the
companionway stairs to the upper deck. Longshoremen
were positioning huge cranes to begin the chore of loading a
cargo of copper cable bound for Puerto Rico. There was
more than enough time to accomplish what he had come to
Florida to do.

Toward the west, high, fat clouds were building. To the
east, rows of palm trees swayed in the gentle breeze like
supple sentinels guarding the eastern approach to the port.
A few sport fishermen in their pleasure cruisers made their
way through port and out toward the ocean cut, oblivious to
the *San Miguel* and its arrival at Port Everglades. Squat and
dirty, with its collection of quonset huts and ugly ware-
houses, the port resembled many of the smaller Pacific spots
that the *San Miguel* had visited last year. Josh had had his
last shore at one of those ports—where there were no

immigration officers, where he could move about without interference.

For the last six months, the *San Miguel* had been working U.S. ports, so he had stayed on board. But he had checked Port Everglades in advance. Security here was practically nonexistent. He had been traveling on an English passport he had bought in Hong Kong and he was certain he wouldn't have any problems.

Three years made a difference. He was lean and well-muscled, in top physical condition. Because of his monastic regimen, almost everything he earned went into his savings account. He had built a comfortable, almost secure existence.

Josh let his hair grow unfashionably long; he had a full beard and neatly trimmed moustache. Coupled with the reconstructive facial surgery performed at Tokyo General, he was sure that no one who had known him prior to his last days in Vietnam would recognize him.

After his disappearance from Hawaii, the news stories ran for days. Although the Pentagon had tried to cover up, somehow the details had leaked to the press. Headlines screamed: HERO'S DISAPPEARANCE LINKED TO SYNDICATE HIT MAN.

Josh had been right about the man in the alley. He was a hired killer paid by the Canadians. Suddenly, there were no more stories. A coverup. The military had done their job well. From his standpoint, he hoped it would stay that way forever.

He was now in Florida to see Paul MacGregor, the one man he felt he could trust, and to whom he owed an explanation.

The *San Miguel* had deadheaded from Japan to Alaska—then on to San Franciso to pick up cargo, sailing through the Panama Canal to New Orleans and finally to New York. After that they were halfway to Port Everglades before Josh saw that their cargo was marked for shipment to Boca Raton and the Caldwell-MacGregor Company. It was then that he decided to visit his old friend.

Josh had changed some of his habits over the years. Wilhelm Gotz, the *North Star*'s captain, had befriended him. Gotz had kept a small library onboard and shared it with Josh. He stocked Hardy, Rousseau, Conrad, Shakespeare, Thomas Mann, Tolstoi—a dozen other writers. Josh's appreciation of literature was born. Josh was nicknamed "the professor" by his peers, but the crew didn't use it derogatorily. They didn't dare to. Many had seen Josh's darker side. They knew that he was not a man to fool with.

The first truckload of pipe bound for Caldwell-MacGregor was ready to roll. Josh ambled down the gangway. He called to the first mate who was supervising the offloading—"See you in a couple days."

"Hoist a few for me . . ."

The mate had arranged for Josh to ride with the first truck up to Boca Raton. Josh climbed into the cab of a stake-body International that had seen better days. The driver geared down the truck and roared out of the dockyards. U.S. 1 in Ft. Lauderdale was lined with small hotels, a few restaurants and lots of bars. They passed through the tunnel under the New River. A few large buildings and hotels comprising downtown Fort Lauderdale appeared to Josh's left.

The trip to Boca Raton only took thirty minutes. Josh took in the Florida countryside. Traffic was almost nonexistent once they were beyond Pompano Beach. Just past Camino Real, the driver pointed out the Boca Raton Club. "Big bucks there." And then, pointing just beyond the club, "Over there's Caldwell-MacGregor."

Josh clambered out of the cab. "Thanks, pal. See you around."

Seabag slung over his shoulder, he strode across the lawn to the double doors of an unimposing two-story building. Over the glass doors was the simple, gold-lettered sign: CALDWELL-MACGREGOR, INC. ESTABLISHED 1918.

He pulled open the double entrance doors and stepped into whispered air-conditioning—a large, austerely furnished reception area. Two ceiling fans whirred on long steel poles from a high domed ceiling.

"Young man, the delivery area and employment office are at the *rear* of the building." An old-fashioned plug switchboard was at the receptionist's right elbow, and a headset adorned dyed blond hair. She was thin and unattractive. He approached her slowly, enjoying her discomfort. His attire—washed out jeans, blue, short-sleeved work shirt and sneakers—was fine for a seaman, but combined with his long hair and full beard, not at all appropriate for a business call. He lowered his bag to the floor at the front of her desk. She sat, plug held in her hand, poised as if it were some sort of weapon. Warily she eyed the terrible apparition standing before her. Josh, sensing the game had gone far enough, smiled as winningly as he knew how.

"Sorry to bother you, ma'am. I'm here to see Mr. MacGregor."

"Mr. Paul MacGregor?" Her questioning voice filled with disbelief.

"Yes, ma'am . . . if you'd just see that he gets this envelope, I'd appreciate it."

She eyed the wrinkled envelope as if it were poison.

"I suppose you're going to tell me that Mr. MacGregor is a personal friend."

Josh ignored the sarcasm. "I'm sure he'll see me."

She acquiesced grudgingly. "Take a seat over there." She indicated the chair farthest from her desk. "I'll call his secretary."

Josh had been seated only a few minutes when a door at the rear of the room opened. A striking woman stepped into the reception area. Her tailored clothes fit her like a fashion model; dark rimmed glasses rode over her high cheekbones in a face sculpted like a Dresden figurine. Her hair was pulled back tight against her head and highlighted by silver streaks. He judged her to be in her mid-forties, but with a less severe hairstyle she could have passed easily for thirty-five.

She approached Josh, smiling, hand extended.

"I'm Hallie Norton, Mr. MacGregor's secretary. You seem to have given our receptionist quite a start. You don't look all that bad to me." She exuded warmth, yet was businesslike. He felt at ease with her.

"I should apologize." His hands moved from his ragged beard down to his clothes. "Can't blame your receptionist—I hardly look the type to be calling on the owner of a company."

"She'll get over it. May I ask what you wish to see Mr. MacGregor about, Mr. . . . uh . . . ?"

Josh, constantly on guard, didn't offer his name. "It's rather personal, Miss Norton. I met the general in Vietnam. If you'd give him the envelope, I won't take up much of his time."

At the mention of Vietnam, her attitude changed. She took the envelope. Her tone was solicitous. "Why don't you make yourself comfortable? I'll be back in a moment."

Josh dropped into the easy chair; the receptionist eyed him uneasily. He picked up a copy of *Newsweek* and began thumbing through it. He didn't get past the first story before Hallie Norton returned.

"Come with me. Mr. MacGregor is anxious to see you," she said loudly.

Josh noticed the beginning of a grin which Hallie Norton suppressed. He sensed a kindred spirit.

She led him by a stairwell toward a door marked "Utility" that appeared little used. It was locked, and she inserted her key, opening it quickly. To Josh's surprise he found himself in a small elevator. Anticipating his question, Hallie Norton smiled. "It's MacGregor's escape hatch. I'm really happy to meet you, Josh Williams! I've heard so much about you. We owe you a lot."

Josh grinned. "I owe *him*, too."

The elevator ground to a halt and when the door opened, MacGregor grabbed Josh's arm, jerking him out of the cage, embracing him in a bear hug that literally forced the wind out of him.

"So you finally decided to come see me!" Mac's welcome was warm and genuine. "Let me look at you!" Standing back to get a better view, Mac squinted, frowned, first looking at Josh, then at a framed picture hanging over a monstrous desk cluttered with papers. Josh followed Mac's gaze to the picture. It was the *Time* story. It was a poignant moment, seeing Karen in the picture. He had thought of her often in these last few years.

Then he realized the reason for Mac's controlled confusion. He touched his face. "Of course you don't recognize me. My face got kind of scrambled—remember?"

Mac nodded. "I just forgot how extensive the damage was. But you look fit. How's the leg?"

"I limp a little when it rains, but everything else is better than ever."

Hallie spoke. "If I can butt in, it looks to me as though the surgeons did an amazing job. Without the beard he'd be the closest thing to Steve McQueen."

"Women," Mac said warmly, "can't help thinking about how to improve men. I think our friend could use some chow in place of the flattery. Hallie, cancel everything for the next two hours. This is an occasion—a very special occasion."

12

MAC AND JOSH sat at a small, elegant antique table, finishing their lunch—simple conch chowder and hearty, rare roast beef sandwiches. Throughout the meal Mac had been offering his guest a running commentary on the projects and holdings of the company, carefully avoiding any mention of Vietnam.

Josh was fascinated by what he heard, and amazed at the difference in the man he had last known as Colonel MacGregor. Here was someone in control not only of his own destiny, but the destiny of hundreds who worked for him; he touched the lives of thousands who would buy homes and live in communities built by his company.

"Just listen to me!" Mac said at last. "Hallie claims that once I get going it takes a court order to shut me up."

"But you're not boring me," Josh said, smiling. "Compared to this, everything I've done in my life seems inconsequential."

"Nonsense. Remember what I was doing when we met? I was a fifty-two-year-old man playing at war. In fact, some of the things you said to me back there in Nam made me realize just how important this is. So . . . tell me about you."

Hallie Norton returned. "Two hours are almost up. What about your schedule?"

"Cancel everything for the rest of the afternoon. We'll fit

it in during the week. I'll make the dinner at six and the zoning meeting later." Mac, pleased with himself, turned to Josh. "We've got all the time we need."

He leaned back in his chair, propping his feet, careful not to knock over the piles of paper stacked on his desk. He gestured Josh to a chair at the front of his desk.

Josh stared at the floor for a moment. "I don't know where to begin." He looked up at Mac. "I didn't think it would be this hard to tell."

Mac smiled. "I've got a pretty good handle on you from Vietnam to Hawaii. Before and after . . . nothing. Tell me what happened in Hawaii."

Two hours later, Josh finished. He covered it all: the rape-murder in Canada, what happened to his woman in Lang Vei—then Hawaii. Mac had known about the hired killer. He also seemed fascinated by the three years at sea following his escape on the *North Star*.

"That's quite a story, my boy. You've packed in a lot of living. What do you plan to do now?"

"My ship sails the day after tomorrow. Until something better turns up, I'll stick to the sea."

"You can't do that forever." MacGregor's tone grew serious. "You've got to stop running, Josh. Got to make a life for yourself. Up to now, because of a crime you didn't commit, you've been always looking over your shoulder. I've got a couple of ideas." He hesitated, looking at Josh squarely. "Interested?"

"I might be. Sure, I am."

"First, do you want to go back to Canada?"

"No, it's not worth it."

"All right. Let's think this through. The Army," he mused. "They were pretty pissed off over their AWOL hero. But you'd have received a medical discharge. Chances are, they're not really interested in you anymore. If they are, I can pull a few strings. But that stuff about the hired killer, that bothers me. Your Canadian friends were awfully anxious to have you eliminated. Maybe the police back there aren't as convinced about your guilt as you think."

Mac leaned forward. "I've got a proposition for you. As I said, sooner or later you're going to have to settle down. You're intelligent and, from what you've told me and what I know about you, you're certainly resourceful. What about working for me? I'll give you a year out in the field working on our projects. If you like it, we'll talk about bringing you inside . . . maybe as my assistant."

Josh mulled over the proposition. "What if this thing about my past life blows up again? It could cost you, especially now that you know all the details."

"You forget that I was with the OSS during the war. I'm more devious than you know, and I've got an idea that may take care of your problems once and for all. What do you say? Give me a week to work it out. If I can't, you can rejoin your ship at its next port of call."

Josh shrugged. "What the hell. I need a vacation anyway."

Mac punched the intercom button. Hallie entered his office within seconds.

"Hallie, take Josh over to the Boca Cabana and check him in under my name. I don't want any record of him there at all."

He turned to Josh. "The beach isn't crowded this time of year. Keep to yourself as much as possible. Don't make any contact with the people at the hotel. Hallie will make sure you have enough money and some decent new clothes. So for now . . . get the hell out of here."

Hallie was gone only an hour. As she walked into the office, MacGregor was just hanging up the phone.

"Well, what do you think of our hero?"

"Very impressive. But he does need a haircut and a shave."

"Well, you're nominated."

"For what?"

"Temporary motherhood. I'd like you to check on him

regularly, make sure he's comfortable. Let me know if he seems upset for any reason, any change in his attitude." Mac proffered a small cassette. "I want you to transcribe this tape. Just pick out the pertinent stuff, then destroy the cassette. Send a copy of the transcript to Sam Goldman. I've already discussed this with him and he knows what to do when he gets it. Make a file on Josh and put it in my personal safe. Only three people will know about it—you, me and Sam Goldman." Mac paused, eyes shining, excitedly.

"I feel good about this, Hallie. Maybe I can give him the life he deserves . . ."

"I have a funny feeling . . ."

"About what?"

"I know you, Paul. There's always a reason . . . an ulterior motive. Or does my so-called woman's intuition betray me?"

Mac grinned sheepishly. "You're right . . . you know me too well."

The four days Josh had been on the beach was the longest time he had been away from the ship since Hawaii. His hotel was located south of the inlet leading to the ocean from Boca Raton. The city had received its name from early Spanish explorers who, because of its shape, named the inlet "the Rat's Mouth." It hardly seemed an appropriate name for such an idyllic place. Although there were a few apartments near the line separating Boca from Deerfield Beach, there were stretches of beach where it was wild and unspoiled. Josh shared them mostly with the sea birds. Even the road that was some two hundred yards away was obscured by palmetto scrub and sand dunes. Each day he walked north from the hotel to the inlet and then south to the pier in Deerfield. Walking the sand was the best exercise possible for his leg; despite the doctor's grim forecast, he felt that he had recovered almost full use of the badly scarred limb. Each day he reveled in sprinting the last quarter mile into Deerfield. The leg did not betray him, and as a reward he treated himself to a couple of frosty mugs of beer at a rustic little tavern. Josh had discovered from two consecutive soakings that it rained every afternoon—you could practically set your watch by it. Usually the downpour lasted just long enough for him to drink two draft beers. He liked the routine. His appearance, following a shave and hairstyling prescribed by Hallie Norton, had been altered, and his daily exposure to the sun had tanned his body and his face where his beard had been.

His new wardrobe—another one of Hallie's touches—was icing on the cake. She had been wonderful. They had decided somewhere in the midst of their shopping spree, and without discussing it with one another, that her role was to be that of the rich widow and his the kept man. They enjoyed the discomfort and consternation of a succession of salespeople.

He checked the sky; today would be no exception to the predictable rain. But he had delayed too long watching a large yacht negotiate the inlet cut. He was about halfway through his final sprint when he felt the first heavy drops. He burst into a dead run, head down, trying to make the overhang of the bar's roofed entrance before it really poured. He looked up just before he collided with a raincoat-covered figure coming from the opposite direction. He bounced against the wall, temporarily off balance. He grabbed backwards, his fingers catching the rough brick wall and steadied himself. The person he had run into had been less fortunate and sprawled at Josh's feet in front of the door.

He extended his arm. "Here, let me help you. I'm sorry . . ." He stopped. He was looking into the greenest eyes he had ever seen.

"You stupid son of a bitch! You schmuck! Why don't you watch where you are going!" She refused his hand, struggling angrily to her feet, shaking the water off her coat. She was as furious as she was beautiful.

"Miss, if you're going to cuss me out, why don't you do it inside where it's dry?"

It had begun to pour in earnest. Josh fought to suppress a grin as he opened the door to the bar. "Here," he said, handing her a towel he had wrapped around his neck. "Dry off. What'll you have?"

"A draft," she answered, still miffed—but her voice carried a less strident tone.

The bartender drew two Michelobs and Josh carried them to the table where she sat drying herself with the towel. He studied her as she stood at the bar and as he approached the table. She *was* beautiful. A strawberry blonde, a little over five feet and no more than a hundred and ten pounds. She appeared almost fragile.

"I'm sorry about my outburst," she said. "It's just a damned embarrassing way to meet someone—falling on your ass that way. Not very ladylike. She looked at him, smiling for the first time. "Truce?" she asked, hand extended. Her grip was surprisingly strong; her hand, he noticed, was roughly calloused, contradicting his initial impression of fragility. She answered the question that he wouldn't ask.

"I'm a gymnast," she said. "Actually more an instructor now than active participant. I'm also into judo. The two don't leave much room for soft hands. And my name is Beth Sheldon."

"Josh Williams," he responded, ignoring MacGregor's admonition. With that out of the way, he raised his glass. "To no more pratfalls in the rain." He took a long pull on the ice-cold beer.

"And you, Josh, what do you do for a living? No, let me guess. Something crazy. You're young and handsome. You obviously spend your days on the beach. I've got it," she said, laughing. "You're a gigolo!"

Josh sputtered. He was thinking of the roles that he and Hallie had played just a few days before.

"Here . . ." She laughed at his consternation. "Dry yourself off. We're even. Now, what do you really do . . . I mean besides pick up . . . and I mean literally pick up broads on the beach?"

He spoke about the sea and she about her life. She was an Army brat—more of a tomboy with her bent for sports than either of her parents had wanted. Josh looked out the window—the sun was blazing again. "Rain's stopped," he said. "Can I walk you back?"

"Hell . . . can't you do better than that?"

He was nonplussed. "What do you mean?"

"First you knock me on my ass. You pick me up, buy me a couple of beers—then you drop me like a hot potato! I must be losing it." She looked at him almost coyly. "Dinner, idiot! If you think I'm going to let the only decent thing in pants I've seen all week get away from me that easily, you're crazy. I've got a car. I'll pick you up at your hotel about seven, and we'll do Palm Beach."

A few minutes before seven o'clock he stood waiting in front of the hotel. He was grateful to Hallie. He wore tan slacks, a pale blue shirt and a madras jacket. He had tried a tie, but it seemed some things would take a little longer to get used to again.

She pulled up on time in a bright red Mustang convertible, top down. Her blond hair cascaded shoulder length. Her white slacks were worn tightly enough to reveal her athletic figure. A green halter top complemented her eyes, making them an even more vivid green. A strand of pearls rode the gentle swell of her breasts.

"Hey," she said, taunting him. "Close your mouth and get in . . . you clean up pretty good yourself."

By twelve o'clock they had eaten at La Petite Marmite—and had a drink afterwards at the Taboo on Worth Avenue. They had explored the catacomb of alleys that lined both sides of that famous street.

Beth pulled the Mustang to a stop on a deserted section of beach, just south of Lake Worth. "I'd like to walk." She reached in the back seat for a large beach towel. "Just in case you get tired."

The air was filled with the scent of night-blooming

jasmine. A waning moon cast a pale glow over the ocean.
The waves broke gently on the shore, creating an iridescent
border between the sand and the sea. He looked at her
standing in the moonlight, her hair billowing—the outline
of her breasts and her nipples taut in the soft ocean breeze.
He realized then that he wanted her badly.

He dreaded it. His only experience with women since his
years with the Montagnards had been occasional encounters
with bar girls and brothel whores during brief periods of
shore leave. Those brief liaisons left him feeling empty.
They lacked meaning. And here he was with a woman
unlike any he had ever experienced—yet, he sensed, one
who was far more worldly than he.

Beth, however brash and outspoken, had read Josh's
reluctance and gathered more from what he hadn't said that
there was in him a certain innocence . . . a fear. If the
barriers were to fall between them, she realized, it was up to
her. Her arms were around his neck, her mouth on his.
Slowly she moved tightly against him.

She spread the towel. Loosening her belt, she slid her
pants down, kicking them away. She pulled him down
beside her, whispering softly in his ear, "I'll do the rest."

They lay locked together for a long time. Beth finally
lifted her body off of him; their separation made a soft
sucking sound. She turned and ran toward the ocean.

They were inseparable for the next three days—swimming, eating, dancing and making love. And then it was
over. Beth's time was up.

They stood on the beach across from the bar in Deerfield
where they had met. Her car, parked in the street, was
already packed for the trip back north.

She stood on her tiptoes, kissing him warmly. "Josh . . .
I'll never forget you. I've never had anything like the last
three days."

"Beth," he said sadly, "you make it sound as if we'll
never see each other again."

She hesitated, biting her lip. "I'm afraid we won't, Josh. I've been wanting to tell you . . . but I couldn't. But I've come to really care about you, and you deserve the truth. I'm married. My husband's in the Army. We haven't been getting along. We've been thinking about a divorce. He gets his discharge in a few months and he wants to move to California. He thinks that if we make a new start our marriage will last. I came to Florida to get away from it for a while. Maybe subconsciously I wanted to have an affair . . . a fling, if you like. But then I met you. I realize that if I don't leave now, I probably never will. Josh, please don't think badly of me. I owe it to my husband to give it another try."

Josh looked down at her. She had never been more appealing or more vulnerable. More than anything, he realized, she needed his approval and his understanding. His feelings weren't important.

"Beth, don't worry, I do understand. I've spent the last eight years of my life running away from reality. And I haven't learned to face it yet. It comes hard." He reached out, hands cupping her face. "I'll never forget you either. Goodbye and good luck."

He turned and began walking down the beach, not trusting himself to look back. When he opened the door to his room, the telephone was ringing.

"The boss would like to see you. How soon can you be packed and ready to go?"

"Give me about a half hour, Hallie. I'll meet you in front of the hotel."

When she drove up thirty minutes later, Josh was waiting for her. "What's up?" he asked. He got into the car and threw his gear in the back seat.

"Even if I knew, Mr. MacGregor would kill me if I told you. Just be patient. Let him tell you in his own way."

They entered through the back entrance and took the private elevator to the second floor. "Make yourself comfortable," Hallie said.

MacGregor stormed into the room, exuding his usual energy and confidence. Josh, whose spirits had been sagging since he left Beth Sheldon just an hour before, felt himself reviving. Mac set a large manila folder on his desk. For the next few moments he was absorbed in the ritual of lighting a six-inch Havana.

"Have a good stay on the beach?" He winked knowingly. "This climate does something to people," he said around his cigar. "Especially to short-timers. Lowers the barriers fast. Been bitten by the bug more than once myself. But a good woman is the best tonic in the world . . ."

He flipped the file folder open. His mood changed completely.

"Caldwell-MacGregor," he said, "is a big, well-respected business. But we operate in a small town. We can't afford to have anything happen that would jeopardize our reputation. I hope you understand. Under the circumstances, it was necessary for me to do some digging."

Josh was subconsciously girding himself for the inevitable. He opened his mouth to protest, but MacGregor cut him off.

"Hear me out. When you left my office, I contacted a friend of mine who was with me in the OSS in Europe. He's still active in the worldwide intelligence community. His name is Sam Goldman. I'll tell you about him some other time. Anyway, his people went over your story. First, the file on the murder case in Canada is still active. Oddly, however, all the evidence in the police files disappeared a few years ago. The explanation was that it was misplaced during microfilming. You and I know it's the work of your friends . . . pretty powerful fellows.

"One of Goldman's people was able to contact the detective who originally investigated the case—he's retired now—under the guise of a newspaperman interested in the case and checking on further theories, if any, on suspects. He came away with a curious impression. You're still wanted for questioning, but the detective has always had doubts as to your involvement. He believes that you were set up, but he couldn't prove it without your testimony . . . and you were gone.

"Then we have the military. Your record there was excellent. Of course, it reflects that you went AWOL. But some shrink helped you out there—he documented a file with an explanation that they suspected some psychological disorders as a result of your wounds. As a result, they actually blame themselves for your disappearance."

Mac continued. "Improper diagnosis. No therapy. The guy you killed in Hawaii has a police record a mile long. He was a fairly big-time hit man. The case is closed. What we know is that you've got no problems with the authorities, military or civilian. And anyone who knew you before Vietnam wouldn't even recognize you now."

"What are you driving at?" Josh asked.

"It's time for a fresh start. I can give that to you . . . heading in the right direction, for a change. Satchel Paige said it best: 'Don't keep looking over your shoulder, something might be gaining on you.' What I'm saying is you don't have to look back anymore. For a change, you can start looking ahead."

Mac paused a moment, letting his advice sink in.

"Now just sit back and listen. The first day you were here you told me a story . . . one that included a lot of tragedy. Somehow I think tragedy is just another one of God's tools to make us better people, to make us realize how vulnerable we are. No one, rich or poor, is immune. But I'm convinced that there's always a reason. While it seems impossible at the time, if you're patient, the reason eventually shows up."

For a moment, Mac stared up at the ceiling.

"Very few people remember that I had a sister . . . Laura. She ran away from so many private schools that my mother lost count. She wasn't suited to the Caldwell-MacGregor image. As a teenager, there were juvenile pranks. As an adult, affairs—pregnancy—abortion—annulment. She drove my mother half-crazy. She ran off with an oilman from Texas . . . a poor roughneck. They traveled from drill site to drill site. But that's what she wanted. They were married and she got pregnant. Laura had always stayed in touch with me and really wanted to make peace with Mother, who by then had disowned her. I arranged a meeting. They thought they met by accident. I'll never forget Mother coming home and calling it divine intervention. Owen, Laura's baby, was born in April of 1947. No one else in the family knew anything about her marriage, much less about the baby. Then . . . they were on their way to Florida by car. There was a grade crossing accident. Laura, her husband and little Owen were killed. My mother never got over it. It was as if someone had sucked all the life out of her." His voice was strained by emotion. "She died not long after that." Mac stopped clearing his throat, but obviously the hurt was still there.

"The reason I told you that story is because in some oblique way, out of Laura's tragedy there may emerge a solution to your problems. Look at this."

Mac pushed the folder across the desk to Josh, who picked it up and leafed through the papers inside. It contained a birth certificate for Owen Caldwell Hunter, born Amarillo, Texas, April 10, 1947; a Social Security card; credit card applications; school records; a complete identity; and a check for $5,000 made out to Owen C. Hunter and signed by Paul MacGregor.

"I pulled some pretty long strings in Washington for all this. Cashed in some markers."

"I don't know what to say . . ." Josh struggled, harder than he would have believed possible, to express himself. "This is the first time anyone has ever believed in me."

"Before you take on your new identity, if you do, I should explain my motives for all this. I want to repay you for what you did in Vietnam, but there's something else. I have a feeling about you. I always follow my instincts. My gut tells me that you can be a valuable asset to me and this company. With the right start, it'll work out. Let's just call this an investment in the future . . . yours and mine."

"I'd be a damn fool not to accept, Mac. You and Hallie have been the closest I've ever had to family."

A grin split Mac's face from ear to ear. "Good." He stabbed at the button on the intercom. "Hallie," he barked, "get in here." He added, "Please."

Hallie entered, bottle of champagne in hand.

Mac popped the cork. He lifted his glass, with Josh and Hallie following suit. "To Owen Caldwell Hunter, my long lost nephew, and to his future." Glasses clinked and champagne was sipped.

For Josh, there was finally a light at the end of the tunnel.

It was Monday, and Owen Hunter, aka Josh Williams, born Edward Villard, was thinking back to the scene in Mac's office. They'd had their champagne, but Mac didn't waste time in getting back to business.

Setting his champagne aside, he said, "I've got a job for you. We're having a problem with one of our subcontractors." With that, Mac launched into a half hour overview on how the company operated.

Caldwell-MacGregor, with the exception of its land sales operations, subcontracted all of the other functions. These included dredging land, draining it where it was swampy, and the installation of utilities, waste treatment systems, roads and sidewalks, all of which had to be in place before the land could be sold. One of the areas causing the greatest amount of concern was cost overruns by the Matson Company, which was involved in sewer installation and waste treatment systems. The company was run by Ollie Matson, a lifetime family friend.

Owen Hunter was to start to work on Monday as a laborer with Matson.

"Keep in touch with me on a regular basis through Hallie. Keep your eyes open. Anything that looks out of order, make a note of it. Hallie and I rented an apartment for you. She has the keys. If you need anything, she'll help you."

Mac rose, extending his hand, and they shook.

"Well, Owen . . . a new beginning. I want it to work."

"So do I," responded the newborn Owen Hunter. "I'll try not to let you down."

13

IF JOSH WILLIAMS harbored any concerns about preferential treatment as Owen Hunter, nephew of Paul MacGregor, they were dispelled early Monday morning immediately after arriving at the Matson site.

Matson snorted, looking at him through bloodshot, rheumy eyes.

"Start down there." He pointed to a deep trench. "That's what separates the men from the boys."

Matson was a huge, florid-faced man, spreading to paunch in middle age. His arms were bearlike, his hands large as hams. But he was still a physically powerful man.

Owen was surprised to see a bottle of Old Granddad standing conspicuously on a rusted and dented file cabinet next to Matson's desk in the construction shack. Matson made no effort to disguise his drinking throughout the day. The more he drank, the harder he drove the men. Owen didn't escape Matson's slurred tongue for very long.

"Boys," he addressed the dragline crew, "this here's Owen Hunter, Mr. MacGregor's nephew." He continued, sarcastically, "I want you to show him how we lay this pipe . . . but don't be too hard on him." Cynical laughter erupted from the assembled crew.

Owen fought to control his anger. He would have to prove himself.

He started "in the hole," as the crew referred to it, laying

drainage pipe in airless trenches excavated by draglines. He
was to guide pipe lowered by crane to the workmen
connecting it. The temperature often reached well over a
hundred degrees; there was high ground water and constant
cave-ins. It was dangerous, grimy and strenuous work. Heat
prostration was common among the men. The mosquitoes
were vicious, and occasionally the dragline bit into a shovel
full of moccasins. The snakes were one thing universally
feared.

It was damned uncomfortable, but next to Nam, Owen
thought, it was heaven. No maiming mines. No Viet Cong.
Here, at five p.m., he merely rode the crane up, showered
and went out for a cold beer. He worked hard, doing more
than his share, and he was quickly accepted by the crew. He
found that, almost to a man, they despised Matson and his
methods.

He made his identity transition rapidly. Josh Williams
was becoming a memory. He was Owen Hunter.

As the days passed into weeks, and then became his first
month, Matson sensed that the men respected him; he put
Hunter in charge when he left the site, which, Hunter noted,
was frequently. The men viewed Hunter as a natural leader.
He mastered each phase, including the handling of every
piece of heavy equipment. If someone needed a break,
Hunter filled in. If there was a cave-in, Hunter was the first
in the hole.

Hunter also started working inventory. It was during the
unloading and inventorying of new supplies that he first
noted irregularities. Knowing the marine and stevedoring
business as he did, he put the shortages down as breakage at
that end. But the problem persisted and nagged at him . . .

His last act as Josh Williams was to close his bank
account in New York City that had been set up by his friend,
Captain Wilhelm Gotz. The money—now over $35,000—
rested in an account in Florida along with the $5,000 Mac
had given him. His books, sent to him in Ft. Lauderdale,
were now placed neatly on shelving Owen himself had built
for his apartment. It was a decent life—one he had never

expected and one, he swore, that nothing was going to overturn.

He occasionally stopped in a small bar in Deerfield for a beer. But as a matter of habit, he kept to himself. Hallie called him now and then to inquire after him.

In his months with Matson, he acquired a working knowledge of what it took to get raw land ready for sale. Although these were far from the glamorous aspects of the business, they were its staples—integral parts of the success of any company. It was impossible for any company to succeed without the land being sculptured properly. The more he learned, the more Hunter wanted to know.

It was this immersion in the business and the nagging concern over the ongoing inventory shortages that triggered his first suspicion that something was wrong with Matson's operation. He found that while a crew of twenty-eight to thirty men punched in and out each day, there were rarely more than fourteen or fifteen on the job. At first he believed that there might be another project on the property where these additional men worked; but this was dispelled after an inquiry to Hallie.

Another thing that bothered him was that the construction schedule posted in the shed called for much heavier equipment than was in evidence; each time a new load of pipe and tile was delivered and stockpiled, it disappeared more rapidly than it was going into the ground.

Through some of the material he was reading, Hunter got his first insight into what was happening. Matson, as did all other subcontractors of Caldwell-MacGregor, worked on a cost-plus basis. The company reimbursed Matson for labor costs, paid for equipment rental and raw materials ordered by him, then paid him a specified percentage over and above this as his profit. Hunter began to realize that he might be treading on dangerous ground. Matson's relationship with MacGregor went back a lifetime. He, Hunter, was the newcomer. He had a gut feeling, however, and his instincts drove him ahead.

He knew no one he could trust. He was on his own. He

began working day and night, marking pipe, taking pictures, following the men and the cars. It was a painstaking and dangerous business. The more he learned, the more he realized the scope of what was going on, and the amount of money involved.

One morning he approached Hallie Norton at the offices of Caldwell-MacGregor, two files tucked under his arm. His face was deeply tanned, his body slimmed and hardened by months of hard physical labor. His hands were calloused. He wore gray slacks, blue pinstripe shirt and navy blue flannel blazer.

"Hi, Hallie. Is he in?"

Hallie was surprised to see him. "What's on your mind? That's hardly a Matson outfit. Got the day off?"

"Matson thinks I'm sick. I need to see Mac. It won't wait."

Hallie checked Mac's appointment book. "His schedule's crammed. He's a real mean man when it comes to interruptions. Are you sure you want to take the chance?"

"Yes, Hallie."

"Okay, but I warned you."

Hallie ushered Owen into Mac's office. Mac glared at them, irritated. What I've got to say, Owen realized, isn't going to make him any happier.

"In the future, young man," Mac said gruffly, "I'd appreciate it if you'd extend me the same courtesy as the president of my bank. In other words, make a goddam appointment." Mac checked his watch. "You've got ten minutes."

Owen laid the two files on Mac's desk. "Your subcontract with Matson is on a cost-plus basis. On this basis, Caldwell-MacGregor is getting screwed. He's phonying up contracts and payrolls. He's robbing you blind."

Mac leaped out of his chair, bellowing at Hunter. "You better have some goddam good proof of this!" Veins protruded angrily from his forehead. "My relationship with Matson goes back a long way."

"All the facts are here." Owen pointed to the file.

"Let's have them!" Mac paced back and forth like a caged tiger. He was trying to control his temper. He continued to pace as Owen ticked off the facts.

"First, *manpower*. An average of twenty-eight people per day punch in and out at the job site. An average of fourteen people actually work at the site. The rest work at another site, not Caldwell-MacGregor, in North Palm Beach.

"*Equipment*. Only sixty percent of the equipment that you've been paying for has actually turned any Caldwell-MacGregor ground. The rest of it is at the same North Palm Beach site.

"*Materials*. Each night for a week, following every delivery from Port Everglades, materials of every description are pulled out of your yards—on equipment that you are renting—then delivered, again, to the North Palm Beach site.

"I took photographs." He handed them to Mac. "Check the markings on the pipe and the dates in the pictures. Do you want me to go on?"

Mac nodded.

"I've had someone whom I consider damned competent go over these figures, without identifying names. His conservative estimate is that Matson has stolen almost a quarter of a million dollars in materials, equipment and man hours. On top of that, Matson's been hammering you an additional fifteen percent for the mark-up portion of the contract. God knows how long this has been going on."

MacGregor clenched and unclenched his fists. "How in the hell could he get away with it?"

"Very simple. Someone here is helping him . . . has been for a long time."

"Jesus!" Mac was incredulous. "Who?" For the first time he spoke quietly.

"Alex Wykoff, your senior accountant."

Now Mac roared. "I don't believe it!"

"Check it out. Wykoff has a problem. He likes the dogs. I made two trips to the track with him and he dropped a bundle each time. Big bucks, not small change—$1,000 a crack. That's hardly a normal past-time for an accountant. Plus, he's into the bookies.''

"Jesus Christ . . . a quarter of a million dollars in three months? Son of a bitch!"

MacGregor galvanized into action. He wrenched the intercom switch, barking into it, "Hallie, cancel my schedule for the rest of the day. Get Ollie Matson. I want him here ON THE DOUBLE! . . ." He paused. "On second thought, send two of the biggest and meanest security guards we've got to get Matson. *Now*."

He turned on Hunter. "You stay put. You call a man a thief, you've got to do it face to face."

He hit the intercom again. "Get Leo Birch on the phone. Tell him I want him here within the hour. Don't take no for an answer—tell him I'm calling in a marker. I don't care if he's screwing Raquel Welch, I want him here. If he doesn't show, it's his neck."

They both sat, unspeaking. Mac's dark rage was too thick to penetrate.

Matson was manhandled, practically thrown into Mac's office by two guards—both Matson's size, but younger.

Matson roared, "You pompous old son-of-a-bitch! Who the hell you think you are sending these goons to pull me off the job?"

Matson's face darkened as he spied Hunter. It was obvious from his rumpled appearance that he had put up a fight. His shirttails hung half out of his pants and one of his shirt sleeves was torn. He was sweating heavily. Hunter tensed, relishing the thought of repaying Matson for five months of abuse.

Mac was relatively calm, which surprised Hunter, but his voice was steely with anger. "Sit down and keep your mouth shut."

Matson eyed Hunter coldly, disdain written all over his face.

"What the fuck is going on? He calls in sick, and there he stands dressed up like a deacon's dick. Mac, you and I have been friends a long time . . ."

Mac spoke, his voice controlled now. "Friends don't steal from each other. How long, Ollie? Six months? A year?"

Matson's mouth fell open.

"Oh, we'll find out. We'll do a complete audit covering the term of your contract with my company. Quite a scam, Ollie. Overcharge for my labor. Rent equipment at my expense and use it somewhere else on one of your projects. Steal materials, then add fifteen percent on top of that. It only cost you some nickels and dimes to pay off one of my staff to cover up for you." He leaned down to Matson, eyes only inches away from him. "It will make me very happy to see you do some hard time in Raiford. You know Raiford, don't you, Ollie? That's where they lay pipe . . . up your ass."

Matson reacted out of reflex, not thinking. "How the hell . . . who told you?"

Then the veins in his head twitched as he wheeled on Hunter. "You fucking little asskisser. I knew you were trouble first time I laid eyes on you." Matson's usually florid face was even a deeper red. "I'll stomp your ass into the ground! Working for me and all the time looking to bust my balls!"

He jumped out of his chair. "I'll kill you . . ."

"It's been tried before," Hunter replied quietly.

"Sit down, Matson," Mac shouted, "and shut up!"

Matson ignored MacGregor, totally immersed in his hatred of Hunter. They squared off like animals ready to battle over their domain. But Matson was surprised—where he expected fear, there was none. Rather, he felt fear; he sensed danger and was chilled. Finally he slumped back into his chair, a wornout rhino, confused, defeated . . . drained.

Mac pulled out a tape recorder, ejected the small cassette and laid it on the desk top—a silent witness to what had just transpired. He punched the intercom. Hallie entered silently. Mac handed her the file and the cassette. "I'll need a transcript of this tape. Where's Leo Birch?"

"On his way, Mr. MacGregor."

MacGregor turned his attention again to Matson. "You have a choice, Ollie. Restitution or criminal charges. We have enough here for the judge to lock you up and throw away the key."

Matson seemed to shrink. With downcast eyes, he said, "How can I pay you back? I got no money. All my cash is tied up in that property."

Mac paced, stopping at Matson's chair. "What's it worth right now?"

Matson's brows furrowed deeply. He was still sweating, even though the office was comfortably air-conditioned. Haltingly, he said, "The property is nearly two hundred acres . . . at about five thousand dollars per acre . . . plus improvements . . ." His voice dropped, becoming almost inaudible.

"For Christ's sake, Matson, speak up!"

"I said," he repeated, loudly, "plus improvements of about $750,000—about a million-five to a million-seven, I estimate."

MacGregor's reaction was a low whistle. "That might just do the trick. Let's call it a firm million-five." He was enjoying himself, watching Matson squirm.

Hunter sat quietly. He was a spectator, observing a contest of motives and wills. It was different from what he had expected. Matson was a thief who fully expected police and criminal charges—legal retribution. The encounter, however, had taken on an air of a business meeting. Two men, the victim and the thief, were discussing a proposed commercial transaction. MacGregor was conducting the meeting with the gusto of a maestro holding a baton.

The intercom lit up. It was Hallie Norton. "Mr. Birch is here."

Nothing anyone could have told Hunter would have prepared him for Leopold Quinn Birch III. Birch skipped into the room, right hand extended, pumping Mac's hand firmly, left arm gripping him in a hug. "Paul, how are you?

I came as quickly as I could. Hallie said you had a problem."

Birch, to Hunter, seemed a cross between a Dickens character and a fashion model from *Gentleman's Quarterly*. His dark blue pinstripe suit was accented by a light blue shirt and a regimental striped tie. A scarlet handkerchief puffed in a perfect cascade from the breast pocket of his jacket. A gold watch fob draped his vest pocket. Black Gucci shoes shone to perfection.

"Leo, do you remember Ollie Matson?"

Birch turned to the still perspiring Ollie. "The Magnificent Mud Mover. Don't get up on my account, Ollie. Remember, we agreed to dispense with any cordiality a long time ago." Birch's voice oozed scorn.

"Our friend here has just admitted that his firm has been involved in some pretty substantial cost overruns. Perhaps that's the best way, for the moment, to describe Ollie's actions. By the way, you haven't met Owen Hunter."

Hunter and Birch shook hands. Hunter was impressed by the strength of Birch's grip.

"Owen is responsible for uncovering Mr. Matson's secret activities." Mac handed Birch the file that Hunter had prepared. "Look through it while I have Hallie bring in some coffee."

It took Birch only a few minutes to review the information. He grunted verbal exclamation points several times and, when he was finished, replaced the file on Mac-Gregor's desk. He sat on the edge of Mac's desk, facing Matson squarely. He began slowly, gravely, "Caught with your hands in the cookie jar. I haven't dealt in the criminal arena for some time, but a third year law student could tell you that you can look forward to . . ." He stopped as if pondering the importance of his statement. ". . . at least to five counts. A long time, Ollie. And Raiford's a rough place. You were forty-two when I handled your wife's divorce—that's almost three years ago—so you're forty-five now. With time off for good behavior, you might make it out of there by fifty-two." His tongue made a clucking noise.

"I need a drink." Matson's voice was barely a croak.

"A drink, is it? Mr. MacGregor, can we help this man out? Bourbon, neat, as I recall."

Mac furnished the bottle and the glass. Birch was slow in opening the bottle. Matson's eyes followed his movements. The drink was poured. Matson could barely hold the glass in his shaking hands, spilling half the liquor down the front of his already stained shirt. Birch nodded imperceptibly at MacGregor.

"All right, Matson, here's what I want from you." Mac's tone was almost appeasing. "A full statement verifying the cost overruns. A signed bill of sale for the cost of the total. We'll leave the amount blank and fill it in after a full audit. Then I'll need a statement from you outlining the arrangements you made with my accountant. Agreed?"

Matson dumbly nodded in approval.

The two security men were summoned. "Get him out of here," MacGregor ordered, "and hold him downstairs." Matson, stumbling toward the door, was escorted out.

MacGregor turned to Birch. "Leo, I'd appreciate you working with Hallie to draw up all the papers. Have an extra set ready for Matson's lawyer. He'll be here a little later today."

"Paul . . ." Birch hesitated. "Do you realize you're suppressing evidence of a felony?"

"Why the hell do you think I called you? Who better to take care of this than you? Everyone knows you don't handle anything but juicy divorces. Even if Matson wants to tell the story, no one would believe him. But maybe you're right, Leo. I should cover all the bases. I'll call the sheriff this afternoon and explain what happened. Certainly there's no harm in a little overcharging as long as it's paid back. Hallie," he said, "I want you to help me wrap up some loose ends. Arrange for security to escort Alex Wykoff out of here immediately. If he gives anyone any trouble, have him arrested." He hesitated.

"Anything else?"

"Make reservations for dinner for four at The Embers On

The Beach for tomorrow night. Leo, can I count on you to arrange for some suitable company for Owen? He's been working far too hard lately. He deserves a little relaxation."

Hunter missed the exchange of expression between Birch and MacGregor. He had been concentrating on Hallie Norton. He sensed her disapproval, but he was looking forward to an evening with Leo Birch.

Birch and Norton left. MacGregor's mood was ebullient. He had the full-bellied look of a tiger after a kill. He paced the room, rubbing his hands together. "Owen, we've just made a cool half million dollars profit, thanks to you."

"Mac, I'm confused. Maybe you can help straighten me out. You've just found out that one of your best subcontractors has been stealing from you—and not on a small scale. You know he deserves to be in jail. Yet, you're deliriously happy."

Mac stopped pacing. He smiled. "I think it's about time for your first lesson from me, young man. Just suppose I had called the sheriff and had Matson put in jail on criminal charges. Can't keep it from the press, right? Here's your headline. 'Caldwell-MacGregor Bilked Out of Millions.' By *one* subcontractor. So . . . how many other subcontractors have done the same thing? Can the company stand the loss? Caldwell-MacGregor loses its credibility—its sales drop. On top of that, Matson and Wykoff are publicly branded thieves, so neither of them can work to support their families . . . and we lose any possibility of restitution. Now, you tell me—which is the better way to go?"

Hunter didn't have to think about it. "Case closed," he said.

By late in the afternoon, Hallie Norton and Leo Birch had finished all the documentation. The sheriff agreed with MacGregor. A simple land sale . . . value received for services rendered. Hunter was learning.

"Mac, I know you must be tired, but now that we've got all that out of the way, could I finish talking to you?"

"Haven't you had enough for one day?"

"Sure, but there are some things I'd like to discuss. You've been so happy about acquiring that land. You haven't thought beyond this afternoon."

"Is that so? You put a shirt and tie on a guy and suddenly he's an expert. Come around here—I want to show you something."

Hunter moved around the desk while MacGregor unrolled a large map of Palm Beach County. Mac's finger moved quickly to a spot in the northern part of the county. "This is the property we just acquired."

"Sure . . . but how do you know exactly where it's located? You can't tell from the plat."

Mac grinned. "I knew where it was the day Matson bought it. Every transfer of property in this county, over a hundred acres, is reported to me on the day of closing. I record those transactions on this map. You might say it helps me to keep my fingers on the pulse of things." Mac continued, "Our property is adjacent to Interstate 95 . . . the last stretch that's going to be completed. In five years, maybe less, it should be worth at least five times as much as it is now. We simply inventory it and watch the price go up. Now you understand why today was so important?"

Hunter was impressed; Mac was a clever old bastard, always two steps in front of everyone else.

"So, what do you want to discuss that's so important?"

Hunter decided to plunge. "What you've overlooked is that as of right now your operation is dead in the water. You can't sell a damn thing unless the property is ready. All of your sales and construction schedules are going to lag behind—and if I'm not mistaken, a lagging cash flow will soon follow."

Now it was Mac's turn to be impressed by his protégé. "You *have* been doing your homework."

"I told you I had someone check the numbers. Your accounting staff is going to find out that the overcharge estimates are damned accurate. Let me tell you why."

• • •

It took Hunter nearly a half an hour to explain. There were no interruptions from MacGregor.

Hunter finished. "The bottom line is that if you hire another subcontractor, you risk repeating what just occurred. Some people say, 'The devil you know is better than the devil you don't know.' But you have an alternative."

"Such as?"

"You start your own company, a subsidiary of Caldwell-MacGregor. It would be responsible not only for dredging and drainage, but all heavy construction as well. Take a look at this." He placed some papers in front of MacGregor.

"Here's a company owned by Andy Duncan in Delray Beach. He owns his own equipment, but he's in hock up to his neck. His biggest problem is that he always submits an honest bid and lives up to the letter of the contract. If he makes any mistakes, he absorbs the losses personally. He's for sale right now. Make him a quasi-partner. Give him a salary, plus bonuses for bringing jobs in on schedule. Based on Duncan's numbers, you could save the company over half a million dollars in the next two years. Plenty of tax advantages, but most importantly, you control it. If you decide to, you can subcontract for other developers."

MacGregor sat back, pensive. "We save money and create a profit center. Damn good idea. Let me look over these numbers. See me at ten in the morning . . . and take the rest of the day off, Owen. Tomorrow you start working for *me*. You're too valuable to be out playing around in the mud."

It was 9:45 when Hunter arrived in Hallie Norton's office the next day.

"A little early, aren't you, handsome? You're not due until ten."

"Guess I'm a little anxious. Mac says he wants me to start working with him today." He pointed to the window. "Out there, I'm okay, but I don't know whether I'll be able to handle it in here."

"Don't worry. It took a lot of guts to do what you did yesterday. After that, the rest of it will be a piece of cake. That Duncan idea really has Mac fired up. We were all here until after midnight last night. Lou Rosenthal, our comptroller, worked all night. He's in with the boss right now."

The intercom buzzed. "Hallie, is Owen here yet?"

"Yes, Mr. MacGregor . . . a few minutes ago . . ."

"Send him in."

MacGregor sounded in good spirits. Hunter entered. In Mac's office were Lou Rosenthal, Bruce Whalen of the legal department and Harris Smith, head of land sales.

After introductions, Mac said, "Owen's presented us with an interesting concept. We have long been aware of the dangers we face in dealing with subcontractors. Up to this point, we've accepted it as a fact of life. Now we have an alternative solution. I'm recommending that we acquire an operator-owned subsidiary, both as a method of cost control and to develop additional profit centers for the company. I realize this is a drastic departure from the philosophy we've operated under for a good many years. But I can see the need to open up areas of expansion for the company as well as areas of diversification. I'm just sorry that we've ignored these possibilities for so long. Your instructions are to open negotiations for the acquisition of the assets of Duncan Heavy Equipment Company in Delray Beach. You're to place Andrew Duncan on a job contract to run it for us. We'll no longer subcontract any work in this area and we'll instruct Mr. Duncan to expand the company to enable us to bid other jobs up and down the coast. That's the concept. I want you to consider any other areas of construction. Hotels, even banks. The scope of our diversification doesn't have to be limited in any way. The most important thing we need is competent, trustworthy people. This is to be the future direction for Caldwell-MacGregor. Any comments? Any questions?"

There were none.

MacGregor had spent time instructing each of his key

people on the new direction of the company. This was merely the formal announcement.

"Okay, gentlemen. Get to work. Owen, would you stay for a minute?"

As the other three men left, Hallie brought in an envelope and placed it in front of MacGregor.

"Owen, yesterday was a real eye-opener for me," Mac confided. "It showed me just how vulnerable this company has been. We've all been sitting on our asses, milking the land for all it's worth. No one around here has had an original idea in five years. Then you walk in. You showed me how we'd been cheated . . . you handed me a big problem. Better yet, you gave me a solution."

"You're the one that thought of the land deal for restitution," Owen said.

Mac raised a hand. "I didn't mean that. I was talking about acquisition of the Duncan Company. We've taken the first big step toward becoming a real operation . . . not just buying land at one price, but throwing in some improvements and selling it for a profit. Think about it. Working from the concept to the completion and then providing services—building and creating communities. It's a new world for us. I may be getting carried away, but until yesterday I considered this company just a land sales operation. Now I perceive a land company as the basis for the development of a far more diversified company . . . a conglomerate . . . with each part feeding the other." He paused. "I want you to be part of all this. Starting today, you'll work as my special assistant. Your first job will be to coordinate the acquisition of Duncan. What I'm interested in from you is the human side. Relate the numbers and the people and you always get the real story. Hallie will help you get oriented . . . any spare time you have, just walk in this office. Sit down. Listen. That's the best way to learn."

MacGregor fingered the envelope in front of him. "I have a couple of things for you." He withdrew a check from the envelope. "Consider it as appreciation for uncovering the Matson situation."

Hunter was flabbergasted. "$10,000? . . . This isn't . . ."

". . . necessary? The one thing you're going to have to learn around here is that *I* decide what's necessary. Here's something else I think you'll enjoy, maybe even more than the money . . ."

He threw a set of car keys at Hunter. "It's a Mustang convertible. It's out front. Consider it a gift from a grateful uncle. One more thing, you're having dinner with Leo Birch. Get to know him. He's a brilliant son-of-a-bitch. He also gets more women than the law allows. Now, get the hell out of here. I've got work to do."

The setting sun of the late summer evening bounced off the high clouds far out above the Atlantic. The gentle trade winds moved in, pungent with the aroma of salt and the scent of night-blooming jasmine.

Owen pulled off the road at the Embers, parking carefully toward the back of the restaurant lot. He sensed danger . . . then saw them.

The doors of a jet black Cadillac directly between him and the rear entry of the restaurant opened slowly. Two men got out, in the darkness, blocking his way.

"Well, if it isn't Paul MacGregor's little nephew . . ." one of them sneered.

Hunter recognized the slurred voice immediately as that of Ollie Matson. He had been drinking heavily. Hunter assumed the other man was Jim Harris. Harris and Matson were inseparable. They both advanced toward him, each brandishing what appeared to be a steel spanner wrench. Hunter's eyes flicked around the area. They were alone in the lot. He was trapped between his car and an eight-foot wire fence.

"You sneaking, no good son-of-a-bitch . . . I'm going to kill you. No one does what you did and gets away with it." Matson growled at him from ten feet away, advancing slowly and flat-footed like a gorilla.

Hunter stood absolutely still. At worst, they intended to kill him—at best maim him. It was Nam all over, but this time in a parking lot in Florida.

For the second time in two days, Matson expected fear. Again, there was none. But Matson was too drunk to sense the danger he had been so aware of the day before in MacGregor's office.

He charged Hunter, swinging the spanner wrench in a long arc toward the head. Hunter shifted to his right, easily avoiding the blow, leaving Matson off balance. He kicked out, slamming the toe of his left shoe into Matson's knee. He heard a crack as bones shattered. Matson collapsed, crying out in pain, dropping the wrench.

Hunter dove for it, anticipating the second man's rush. He drove the wrench hard into Harris' crotch. Harris sagged to his knees, vomiting. Hunter brought the wrench down on the side of the kneeling man's head, tearing the top half of his ear away. Harris slumped to the ground, unconscious. Hunter quickly shifted his attention back to Matson, turning the wrench around in his hand. He thrust the handle, full force, into Matson's half open mouth. Teeth snapped off with the force of the blow, blood and spittle sprayed the asphalt. Hunter threw the wrench at Matson's feet.

He leaned over and spoke very quietly. "Don't ever come near me again."

He turned away, disgusted, slowly heading to the bar. He had come close to killing them both . . . why he had stopped, he didn't know.

But thank God I did, he thought.

The front entrance to The Embers opened to a hallway leading to a large dining room. Down several stairs, a bar ran the length of the building; it was there that Hunter located Leo Birch by the sound of his rich baritone voice. He was dressed almost totally in white, just a breath away from formal, with a ruffled pink shirt and a scarlet ascot adding the only blushes of color. He was deeply tanned, adding to the effect of his plumage.

The two females with Birch were both close to tens on anyone's beauty scale. Hunter finally caught Birch's eye. Birch left the women and approached him.

"Good to see you, Owen . . . Jesus! What happened to you?"

Hunter looked at the back of his hand. It was spattered with blood. Starting self-consciously, he reached for a handkerchief. "I ran into Matson and one of his goons in the parking lot. We had a difference of opinion."

There was a disturbance behind Hunter. An out-of-breath patron was imploring the bartender to "Call the police . . . get an ambulance . . . two guys are laying out there." He jerked a thumb at the back parking lot. "They're hurt bad . . ."

Birch turned, flipping his car keys to one of the two young women. "There's been a slight change in plans. We'll meet you at my place in a half hour." He turned to Hunter. "What kind of car are you driving and where is it parked?"

"A Mustang convertible. In the back, next to the wall."

"Give me your keys and meet me out front." Birch tossed two ten dollar bills to the bartender. "Keep the change, and forget you saw me here tonight, Al. That goes for him, too." He pointed at Hunter. "Deal?"

The bartender nodded, pocketing the money.

Hunter slipped into the men's room to wash off the blood. He was lucky. There were no bloodstains on his clothing.

He emerged from the front door just as Birch pulled the convertible around to the entrance of The Embers. As soon as Owen closed the car door, Birch had the car in motion, burning rubber as he screeched onto A1A.

"You're one cool son of a bitch. You walked across the parking lot like you were on your way to church. Those guys looked like they'd been run over by a truck. What'd you hit them with, a baseball bat?"

"Maybe I am a bloodthirsty son of a bitch but don't

worry about Matson," Hunter said. "The last thing a guy like him can afford to do is admit he's been whipped by just one man. When he tells his story to the police, it'll be six goons who jumped him. I'm not happy with what I had to do . . . but they won't try again."

"I believe that, too," Birch said solemnly. "Well, kid, let's go celebrate."

14

AN INSISTENT BUZZING roused Hunter from deep sleep. He couldn't seem to get a fix on the source of the sound. Wakefulness came quickly as he finally recognized that his beeper was sounding. He glanced at his watch—it was only 7:30 a.m. He quietly slid off the bed, careful not to disturb his companion, then dialed his office from the kitchen phone.

Hallie Norton answered on the second ring.

"What's up, Hallie?"

"It's Mac, Owen. There's trouble at the boat. He wants you there right away." Hallie was never one to lose her cool easily, but Hunter could detect the concern in her voice.

"Hallie, I'm at Leo's place in Lighthouse Point. Call Mac back and tell him I'll be there in about fifteen minutes tops. Try to find out what's going on. I'll call you from the car."

Hunter showered quickly. He wanted to erase the odor of last night's lovemaking—perfume mingled with the musk of sex. He toweled quickly and returned to the bedroom to dress. Her name was Donna, from Darien, Connecticut— the most intensely sexual woman Hunter had encountered in some time. A gift from Leo Birch . . .

In the years since what they had come to call "the Matson Affair," Leo had indeed become Hunter's friend and confidant—and far more. Hunter had soon discovered that Leo took pleasure in the fact that he had, by the age of

133

twenty-six, partaken of sex in all of the known positions of the Kama Sutra; and now, twenty years later, he was wont to suggest several others to anyone—preferably female and under thirty-five—who was willing to listen. His extensive law library was dwarfed by his collection of erotica: literature, art, devices, games, magazines, slides and movies, all continuously updated. Leo lived for sex. In Hunter he had found a willing junior partner.

Donna from Darien was the newest acquisition to what Hunter privately thought of as Leo's stable, and Hunter had been awarded the task of servicing her. It had not been easy.

"You're leaving? So soon?" Donna's arms stretched toward him. Her blond hair tumbled over her upturned breasts. She was ready again.

Hunter felt the stirring of desire and silently cursed Mac for his early morning call. He tucked in his sports shirt and reached over, planting a kiss on one nipple.

"Don't go away . . . I'll be back as soon as I can . . ."

The Corvette's engine roared to life instantly. Hunter shot out of Leo Birch's driveway, heading west toward U.S. 1. He reached for his car phone, hit the highway and turned right heading north, flooring the accelerator. The speedometer reached seventy as Hallie answered his call.

"Anything new?"

"No, just that they're having trouble with one of the crewmen on the boat. Apparently he'd been drinking all night and now he's threatening everybody."

"On my way. Should be there in about five minutes. Tell Mac to sit tight and don't worry . . ."

"I'll feel a lot better when you're there . . . but don't do anything foolish."

Trouble at the boat, he thought. Hell, it had been nothing but trouble all along.

As he sped northward, his thoughts traveled back to the day after he was named Executive Vice President of Caldwell-MacGregor. The years had passed quickly, with Hunter immersing himself totally in the running of the subsidiary corporations. He had also recruited a new staff for Mac's newest and biggest project west of the city. With all of his reservations, Hunter had still been too optimistic about timetables. It had been late in 1977 that Mac came to him, clearly troubled. Age had begun to take its toll and MacGregor's fatigue was evident in his voice.

"I'm concerned about the western project. Nothing seems to be coming together the way I wanted it to. I just thank God for the profits you've been pulling out of the rest of the operation."

"Mac, I think we were both guilty of a little too much optimism. But even with our land costs, with appreciation alone we're sitting on an $8 million capital gain. We could realize that much even if we sold tomorrow." He grinned warmly. "That ain't all bad."

"I wish you could give me a shot of that eternal optimism," Mac said, chuckling. "Maybe the problem is me. Maybe I'm just too damned old."

Hunter hesitated before speaking. His benefactor's age always had been a sore subject. He thought out his words carefully.

"Mac, we've never pulled any punches with each other, and I'm not about to start now. Sooner or later everybody has to think about slowing down. You've been working at a pace that would kill a man half your age. Besides, you've been trying to do it all. It just won't work that way."

Mac sighed resignedly. "So what the hell do we do?" In response, Hunter allowed just a hint of a smile to cross his face.

MacGregor leaned back, lighting a cigar, and said, "Am I right in thinking that this is going to be a long conversation?"

Hunter began. He had, as usual, been anticipating the problem. His plan called for revising the corporate structure: a new holding company which would be an umbrella for all of the subsidiaries, central control, better defined lines of communication, better use of manpower, greater efficiency. Most importantly, more black ink at the bottom

of the financial statement. In the end Mac had agreed. A
delicate transfer of power. The ball was now in Hunter's
court.

When Hunter had become involved with the company's
reorganization, he had turned over the western project (as it
was then called) to a new land-planning subsidiary. He had
spent many hours of the next two years working with them,
overseeing a master plan for a self-contained resort community: five thousand acres planned down to the last shrub.
Golf courses, tennis courts, clubhouses—a developer's
dream come true. Three-dimensional plans had been built
and set up in the large conference room next to Hunter's
office, later to be reassembled in the sales office. Hunter had
a smaller mock-up set in his office. He was finally ready for
MacGregor.

He had placed a large auditor's portfolio on Mac's desk.
As the door opened, the older man walked in.

"What's up, Owen? Hallie says you've got a surprise for
me. It's not smart to surprise the Chairman of the Board."
Hunter opened the door leading to the conference room. It
was a large room, used in the past for meetings with real
estate brokers. Mac had been told that it had been converted
into a storage room.

He seated MacGregor at the back of the still-dark room
and switched on the slide projector. A split-screen show
with three screens spread across the end of the room. It
opened with "Welcome to Indian Trace—the newest concept in planned living offered by Caldwell-MacGregor
Enterprises."

Indian Trace was the name of Teresa MacGregor's
magnificent home in Boca Raton, still a local landmark.
The slide presentation lasted fifteen minutes. MacGregor sat
quietly as it ended. Hunter turned on the room lights,
adjusting the rheostat to its lowest level. He moved quickly
over to an elaborate control board, and again a small neon
sign over the three dimensional plan lit up: "Welcome to
Indian Trace."

MacGregor gasped as Hunter brought the lights up revealing the display. He moved toward it.

"Owen, it's fantastic! Exactly what I had in mind! How did you do it?"

"Hallie and I dug up every note you ever put in the file on the western project. What you see here is an amalgamation of all that, with a little extra thrown in. Indian Trace represents all of your ideas. I hope you like it."

"Like it? It's all I've ever dreamed about."

"Then we can break ground any time you'd like . . ."

"How about tomorrow?" Mac shouted enthusiastically. "This calls for a celebration." He moved toward the phone. "I've got to get Hallie down here. I want her to see this. It's fantastic."

"Whoa, Mac. Can we talk first?"

"Sure . . . any problems?"

"You better sit down," he said to MacGregor, as he hefted a large portfolio. "You're not going to like this. Do you want me to read all of it or should I just give you the bottom line?"

"The bottom line will do," said MacGregor, with some dread in his voice. He had known the auditor's report was forthcoming.

"Mac, the auditors have just completed a six-month study of all the company holdings. The bottom line is that if anything were to happen to you today, the tax liability facing the company would be so great that we would have to liquidate completely. Any ongoing projects would have to be stopped—immediately. Financing in every area would be tied up. A project like Indian Trace would just have to be forgotten. Sold off, piecemeal. Mac, I'm sorry it had to be me to tell you."

Mac interrupted him, waving his arms as if to silence him. "Don't be sorry. I've been a stupid old man . . . living in the past. An anachronism. But it's been easier to keep my head buried in the sand hoping it would just go away, when all the while I knew it wouldn't." He stopped to draw a deep breath. "What are the recommendations?"

"Really only one, Mac. We've discussed it before. Look for someone to acquire the holding company, hopefully using a taxfree exchange of stock."

"Spare me all the gory details. Is anyone interested?"

"That's the good news. I've spoken to a company—Comtec International. They're not just interested—they're eager. It's an international conglomerate—big bucks. John Hammer, their Chairman, wants to see us in New York next week. They even want to provide some of the long-term financing for Indian Trace." As usual, Hunter had saved the best for last.

Mac looked up at him, his eyes beginning to sparkle again. "You son of a bitch! You've done it again! So what the hell are you waiting for? Set it up! Meanwhile, it's still time for a celebration. I want everybody to see my new toy."

Hunter shook his head. It had seemed easy, he thought. But it had taken years. As usual, timing was everything.

He would never forget the meeting that opened negotiations between the two companies. Mac, by far the wealthier of the two, the epitome of success in what had begun as a family business—Hammer, the polished Madison Avenue man, an international business executive, a *Fortune 500* candidate. Notwithstanding the contrast and the age difference, the meeting had gone well. In Hunter's mind, the deal had been made in the first half hour. After the completion of the preliminary discussions, Mac and Hammer had gotten into some playful bantering about one of their common enemies: the IRS. Hammer obviously respected MacGregor's opinions, and they shared an instinctive dislike for the Federal Government and its intervention in business.

The conversation drifted . . . Hunter couldn't remember who brought up the subject of Comtec's company yacht. But before he knew it, both Mac and Hammer were immersed in a conversation about sailing.

Hunter began to feel like an outsider. He excused himself briefly to call Hallie and returned in time to hear Mac say,

"John, if you give me a week with that problem, I think I can solve it for you."

"Paul, that would be great. Our CPAs will love you forever."

Mac seemed pleased with himself during the limousine drive back to the airport. "That went well," he said. "I like Hammer. He's a straight talker. Some of the guys with big jobs in big companies are pompous assholes. And the potential . . ." He let his voice trail off. Hunter could practically hear the wheels turning. Then Mac said, "You're going to like our new boat."

Hunter was taken aback. "What boat?"

"Sometimes I wonder if you pay any attention, Owen." Mac's tone was mischievous. "Hammer's company has a yacht and a tax problem—right?"

Hunter nodded affirmatively.

"Okay . . . we have a solution to his problem."

Hunter had seen him in action before; he knew that Mac loved an audience.

"How much land have we set aside at Indian Trace for the Catholic church and college?"

"About three hundred acres."

"What's the inventory value of that land now?"

"About $200,000, give or take twenty grand."

"Then that's our trump card. I thought I was just about right on the numbers. Let's say we schedule to turn that land over to the church as a donation—sometime next year, which is when the Archbishop says they'll be ready to build." Mac was rubbing his hands together. "Comtec's boat is worth almost a million dollars, but they've depreciated it down to a book value of $200,000. If they sell it at market value, they've got to pay taxes on the difference. If they give it away or donate it, they can only deduct the book value from the taxes."

"That much I understand," said Hunter. "What are you driving at?"

"Just this. Suppose we take the three hundred acres set

aside for the church . . . and trade the land to Comtec for the boat.''

Hunter protested, but Mac cut him short. "What do you think the retail value of that property is?"

Hunter thought it over for a minute. "Assuming that everything doesn't go to hell in a hand basket, I'd say about a million-two . . . maybe a million-four."

"That's what I figured."

"So, Comtec trades the boat for the land, even up, and Uncle Sam can't tax us?"

"He can't tax an even trade now, can he? Comtec agrees to make a charitable donation of the land to the church when they're ready to build in 1982. Here's the beauty of the whole scheme—when Comtec makes that donation, it will be made at the fair appraised market value, which according to you will be somewhere between a million-two and a million-four. That's what they get as a tax deduction for a charitable contribution." Mac relaxed against the car seat. He had assumed the pose of a saint.

Hunter burst out laughing.

"You just figured out a way to get a million dollar boat for nothing, screw the government out of at least three quarters of a million in taxes—and you figured all that out with a look on your face that would do justice to the Pope. It looks to me like I better do some homework on yachts . . .''

Hammer and his company had been ecstatic about the deal. The accountants and tax consultants approved whole-heartedly. Mac was looking forward to his new toy . . . and it was then that the trouble began.

The boat had been in the Mediterranean on a cruise when the news of the sale reached the crew. They docked the boat immediately in Cannes, informing Hunter they were terminating their employment. After a number of trans-Atlantic calls, a new crew was hired through a ship's chandler in London. The idea was to return the boat to Boca Raton and fly the temporary crew back to England. Then an engine blew, followed by problems with the electronic gear. Hunter wished that he had never heard of the damn thing. Now this.

He sideslipped the Vette and skidded to a stop in the marina near where the yacht was berthed. The first thing he saw was Mac yelling and gesticulating, crimson with anger. Hunter reached into a specially-built compartment below the glove box and pulled out a snub-nosed .38 revolver. He stuffed the gun into his belt and closed his jacket to conceal it as he hurried to Mac's side.

"Christ, I'm glad you finally got here! The son of a bitch is threatening to sink the boat! Get him down from there."

Hunter looked up. The deck was a good twelve feet above the dock. At the head of the gangway was a muscular, heavyset man. He was at least six feet tall and appeared to be well over two hundred pounds. The fire axe he brandished made him seem even bigger. It was apparent that he had been drinking.

Hunter turned to the dockmaster. "Charlie, fill me in and make it quick."

"The Englishman up there says he was promised two weeks' paid vacation in the Bahamas. But it's not true. When he found out, he got nasty. Then he started to booze it up and got even nastier. He swore at the old man and threatened him with that axe he's holding. Now he says that unless he gets what he wants, he'll scuttle the boat. I don't envy you, Owen . . . he's a mean son of a bitch."

"Thanks, Charlie. Do me a favor, get the old man back to his car before he has a coronary. Have the chauffeur call the sheriff's office from the car phone."

Hunter turned and walked to the foot of the gangway, looking up. "Hey, you! I'm coming up!"

"Bloody fucking hell you are, mate," the seaman yelled. He wielded the axe menacingly, weaving slightly.

Hunter walked up the swaying gangway, ignoring the threat. He stopped about halfway. He judged the man to be in his mid-thirties, muscular, but drunk and out of shape.

He hissed, "Don't come any further, if you know what's good for you."

Hunter reached down and unbuttoned his jacket. He held the pistol close to his body so that it was not visible to anyone but the seaman. His voice was low. "You're in trouble, mate. If you don't think I'll use this, think again. After the threat you made, I can blow you away and still be a hero. Drop the axe."

"Fucking pissant bastard!" Fresh sweat broke from the sailor's forehead.

"Drop it . . . *now.*" Hunter didn't move. After a few moments, the axe thudded to the deck.

"Now, start walking down the gangway."

Hunter could feel the seaman's hatred as he came near. He knew instinctively that he would attack. He could have avoided it by backing away, but he stood his ground.

The sailor was only two feet away. Hunter jumped lightly on the gangway just as the man leaped toward him. Hunter brought his knee up sharply, digging deep into the man's belly. The force of the blow took the sailor's breath away. Momentarily his upper body hung loosely over the side of the gangway. Hunter reached down, flipped the man's legs up and sent him splashing headfirst into the water below.

He looked down at the dockmaster. "Keep him there until the sheriff's boys get here . . . then throw him a line."

Moving down the gangway toward Mac's limousine, Hunter hated what he saw. Mac was in the back seat, his right hand holding his chest, his face screwed up in a grimace. His shirt was soaked, his color an ashen gray. Hunter shouted at the chauffeur as he leapt into the back seat. "Head for the hospital . . . step on it!"

By the time the limo raced through the front gates of the marina, Hunter had ripped open Mac's shirt and was pounding on the old man's chest, again fighting his toughest enemy: Death.

=PART 3=

15

He had finished telling Maggie his story.

A log in the fireplace burned through, breaking with a crack. Flames flared briefly, illuminating the cabin. Shadows softened as the flames began to die.

The years, he thought, go by so quickly . . .

Mac had survived, thanks to a coronary bypass. The Comtec deal had been finalized. Leo was now a respected judge. For Owen Hunter, the company, the deal making, had become all-consuming passions. His work, a jealous mistress.

But suddenly, with Maggie, everything had changed. How far had he come to find real meaning in his life? Now it was he who was waiting for her decision.

He glanced at his watch. It was twelve o'clock. He swallowed the dregs of a brandy he had poured what seemed a long time ago. A record was on the stereo. Hunter lay back. It seemed somehow that the lyrics were written for them.

> And if we must look for heaven
> Then heaven must surely be
> In arms that are warm
> And smiles if they tender be

Maggie had not come into the cottage since they had returned from the beach. He had last seen her sitting, hands

around her knees, staring down toward the ocean. He didn't
know how long she had been standing there before he saw
her. Perhaps it was the rustle of the nightgown as she raised
it over her head that caused him to look. She was silhouetted against the moonlit window. Her breasts gleamed
palely in the half light. She moved over him, touching him
on the lips. He knew that he had his answer.

In the morning a chill fog drifted in from the ocean,
isolating them in their cottage. They lay in each other's
arms.

"I don't really want to go back," she said. "Sounds
pretty irresponsible, doesn't it?"

"Not to me," he replied. "But I don't know if Smitty
could stand a steady diet of me."

"Are you kidding? She adores you. The real problem is
whether *my* diet could stand a steady diet of that German
cooking. But I'd like to come back again soon . . ." She
hesitated. "Listen to me invite myself. Jesus. Be calm,
girl."

"Why not? You could even spend your honeymoon here.
Get fat. Get pregnant."

Maggie bolted upright, fisting the sheet over her naked
breasts. "Do I hear what I think I hear? Are ye daft, mon?"

"Never saner. Let's do it, Maggie."

She dropped the sheet, her arms reaching out to him.
"Yes!" was all she could say, tears streaming down her
face.

He wiped away the tears. "Some hardnosed reporter you
are. When I asked you to marry me, I thought it would
make you happy. Let's get dressed and share the news with
the Queen of the Potato Pancakes. Smitty will be glad to
know I'm going to make an honest woman out of you."

Smitty's immediate reaction to the news was to order
them to sit down so she could fix them a hearty breakfast. It
seemed to Hunter that no matter what was happening,
Smitty responded with a feast of food.

She winked at Maggie. "When you first came, I told you

I thought you'd be good for him. He deserves someone like you. There's something I'd like you to wear until you have a chance to pick one out for yourself. It was given to me a long time ago. It belonged to my husband's family."

Maggie opened the small box, yellowed with age, that Smitty handed to her. An antique diamond ring—one large stone surrounded by several smaller gems, in a square gold setting—shone brightly under the kitchen lights.

"Oh, Smitty, it's beautiful! Thank you!"

"Put it on. It will make it official. It's such a pretty piece. It just needed the right lady."

The two women hugged. Owen watched, oddly at peace. He was committed, at last. He had a future.

16

AT EIGHT O'CLOCK in the morning, Hunter guided his car into his reserved parking space in the garage of Caldwell-MacGregor. MacGregor's long black Lincoln was already parked; so was Hallie Norton's car. Even though he and Hallie had been successful in reducing Mac's workload following his heart surgery, Mac had refused to adjust his schedule. He had always been an early riser; the difference now was that by noon he and Hallie were through and spent the rest of the day on the yacht, *Teresa*.

"Hi, Ginny—" Owen waved to his assistant as he walked to his office. She immediately picked up two files bulging with correspondence and followed him into his office.

"What's up?"

"Just this," she said, placing the files on the desk. ". . . and about twenty calls that you'll have to make today. The rest I've handled. I've separated your mail. The red file is the important stuff. But don't get comfortable. Hallie's been calling since seven-thirty. Mac needs to see you . . . oh, by the way, welcome back. We missed you."

She was gone before he could reply. Might as well get this over with, he decided. As he approached Hallie, he was whistling absentmindedly; his thoughts were on Maggie. They had decided that she should visit Florida as soon as

149

possible to meet his "family." Maggie figured it would take
a week to get her affairs in order and arrange for a leave of
absence. She and Owen had not planned beyond that; they
were in no hurry, content to take things one at a time.

Hallie smiled. "You look good and seem awfully happy.
Are you going to tell me about her?"

"You are a witch, I swear."

"Not a witch. It's written all over your face. I've never
seen you look so happy. Now *are* you going to tell me about
her?"

"I'd love to, but it would take time. How about lunch?
I'll tell you this much—her name is Maggie, and she
reminds me of you." He grinned wickedly. "That's why it's
taken me so long. I've been looking for a clone."

"Flattery will get you everywhere. You know, this is the
first time you've asked me for a date. I'll be ready at twelve
sharp."

Mac had lost weight, at the doctor's insistence and with
Hallie's help. To Hunter he seemed reduced in stature, lost
behind his huge mahogany desk. But he was tanned and
looked fit from sailing. The medical reports were all
favorable.

"Owen, it's good to see you. You look super. The
vacation must have done you some good." Mac was on his
feet, his arm around Hunter's shoulder.

"The week at my place up north really did the trick. I
didn't realize how much I needed the rest." It was then that
Hunter realized they were not alone. An older man sat
quietly, coffee cup in hand, observing their interchange.
Hunter immediately sensed something alien. It wasn't his
appearance or anything else he could put his finger on, but it
was there, lurking.

The momentary silence was broken by Mac. "I'm sorry,
Owen. You haven't met Sam Goldman. Sam, this is Owen
Hunter."

Hunter was surprised at the firmness of the old man's
grip.

"It's good to meet you, Owen. You're all I've heard about for the last ten years. Paul is proud of you."

"Sam and I go back a long time, Owen. He was my first OSS recruit in the Forties. We used to call it Donovan's Yiddish Division. But Sam had to strike out on his own. It's been . . . how long? More years than I care to remember. We stopped working together in Washington officially in 1946. Sam, you make me realize how old I'm getting." Mac touched Hunter's arm gently. "Owen, why don't you sit down? Sam has something to say that concerns you."

Hunter sat at Mac's desk, turning his chair so that he could see Mac and also face Goldman.

"Owen, before we begin, let me explain something," Mac said. "Do you remember when you first got here? I asked you to give me a week while I did some checking."

Owen nodded. "That's one conversation I'll never forget."

"Sam was the man I called . . ."

When MacGregor had been given his posting to the OSS in 1942, one of his first recruits was a young, olive-skinned Jew named Sam Goldman. With degrees from CCNY and Columbia, Goldman referred to himself as "a street-smart sheeney." His black eyes, perpetually ringed with gray circles, were topped by ebony brows. He rarely smiled. Toward the end of the war he requested permission to travel with MacGregor in Europe—he wanted to visit the sites of the concentration camps. It was also arranged that he, along with MacGregor, would present the OSS documentation to the prosecutors of the Nuremberg Trials. As it turned out, Goldman had an entirely different mission in mind.

In November of 1946 he and MacGregor were sitting in a small café in Munich. They had just finished briefing the prosecutors—tomorrow they were to return to the States. Goldman was sitting, toying nervously with his beer stein.

"Sam, I've worked with you a long time. What's bothering you?"

"You want to know?"

Mac smiled. "That's why I asked."

"All right. It's the Palestinian question. You're not a Jew, Mac . . . you may not understand. Everything we've seen here in Europe—the camps, the atrocities, the hopelessness—are not just a horror. They're part of a pattern that's existed for centuries. That's what troubles me. The pattern has to be broken. But by whom? Not by the occupying powers. They care, but they don't care enough."

"Then who can break it, Sam?"

"We can. Only us. Only Jews."

"And now you're going to confess."

"Confess? To what?" Mac's intuitiveness clearly startled Goldman; his black brows knitted defensively.

"You're going to tell me that while we've been in Europe, you've been sneaking around behind my back doing your own personal work. So what else is new? I happen to know that you've tried to recruit every Jewish operative we've come across."

"You knew?" Goldman was incredulous.

"My mother didn't raise complete idiots." Mac grinned, enjoying himself, "The 'street smart sheeney' got caught with his circumcision on display."

Goldman laughed in spite of himself.

"Sam, let me tell you something—something I've never told anyone else. When Donovan recruited me, I wasn't looked for a cause. Europe was so far from my world that it might as well have been another planet. I was willing to do anything that would put meaning into my life after the death of my wife. That's all. A job. When the war was over, I'd go home and pick up where I'd left off."

Goldman nodded.

"But it didn't work. The first reports of the camps stood my hair on end. I had difficulty believing them, but then I saw with my own eyes. The enemy was defined. All I wanted to do was get over here and kill Nazis. But then I had a better idea. As soon as the war was over, the people responsible for these atrocities would be punished. And we would show people everywhere that we all share part of the responsibility for what happened. And maybe—just maybe—by sharing the guilt, we could stop it from ever happening again."

Goldman was silent, grave. Mac reached out and clasped his hand. "The transport leaves at eight tomorrow morning."

"I won't be on it."

"I know. For me the war is ending. For you, it's just begun. Shalom, Sam."

"Shalom, Mac. You've been a good friend . . ." With a grin, Goldman added, "For a goy."

They shook hands and went their separate ways. Now, in Boca Raton, they were together again.

Stunned, Hunter looked into the face of a man who, up until a moment ago, had been a perfect stranger. For the first time in many years he realized that he was not Owen Hunter. A memory returned, sharp as a knife . . . stabbing . . . cutting. His facade had been stripped away. He felt naked and peculiarly alien. He felt like Eddie Villard and Josh Williams.

"So you know all about me? Who I am? Where I came from?" His voice was cold.

Goldman sensed his antagonism. "Yes," he said quietly.

"Why are you here?" Owen's discomfort was evident, and he glanced at Mac.

"Mac, let me." Goldman kept his voice soft, realizing that he was treading on dangerous ground, not wanting to alienate and yet aware that he must be brutally honest. He said two words—a name.

"Regis Bennett."

The name was like a gun exploding. Hunter could see in his mind a look of terror on a young Jewish girl's face. Buried memories came flooding back. They had been there all the time, just beyond his consciousness, haunting him. He had tried to run away, but he had carried his demons with him, and they had waited patiently for the catalyst that would bring them back.

It had arrived in the person of Sam Goldman.

"Owen, let me tell you the whole story. I'm with Israeli intelligence—the Mossad. Several of us left the OSS in 1946. After partition we were able to convince Ben Gurion that he needed a functioning intelligence network. Paul was my boss in the OSS, and he's always been a champion of Israel, raising money, using his influence up on Washington. When you showed up, he called in a marker. No one at the Mossad knows anything about you—who you are—where you are—where you come from. I can assure you of that." He stopped, draining the last of his coffee. "Now let's put our cards on the table. *Tuchas affon tisch,* as we say. You were a Canadian, so you know that there's always been a lot of anti-Jewish sentiment in Canada. During the war, some leading Canadian industrialists actually were in favor of an alliance with Hitler. One of these was Regis Bennett's father. Apparently, a good deal of that has rubbed off on his son."

"And the son is now External Affairs Minister of Canada." Hunter finished Goldman's statement. "I'm aware of the problem. I just don't see what it has to do with me."

"Let me explain. Bennett Industries owns and controls a number of firms through nominees who are heavily involved in the manufacture and sale of military hardware. One of these firms is a subcontractor on certain components of the F-15 fighter-bomber. They manufacture wing tanks. Another of their firms manufactures Shrike air-to-ground missiles, completely compatible with the F-15's." Goldman hesitated, frowning. "Let me propose a hypothetical situation. Suppose these fuel tanks were to be purchased by an Arab country, and the range of their jets increased so they became capable of attacking Israel. That would constitute an intolerable threat. It would force Israel into making a preemptive strike. If, in addition, the same Arab nation supplies a major portion of the oil used by the United States, then Israel is in trouble. A no-win situation."

"That's a hell of a lot of supposing," Hunter said. "Why don't we cut out the pussyfooting? I read the newspapers.

Saudi Arabia already has sixty F-15's ordered. They've already started taking delivery. They've been looking for long-range capability ever since they placed the order. Hell, we're ready to give it to them now."

Goldman's expression darkened. "The U.S. won't have to. All the jets that have been delivered have already been equipped . . . secretly, of course. Unless we can document what has happened, it could mean a bloodbath that could easily trigger a nuclear war. We're all aware of Russia's intent. And then throw in a fanatic or two like Khoumeini or Khaddafi . . . the lunatic fringe would take over."

Goldman's revelation was a sobering one, but Hunter still didn't understand what it could possibly have to do with him. The answer came quickly.

"The only solution for us right now is to reveal the details of the conspiracy—to have solid evidence linking the Canadians to the Saudis, and whoever else is involved. We suspect Khaddafi, but we've no evidence."

"So, how do you expect to make Bennett talk?"

"Owen, you're the only eyewitness to a very unpleasant incident that involved Bennett and one of his top men, Dale Sommerville. If your story is told, and believed, it could effectively destroy Bennett's career and bring down those around him. We need your cooperation. We need it badly."

"I'm listening," Hunter said.

"We want you to resurface under the name of Josh Williams. Your occupation as a merchant seaman will explain not only your absence since Vietnam, but will provide you the reason for being in the Mediterranean. You'll write a blackmail letter. It will include some of the original investigative reports and hint at additional information, all of which could be extremely damaging when accompanied by eyewitness testimony. Incidentally, since they think they've destroyed all of this material, it should come as a hell of a shock to them. We've a pretty good idea when they've scheduled their next delivery, and we'll try to arrange for you to meet with them on their yacht in the

Mediterranean, off Cannes. We hope your appearance will trigger their first big mistake."

"And what will that mistake be?"

"They'll try to kill you," Goldman replied coolly.

"Jesus Christ!" Mac exploded. "You didn't tell me that, Sam! Live bait! They've already tried to kill him once and failed. They're sure as hell not going to let him live this time. Once he's on the yacht, he's a dead man!"

"I didn't say there'd be no risks, Paul. The risks are enormous. But he'll be wired, and we'll have at least one operative aboard. The blackmail note will hint at another set of documents to be released if Williams disappears."

"That won't mean a goddam thing!" Mac growled. "No newspaper in the world would publish anything like that without a personal statement from the source."

Hunter sat quietly through this exchange, seemingly impassive, his face a mask. He could not have explained it, but somehow he had always known that one day he would have to face what had happened to him so long ago. He had been running for nearly twenty years. Running from what?

Not just them, he realized. From myself.

Not just from what I did. From what I *didn't* do.

I let her die that night in the old abandoned factory. I could have yelled, distracted them, broken a window, fought them . . . saved her. I didn't move quickly enough. I didn't move quickly enough because I was scared. And so she died. And I've been running ever since.

The decision had already been made for him. His statement rendered any further conversation unnecessary. "When do we get started?" Hunter asked.

"Now," Goldman replied. "We don't have much time."

A vortex, with its inexorable pull, had begun to spin. There would be no stopping now.

17

SWEAT STREAMED DOWN Hunter's face into his full beard. Squint marks showed briefly white against his deep tan as he shielded his eyes momentarily from the desert sun. His shirt was stained, his clothes dusty. He had been assigned to an Israeli Commando unit, and for the past four days his group had been in a forced march across the desert—thirty miles a day with minimum rations of water and food. It would be another four hours before they would reach their base camp. He ached for a hot shower, decent food. Even the thought of the Army cot in his spartan cell was comforting.

He shouldered his Uzi automatic and followed the squad out at half trot. He practiced a sort of self-hypnosis, concentrating on the rhythm of his body. It helped to wipe out the reality of the burning sand and blazing sun. Sweat poured from every pore and dried instantly in the desert inferno.

Much of what followed that day in Mac's office had become a blur to him now—another symptom of life out of control. A call to New York to advise Hammer of a forced leave of absence . . . what did MacGregor describe it as? A diplomatic mission? By that time he had already called Maggie to cancel her trip to Florida. The disappointment in her voice turned to disbelief when he refused to offer a coherent explanation.

"But why, Owen? And why *now?*"

"I can't tell you, Maggie. Please trust me."

"Why can't you tell me?"

"I don't want you involved."

Maggie had hung up, crying.

Then there were the hurried conferences with lawyers, a hastily drawn will and legal trusts, just in case he failed to return. With Hallie Norton as his trustee, he was assured that Maggie and Smitty would share the motel property in Northern California.

When he was through he was abruptly confronted with the realization of how little his life had affected other people. There were a handful of friends . . . but not enough, he reflected gloomily. It was a sad realization, but one that strengthened his resolve to go ahead. He had been deprived for too long of any lasting normalcy.

No, he thought, that's a copout. I deprived myself. I ran away, and I kept running, and I've done nothing in my life except run and hide and strike back at the wrong people. The ones I should have struck back at are Bennett and Sommerville, and now I've been given the chance.

He could atone for his cowardice—his initial sin. He would regain the right to live without fear or guilt. He would balance the books.

The girl, Ruth, had been Jewish; she had wanted to emigrate from Canada to Israel. So it was fitting and proper. It was what he had to do.

At early evening the warm flood of sun exited behind the thin clouds that layered the western sky. The wisps of white at the horizon gave way to brilliant deep reds and mauves. Paul MacGregor sat brooding in a deep leather chair beside his perpetually burning fireplace. Some Jim Beam rested in ice in a large snifter he held cupped in his hands. Fatigue had aged him. The loss of weight, a result of his heart condition, continued to shrink him. And yet there continued an inner fire. The only light in his office, the flames from the fireplace, cast everchanging patterns of light and dark across his face.

He was thinking of Hunter. He had allowed Hunter to go forth as a surrogate, a warrior. MacGregor had brought him every step of the way. Hunter had never failed him. Yet now, there was an unsettling premonition that seemed to flood Mac with foreboding.

The door to his office opened and closed quickly. "Is there anything I can get for you, Paul?" Hallie Norton's voice was soft and soothing.

"Just sit for a bit, if you don't mind. I need some company. A little more bourbon would help, too."

Hallie stood at the bar and poured from the crystal decanter. "You're worried, aren't you?"

"Owen's a capable man," he said. "Goldman won't expose him unnecessarily."

"Nonsense," Hallie replied. "Goldman will stop at nothing. Israel is what matters to him."

MacGregor frowned. "I've asked Owen to risk himself before . . ."

"The difference is that this time it's not *you* playing God . . . it's not you pulling the strings. And you know the worst part, Paul? You've finally admitted to yourself that you love him like the son you never had. Now you have to face these next few weeks like the rest of us who care for him. Me . . . Maggie . . . Leo Birch. Love is a powerful emotion, Paul. It carries the fear of loss. Pray you don't lose him before you tell him how much you love him."

She handed him the snifter of bourbon. Her hand touched his cheek with a soft caress. A tear touched her fingers. Paul MacGregor was trembling.

The briefing from Sam Goldman put everything into perspective. Hunter remembered when they had first talked about it, chuckling, disregarding the gravity of the situation. It seemed ludicrous that an entire country might have to count on one over-the-hill, thirty-five-year-old man. But it was up to Owen to help stop a war whose outcome—even as a victory!—could permanently cripple Israel.

He had commented to Goldman, "Sam, if you ever showed the Knesset your trump card in this mess, they wouldn't just have you shot. They'd probably cut off your balls, coat them in chocolate and send them to Yasir Arafat as candied desert."

"Owen, I don't know how in the hell you got to know those old bastards so well." Goldman chuckled. "But first they'd stuff 'em with gelignite."

Then the tone of his voice once again turned serious. "Under any other circumstances, Owen, I'm sure we could have become good friends. But before this is over, you'll probably hate my guts."

They were sitting in Goldman's office, unwinding from the hurried and secret trip from Miami to Tel Aviv by private jet. The jet lag was compounded by the 120 proof rum that Goldman poured steadily. Hunter was feeling no pain.

Goldman handed him the bottle. "You might as well kill it. It'll be the last until you finish your training."

"Training?" said Owen. "You make it sound like I'm going back in the Army."

"The Mossad is a kind of Army. You remember Entebbe? Those boys were our responsibility—getting them in, getting them out, and letting them know what to expect. We were first in and last out. We have to make sure you're prepared."

It was only 7:30 in the morning, but the sun was well on its journey across a cloudless desert sky; it was 85 degrees on its way to 110. The desert to the east was a flat expanse as far as the eye could see, while to the west rocky hills sprang up from the desert floor at a forty-five degree angle, their rugged points rising almost a thousand feet. Scrub and tendoned mesquite hung tenuously to life, while gnarled trees, stunted and leafless, were mute testimony to the quality of life in this harsh environment. It remained for man to creat something worthwhile here, to push back nature's challenge.

Flat adobe buildings squatted at the base of the hills, looking curiously out of place. A first glance would reveal nothing of the true character of the site.

At this particular camp the comfort of its occupants was of the lowest priority. Secrecy was the highest. Survival depended upon it. Huge hangars dominated an underground complex within the hills behind the adobe buildings, and extensive electronic installments lay below the desert floor. The hard-packed sand formed natural landing pads for helicopters, and a long field had been cleared for the occasional visitor flown in by jet from Tel Aviv or Jerusalem.

It was to be Hunter's home for nine weeks. His future would depend upon his success during that time. He faced the prospect with a deep sense of foreboding. It seemed so far from the lush, green land that he had come to love so much. Thoughts of Maggie worked reluctantly through his mind. He felt as if his connection with all that he had come to know had suddenly been placed on hold.

But Hunter had been there before. Mindless exercise without reason . . . killing to survive . . . reacting on instinct . . . finding his way to safety in places as far away and as remote as this. Vietnam had been no different. His mind could wipe away those intervening years as though they were visions seen only through opaque glass. Future or past, they didn't matter. What mattered was here and now. He had a job to do, a commitment to fulfill. He was a willing surrogate.

Hunter's quarters were sparse: a five-foot by eight-foot windowless room, containing an Army cot with coarse green muslin sheets and a single black blanket. On the other side of the room was a reading lamp, table and stool. Bathing and toilet facilities were communal. A locker at the foot of the cot held his few possessions.

He soon learned that the lack of luxury meant nothing. By the time each day's work was finished, he was so exhausted that the quality of life was one of his least concerns. It was all part of the psychology of the training—

deprivation and desensitization. He had begun to acquire a grudging admiration for these people who were his *de facto* jailers. Goldman had been right. They were bastards.

He had spent six hours a day on physical conditioning during his first week. It had started with a complete physical exam and a computerized exercise program designed for him personally—jogging, calisthenics, rope and rock climbing, weights and swimming. An additional six hours of classroom instruction was also initiated.

His various instructors were all experts in their fields, and they tutored him individually. He was, as always, a quick learner. He mastered basic Arabic phrases quickly and he was instructed in conversational French and Yiddish as well. His Vietnam training returned when his teachers worked through courses in navigation, radio and map reading.

Hunter had returned to top physical condition. The daily exercise which had started at six hours a day was increased to eight hours daily during the second week, then nine hours daily during the third and fourth.

He had been studying in his room when the summons came to report to the camp commander's office. Sam Goldman waited for him there.

"Something new has been added," Goldman said abruptly, grinning, gesturing at the full beard that Hunter had allowed to grow.

He had followed Owen's progress closely over the past few weeks, probing for any weakness or indication of lack of resolve. So far there had been none.

"Our main concern has been to get you into optimum physical condition. That, and giving you some basic language and technical skills, have apparently been accomplished. Do you agree?"

Hunter nodded.

Goldman continued. "Up to this point your training has been one-on-one. It was to accustom you to acting alone. Responsible for yourself . . . relying on no one. There's a reason for that. There are other operatives involved in our plan. Each of you will have a separate and distinct plan of action, wholly independent of each other. It's important that you understand that. This week you'll begin your training with an anti-terrorist squad . . ."

"What the hell for?" Hunter demanded. "Come on, Sam—"

Goldman raised his hand, halting him in mid-sentence. "These squads are our answer to the PLO and to Khadda-fi—trained terrorists. The training you're now going to start will be hand-to-hand combat. Silent killing. Knife and garrote, explosives, fuses and timers. We've scheduled you for three weeks with one of our elite squads. Your previous Army training should stand you in good stead."

"What's after that?" asked Hunter, cuttingly.

"Maneuvers. You'll get one week of actual missions with a commando unit. The Lebanese border, maybe the Golan Heights—wherever Arab terrorists are active."

"Sounds splendid."

"We're dealing with powerful men with great resources. They've already tried to kill you. We know this much . . . your survival depends on how well we prepare you. Remember, it was your choice," Goldman said quietly.

"All right," Hunter muttered. "Let's get on with it."

"When you join this unit, the officers in charge will speak to you in English if a situation requires any detailed explanation. Otherwise, their commands will be in Yiddish. You must not—unless an absolute emergency situation exists—speak in English. Understood?"

Hunter nodded.

"Now I have a little surprise for you." Goldman led Hunter down a maze of corridors toward the hangars that had been built beneath the hills. They were stopped by an Israeli commando well over six feet and two hundred pounds of hard muscle, Uzi slung at the ready. Goldman showed identification, and a door leading to a huge hangar opened. Hunter was not prepared for what awaited him.

Stretched out on the hangar floor was a huge cut-away

mockup of a ship. It appeared to be well over a hundred feet long and was set up like a Hollywood stage. Kleig lights set in the roof of the hangar gave the scene a surrealistic quality.

Hunter strode the entire length of her from bow to stern. The transom confirmed his suspicion. The set was an exact copy of *La Contessa*, the Canadians' yacht.

Goldman noted Hunter's amazement.

"This is where you'll spend the last week of your training. Before you're through, you'll be in complete command of your environment. You'll always know where you are and how much space you have to work with. We have trained actors to play Sommerville, Bennett and your brother. Each day they'll act out every possible scenario that you could encounter."

"You don't leave anything to chance, do you?"

"The stakes are too high, Owen."

Hunter's squad contained eight enlistees and two officers. They had paired off—one-on-one—in a realistic exercise with knives. The idea was for a defender to disarm his opponent.

Owen was startled to see that his partner was a Sabra woman. She was almost as tall as he, and deeply tanned. He wasn't prepared to attack a woman. She sensed his reluctance, took instant advantage of it and circled her body inside his knife hand, her right arm clamped down on his wrists. Her left hand chopped into his upper arm, dealing him a crushing blow which numbed his arm almost totally. She twisted it down, back and up, levering her entire weight against its extension. Hunter left his feet and landed heavily on his back, his shoulder and arm suddenly alive with searing pain.

He reacted with instinctive anger. He rolled sideways without thinking, his feet catching her left leg just below the kneecap. She crashed to the ground, crying out in pain. Hunter scooped up the fallen knife; his hand found her thick hair and, pulling her head back, he thrust the blade of his knife at her throat. The point indented the skin. He held the knife to her throat for a moment and then released her head roughly, pushing her face in the sand.

He was stunned at his own brutality, but the members of his squad stood silently for a moment, and then began a slow, rhythmic clap.

The Sabra woman rose slowly. She looked at him warily with new respect, paused for a moment and then joined in the rite. Hunter had been accepted. He was one of them. The transformation was complete. He had forgotten civilized life as he had come to know it. He would learn to kill again.

Hunter trotted toward the camp which was now visible in the wash at the base of the range of low hills. He had spent the time well. The agony of the first weeks had lessened with weight loss and hardening muscles. But it was the final phase that had transformed him—the week of night missions across the border, retaliation for PLO terrorist activities. He had seen the results of the PLO attacks. Women, little children and old people cut to pieces; their bodies bayoneted, guts spilled on the ground. Garroted corpses, their heads hanging by strips of skin, their spines exposed.

Irrational anger had returned to him—the desire to strike back, to avenge. There were times in this last week where he had to be restrained from killing, but he had killed and killed again. Yet his appetite had only been whetted. He was racing toward the base camp. He, who had begun as a follower, delighted in leading. Most of his group were already exhausted. Strangely, he was exhilarated. His war, perhaps his life, was just beginning.

18

EIGHT WEEKS HAD passed . . . eight weeks resembling
hell. Yet it seemed to Hunter that they were the greatest
reality he had ever known. The hot shower water flowed
over his body, massaging his tired muscles, splashing away
desert grit and fatigue.

If there had been any deterioration brought on by years of
sedentary living, the last eight weeks had erased any
vestiges of it. His body was lean, hard and nut-browned by
the sun. His hands once again had become calloused killing
instruments. The transformation was total, he realized,
alarmed. He finished his shower and dressed quickly. He
was to meet Goldman again.

The Jewish Mossad leader was seated behind the Com-
mandant's desk when Hunter entered the office. "Owen, it's
good to see you."

Hunter took the handshake, reacting hesitantly. The
rigors of training had not allowed for social amenities. He
felt strangely ill at ease. His reply was merely, "Sam."

"Sit down," Goldman said, reaching for a file on the
desk beside him. "It seems our people did their jobs well."
He slowly tapped the back of the file against the palm of his
left hand, as if awaiting some response from Hunter. None
came.

"I've heard some disturbing things about you. They're
all in here," he said. He drew a pair of reading glasses from

167

his breast pocket, appraising Hunter carefully. The man before him bore little resemblance to the man he had met in Florida a little over two months ago. His skin was sun-baked mahogany. His tight khaki T-shirt revealed a bone-hard physique. A full beard streaked with gray gave the only indication of his age. His hair was clipped short and close to his head. But the eyes were the same—brilliant blue and cold. Goldman felt as if they were staring right through him.

The change was as dramatic as it was complete, from a middle-thirties-executive in decent physical shape to a hardened warrior with a finely honed instinct for destruction. It was the mental aspect that concerned Goldman. He began to read slowly from the file, as if to himself. "Incursion—Golan Heights, by Ten Squad: PLO encountered: three dead; two killed by Hunter, by garrote and by knife. Incursion—Syria—Ten Squad: PLO encountered: seven killed—four by explosion, one by Hunter, knife. Incursion—Syria—PLO encountered: four dead, one by Hunter, garrote."

In the last week, the man in front of him had gone into life-threatening situations in retaliatory raids against PLO terrorists. He had killed four times.

Goldman continued from the file. "Hunter exhibits no fear even in the most dangerous situations. No visible emotions after killing even at close quarters. Exceptionally skilled with knife and garrote."

Goldman closed the file, placing it back on the desk.

"Wasn't that the intention?" Hunter asked flatly.

"It was," Goldman said. "But I want to be frank with you. You worry me. If you look at the composite of these reports for the last two months, the picture that emerges is that of a cold, emotionless killer. The squad leader has been at this all of his adult life . . . even he says that you scare the hell out of him. He says he's never seen a man better adjusted psychologically to the act of killing than you." He shrugged. "You know, Mac told me something about what he'd seen you do in Vietnam. He said he still has cold shivers thinking about you pulling your knife out of the neck of some V.C. you just killed and wiping the blade on the sleeve of his uniform. He said you reminded him of a butcher slicing meat. No reactions. No feelings. So what we're seeing now isn't a new development, is it?"

"What are you getting at?" Hunter's voice snapped sharply back at him.

"We've had our staff psychiatry people review your record. Not just here, but going way back—Vietnam, the whole bit. No names, just situations. They've come up with rather an unusual theory." Goldman looked at Hunter inquiringly. "Interested?"

Hunter's reply was an affirmative nod.

"On one occasion in your life, in Canada as a youth, you failed to act in a stress situation. It may have been because of indecision—it may have been because you simply were afraid. The end result was that, apparently, you failed to live up to the standards of behavior you had set for yourself. Those standards were likely established somewhere in your subconscious. You're probably not even overtly aware of them. Because of that, whenever an antagonistic situation arises, it triggers a response mechanism. Fear and a wide range of other emotions are eliminated and you proceed without the inhibitions that affect the actions of most of us."

"That sounds like bullshit," Hunter replied quietly.

Goldman continued as if there had been no interruption. "You might be interested to know that the doctors consider your profile ideal for the job that needs to be done."

"Then what's the problem, Sam?"

"It's this. I've come to like you. And when this is over, I want you to go back to being Owen Hunter."

"I'm not so sure that's possible." Hunter paused. "You got all that psychological crap written down, all that gibberish. Maybe it means something, maybe it doesn't. But let me ask you—when was the last time you saw a five-year-old kid sitting against a building, trying to hold his guts in place after a terrorist emptied an AK-47 into him? Or the corpse of a pregnant woman slit from end to end with the unborn kid hanging out? Sure, I've killed. And every time, in some way, I've repaid the bastards for the suffering they've inflicted on innocent people. All in the name of their cause. Some cause! . . . killing women and kids. Okay, Sam, maybe I'm the monster you and your psychiatrist friends describe. But you didn't create me. All you did was put me in a situation that allowed me to recognize what was there all along. And something else. As rotten as the PLO has become, they don't hold a candle to the people that you're after. Those people kill from their boardrooms in their thousand-dollar silk suits, sipping brandy from crystal snifters and smoking five-dollar Havanas. They kill by proxy. They don't care if it's a woman or a kid or a whole people, just so long as there's profit in it. They go home to their families and their country clubs—lily white, pure, their hands clean. And somewhere blood runs into a gutter. So the sooner we begin, the better, Sam."

Hunter stood face to face with Goldman, eyes glowering, chin jutting—possessed. If Goldman had been asked to describe Hunter in one word, that's the word he would have used. Any further discussion was meaningless.

"Tomorrow then," Goldman said. "We'll begin on the boat. We'll reincarnate Williams."

Back in his room, Hunter removed his clothes, folding them neatly across the foot locker at the end of his cot. He lay naked, staring at the ceiling, slowly allowing his fatigue to overcome the anger burning inside him. He needed to sleep, to rest the demons that haunted him.

He was not too sure how long he had been laying there in the dark limbo between wakefulness and dreaming when he was alerted to a sound at the door. He sat upright, coated in sweat. The door clicked open slowly. A person entered.

"Hunter?" It was a woman's voice—Naomi, the Sabra, whom he had fought with his first day. They had been together for eight weeks, speaking little except for the guttural exchanges of Yiddish necessary for their own survival.

He knew what was about to happen. He had waited for it. He watched her in the dark, his eyes slowly adjusting.

As she unstrapped her brassiere, her breasts swung free and heavy. She sought the barrettes holding her hair in a tight bun at the back of her head. Her hair tumbled down thickly over her shoulders. She shook her head and slipped her pants over her muscled thighs.

He started to speak but her fingers silenced the words on his lips. She spoke in heavily accented English. "It is forbidden for me to be here, but I had to come. I do not know your mission, but I know that it must be for the good of my country. It's time that you were paid in advance, even if in only a small way. Let me give you pleasure."

Her hands brushed his chest, moving slowly across his stomach, then began to stroke him to erection. There was no scent of perfume, but the clean smell of soap mingled with the heavier odor of her sex. Her body radiated heat.

An hour later they lay quietly, their bodies melted together. Words were not necessary. They were each fighting their own war. It was inextricably mixed up with the anger, the suffering and the killing. They had used each other well.

Finally she rose, dressed, and left the room. They would never see each other again.

19

HUNTER HAD ONE week to digest the dossiers of the complement on board *La Contessa*. Bennett, Sommerville and his brother were no problem—he had already made a lifelong study of them. But the others were an unknown quantity.

Goldman's men had done an admirable job of assembling data, including photos: at least three in each file. He reviewed them one by one:

Dietrich, Heinrich. Born Stuttgart, Germany, September 1936. Only surviving son of German immigrants, displaced persons of World War II. Graduate Queens University School of Engineering. Graduate degree in Nuclear Physics. Employed Bennett Industries, Auguste Curie Division. Known expertise in nuclear fission technology. Height: 5'10"; Weight: 180; Hair: Dark-brown; Eyes: Blue; Complexion: Medium. Note: Dietrich has been on board *La Contessa* for one week, boarding in Marseilles accompanying sealed containers.

There were only three pictures of Dietrich, none of which gave Hunter a clear straight-on view of his face. A grainy blown-up passport photo added nothing to his impression and supported the final notation in the file. Dietrich, who was assigned to a cabin designated as Portside Two, had remained in his cabin since coming aboard the yacht. Meals were all taken in the cabin and he was guarded 24 hours a day. Access impossible. Known to carry technical papers. Languages: French and German fluent, in addition to unaccented English.

The right height and weight, Hunter mused. Hair color is somewhat of a problem. Complexion definitely a problem.

Hunter had learned the French patois while serving in Vietnam, but he had no knowledge of German. He closed Dietrich's file and moved forward.

The photos in the next file were blowups from a mini-camera with telephoto lens. The face that stared back at him was broad, beefy, slightly out of focus.

Plessiers, Caron. Born Quebec City, Quebec, 1950. High school education. Joined U.S. Marines Special Forces, 1967. Served Indo-China theatre '67 through '70. Dishonorably discharged. Subsequently mercenary activities in Africa, serving several countries. Height: 6'2"; Weight: 225; Hair: Brown; Eyes: Brown; Complexion: Medium. Known assassin with criminal record.

Hunter had seen this kind before. Overwhelming strength and brutality, but upstairs less than a full deck. He continued aloud.

"Plessiers joined Bennett Industries as a bodyguard in 1979, has worked *La Contessa* as a first mate ever since. Extremely dangerous. Small arms and explosives expert. Heavily French accented, ungrammatical English."

After discarding Plessiers' file, Hunter reviewed the file on the Captain: *John Randolph.* At fifty-five he had been at sea since he was sixteen. His work on *La Contessa,* it seemed to Hunter, would be the grand combination of a lifetime of experience at sea: Captain of a 140-foot ship, capable of speeds above 35 knots. But Randolph was clean. A professional doing his job, unaware of the part he was playing in a world-class conspiracy.

Hunter closed the file quickly, putting it back into the box that Goldman had provided him. He wouldn't need it again.

The steward: *Jurgen Krause,* a Bennett family retainer.

His father was SS, an extermination camp officer who had been executed in 1946. Krause had emigrated with his mother to Canada in 1948. His mother was retained by the Bennett family and he had served them since that time. Notation: "Fervently anti-Semitic. Fits Bennett family attitude well."

He came to the last file. He'd spent a lot of time with this one, and he knew it by heart. It was the one on board *La Contessa* that he feared the most. Hunter lay back on the bed and read it again.

Terrence Giles. Psychopath. The photograph showed the raised face of a venomous snake, poised to strike—eyes barely containing the madness that lurked behind them. A pockmarked face, thin lips, hollow cheeks. Saskatchewan-born, about 37 years of age. Activities with Bader Mein-hoff, Germany; Red Brigade, Italy. Believed involved in three to five politically sensitive assassinations. Received training in Moscow. Positively identified with the murder of the wife of an Italian Consul in Germany; corpse identifiable only through dental charts of what remained of the woman's lower jaw. Employed Bennett Industries 1979. Believed Khaddafi Libyan plant. Background unknown to Bennett Industries. Resumé submitted, false. Suspected PLO agent aware of current conspiracy.

The faces swam in Hunter's mind, committed now to memory. The game would begin on a chessboard over which he would have no control. No opening gambits—no rules to govern play—no closing strategies. *Check* and *checkmate* were terminal conditions. The swirl of the vortex could not be stopped. It was June 8, 1982.

He looked at the files scattered on his cot. He wanted it finished. He knew that he was ready—but Goldman and his men were not through with him yet.

Hunter had begun to hate his inquisitors almost as much as he did the enemies in the portfolios that he had studied. More than once he had restrained an urge to reach across the table from where he sat and smash the fact of the fat, young bespectacled Jew who sat there almost taunting him. A projector had been set up on a table and flashed slide after slide for Hunter to identify. Click. Slide. Pockmarked killer. *Name?* Answer: Giles . . . Red Terrorist. Masochistic killer. Click. Slide. *Name?* Dietrich. *What university?* Answer: Queens, Kingston, Ontario. Click. Slide. Click. Slide . . .

Looking up into the darkness of the hangar, he picked up a ballpoint pen which had been laying on the table and hurled it so hard that the point impaled itself in the back of the chair next to the young Jew's head. The man's eyes widened in fright.

Suddenly the scene before Hunter went black; he stood shaking with anger, disoriented. It seemed like minutes but it was only seconds. The huge kleig lights blazed, the noise of their ignition startling him. The mockup of *La Contessa* stood bathed in lights. A small spot focused on a gantry high overhead, illuminating Sam Goldman. He looked down on Hunter, unsmiling.

"It seems," he said, "that we're ready to move on."

Hunter stood there, shoulders slumped, feeling used, manipulated. He raised his head slowly. "Goldman, you son of a bitch. Let's finish it."

Goldman had been monitoring Hunter's activities around the clock, but now he had another concern. He knew, as any other ranking officer in the Mossad knew, that an attack on the PLO in Lebanon had been imminent. Israeli forces had been on alert for nearly three months.

Israel's Prime Minister had been unable to wait any longer. In his open letter to the United States, he had said: *"Dear Mr. President . . . Dear Friends . . . Ten thousand men, women and children remain in shelters day and night. The purpose of the enemy is to kill Jews without regard. The PLO shelling, spasmodic prior to this weekend, has been heavy since Friday."*

So the Israeli juggernaut had begun to roll.

World condemnation again, Goldman realized. But world opinion was not the concern of the Mossad—they were focused now on the reaction of the other Arab countries. The Prime Minister and other leaders had not been briefed on the operation involving Owen Hunter. The possibility existed for a political upheaval in Saudi Arabia and a military attack on Israel. The surreptitious installation of long range fuel tanks on the F-15 wing of the Saudi Force was almost totally completed. Time, or the lack thereof, was critical.

Hunter had frightened them all today.

"Israel Vows Capture of Beirut," the headline of the newspaper screamed up at him. It was the *Los Angeles Times*, dated June 10. It had thus far been a textbook operation. Originally it was to have been a 25 mile incursion, but the Israeli Army was already on the outskirts of Beirut. They had destroyed the Syrians' SAM missiles and the majority of the Syrian Air Force capability. Beirut was now a death-trap for the PLO. Soon the Beirut-Damascus highway would be cut.

"What the hell are we waiting for?" Hunter growled.

Blindfolded, he walked the corridors. Top deck— bridge—midship—fore and aft. He must know his space. There were no lights. Just ultra-violet for the observers. Fourteen hours straight. Two days running. One hundred-forty-foot length, beam twenty-four feet. Four decks. He knew them better than the builder. They took him to the engine room, disorienting him there. Observing him from the cutaway Plexiglassed side, urging him, critiquing him, criticizing him and ridiculing him. In total darkness, he eluded the Mossad operative on board. In addition to the seven Mossad, there were armed guards posted around the ship. They had been posted following his reaction two days earlier.

Goldman, using a director's mike, called to each of them

to report his position. Each of seven responded negatively.
The quarry had disappeared. Goldman, realizing that this
had become a dangerous game, appealed to him directly.

"Hunter, where are you?"

The answer was not long in coming . . . the feel of a
cold, steel wire encircling his neck. Goldman hit the lights.
The wire tightened, then released.

"I'm ready, Goldman," Hunter said quickly in his ear.

Goldman shuddered. Hunter was proving to be exactly
what they wanted. Capable beyond all of their expecta-
tions—perhaps even out of control.

Contact had been made with the Canadians. Hunter was
to be picked up in Cannes for a meeting aboard *La Contessa*
two nights from now. They had apparently bought the
blackmail gambit. One thing bothered Goldman; he had not
heard from his operative aboard *La Contessa* for more than
twenty-four hours.

Beirut was surrounded. Goldman said a silent prayer for
the success of the mission. Tomorrow would be his last
deceit. Hunter had been told that it was necessary to be
hpynotized in order to test his subconscious behavior. Given
only two suggestions, one to stop the trance, Hunter would
be released from hypnosis upon hearing his name. The
second suggestion was that Hunter would recall nothing that
had happened while under hpynosis. Goldman had to know
Hunter's reaction to one shock yet to come.

Hunter entered the main salon for about the hundredth
time. But this time he was not in full control of his actions.
He had been hypnotized. For almost two full days with six
hours of sleep, they had practiced scenario after scenario.
"What do you do if . . . ?" Over and over. In the main
salon, below decks, the confrontation with Giles, the
Snake . . . with Dietrich . . . with the captain. The line
between sanity and insanity was being stretched taut.

The boat rocked gently. The motion was provided by a
mechanism below, similar to a Link Trainer. They were

approximating a light sea, with wisps of fog rolling against the windows of the salon. He was alone, a Scotch-on-ice in his hands. The oil paintings in the salon, the richness of the setting, unnerved him. He was drifting. No love. No hate. His sense of consciousness was altered. He recognized the character of Sommerville. A consumptive. His chest, full of rales, made wet unnatural sounds with each breath.

Hunter tolerated him, knowing that one swift blow could silence him forever.

Sommerville spoke, his tone full of ridicule. "You have caused us many problems . . ."

He had heard the line so many times before that there was a dreamlike quality about it.

The second voice began. It was Robert Villard, his brother. Hunter looked up, mesmerized. From somewhere deep inside him, as searing an emotion as he had ever felt before, rose. He was enveloped by a desire to kill his brother. But almost immediately this emotion was over-ridden . . . he could not jeopardize the plan. He would defeat his brother. He would defeat them all—*his* way.

He did not see the two-inch double-glass enclosure in the middle of the fake salon separating him from his antagonists. He stood silent for seconds, while his trainers observed him. Hypnosis had been imposed to see his reaction to his brother. It was broken on a prearranged signal. "Hunter!" Goldman yelled. Hunter relaxed. The glass was retracted.

The final test had been passed. The attack on Lebanon was several days old. Now Hunter's war, a secret war, was about to start.

They were to leave for Cannes by private jet. Goldman was saddened. He had just heard that his neighbor, a brilliant young doctor, had been killed outside Beirut. The war had come home to him.

They stood together in the desert at dusk. The private jet that would whisk them across the Mediterranean was due at any time. The last hour had been taken up with packing

Hunter's gear. His clothes were a motley collection of work pants and shirts that looked authentically multinational, exactly the wardrobe that a merchant seaman would have collected in his travels.

The word *Williams* stenciled on his duffel bag was heavily scarred. Heavy work shoes, a wool turtleneck sweater and pea jacket, both black, rounded out his belongings.

Goldman's people had again been thorough. A small leather tube, secreted in the center of the bag to avoid detection from other than the most thorough search, contained the tools of his trade. Drugs for any contingency. Syringes, a supply of curare derivative. In proper dosage the drug could render a normal man unconscious within seconds and keep him that way for twelve hours. A waterproof plastic pouch, a long, slim, professionally balanced throwing knife and a voice-activated tape recorder hidden in a multi-band short- and long-wave radio, completed his supplies. They had agreed there would be no firearms. But on his right wrist, a stainless steel chronometer concealed a razor-sharp garrote.

He felt at times as if he were a spectator. The image in the mirror bore little resemblance to him. The training of the last few days seemed to add to his sense of being out of time, out of place and out of sync.

The roar of jet engines canceled his thoughts. The plane taxied to a halt; the door swung open and down.

Hunter and Goldman advanced, boarding quickly. Even as the co-pilot slammed the pressure latch in place, the pilot pushed forward on the throttles.

The letter to the Canadians had been simple, perhaps crude; but effective. Hunter had given the details of his recollections of that night in Canada so many years ago. They had been translated into a rough blackmail demand: a threat to release details to the Canadian press through its Paris bureau.

They had been thorough. His cover story was fully committed to memory—the scenario of his life from Nam until now. Hunter was secretly happy that he had not had to live it.

But the identity of Owen Hunter had virtually been wiped away and the identity that had lived through the end of Vietnam had been resurrected. Eddie Villard had been born again in the persona of Josh Williams.

20

THE SMELL OF good Provençale cooking filled the air. Through an open window in the small hotel room they could hear the sounds of vendors selling snails and oysters in the back streets of Cannes.

Goldman had fussed all day like an old woman. Hunter hoisted the duffel bag over his shoulder and glanced at his watch. "It's time."

Goldman nodded. "Be careful. With luck we'll have you off by midnight . . ."

The tension was broken; from now on it was up to him alone. Hunter moved out of the room and down the stairs.

The lights were coming on in the dock area. Boats lined the quays, bumped gently against the pilings. The last vestige of a spectacular Mediterranean sunset was still painted on the high clouds to the west. It was an idyllic setting—even peaceful. The irony was not lost on Owen Hunter.

He was confident that, so far, everything was working for them. After sending the blackmail threat, they had waited. Had the Canadians wanted to kill him summarily, then their man Giles hardly lacked the talent or the inclination to do the job. But apparently the Canadians either did not want to risk that course of action or they were confident that once aboard their boat, he would have no way to escape. They wanted to hear him out, destroy him at leisure, on their own terms.

Why not?

The plan was simple. He sat in a quayside sidewalk café, wearing a black turtleneck, carrying his sea bag, sipping a glass of red table wine. The café catered to the people who worked the boats and docks. There was little traffic on the square. Twilight was passing into darkness. A breeze off the Mediterranean carried a light scent of salt air.

He went over the possibilities one last time as he waited. Goldman was sure that their plan was to get him on board, ostensibly to hear him out on his blackmail threat. They would then kill him, and dump the body out in the Mediterranean. His request for $200,000 in exchange for silence would be dismissed as that of a bumbling amateur.

He was playing by their rules, but he had the hole cards. His bag contained the voice-activated tape recorder. He was counting on their overconfidence, their arrogance, their willingness to flaunt an admission of guilt in front of him as they finally pronounced his death. Confession would be used by Sam Goldman in his game of ultimate blackmail. There was only one thing that nagged at him. The missing operative. Sam was equally concerned.

"The last thing we want to have is for them to tie you into us in any way. If that does happen, they'd probably dispose of you without even talking to you. So if you think they've caught on to anything, delay them. Tell them all you know. It's a last resort, but it will buy you some time."

He watched the big man striding across the square toward where he sat sipping wine. He recognized him immediately. The stupid one, Plessiers. The background information ran through Hunter's memory.

Plessiers approached cautiously, letting his eyes roam in all directions as he cupped the lighted match to the cigarette in his mouth. He studied Hunter carefully. Apparently satisfied, he lowered his hands, discarding the match. He crossed quickly to Hunter. "Williams?"

Hunter nodded.

"Let's go."

Hunter stood, slowly hefting his bag. He followed the man across the square. A launch was running, rocking slowly against its moorings in a light chop from passing boat traffic. Terrence Giles manned the helm. The dossier had not done him justice. His face radiated cruelty.

"Plessiers, take over. You," Giles said to Hunter, "just in case you have any ideas." He pointed to a 38 Smith & Wesson jammed into his belt.

He completed a thorough body search. His hands probed harshly, so that Hunter had to restrain himself from retaliating. His search of the bag was more cursory. He seemed satisfied that Hunter was weaponless.

The thirty-foot launch pulled alongside *La Contessa* just fifteen minutes after leaving the dock.

She was a magnificent ship, long and sleek and fast. Davits were swung out of the portside of the aft deck. The cables that dropped down were attached and the launch was winched to the cradles on the aft deck. Hunter noticed that the bow anchor winch was running at the same time. Christ, he thought, they're not wasting any time. The captain was good. By the time the launch was secure, *La Contessa* was making flank speed out into the Mediterranean.

"All right, Williams. Follow me."

Steps led down from the bridge to the main fore deck. Plessiers opened the door that let into a large salon.

As Hunter entered, the door slammed shut behind him. He surveyed his surroundings. It seemed as if he were home. The mockup he had worked on for a week had been identical, down to the glass wall behind the bar and the oil paintings. He placed his sea bag where the voice-activated recorder would pick up any conversation in the room. An octagonal mahogany table, inlaid with ivory, sat in the left center of the salon, facing a settee. At the end of the couch, a semicircular bar jutted out at an angle into the salon.

Plessiers stood guard outside the doors, his presence foreboding, yet reassuring. They were being just cautious enough. They were convinced that Hunter was what he had presented himself to be.

"Good evening, Mr. Williams. I've been asked to make you comfortable." Jurgen Krause stood before him, white-jacketed, properly subservient. Click. Slide. The Nazi.

"A drink, perhaps?"

"Sure," Hunter answered. "That would be fine. A Scotch." He continued to talk as Krause poured a Glenlivet into a shot glass. "Pretty fancy." Hunter whistled. "Compared to a freighter, this is like a Chinese cat house."

Krause pursed his lips. "She's one of the finest ships ever built." He extended a tray which held a single Scotch. Hunter reached for it and drained the glass dry. He gained the reaction he had hoped for: Krause thought him a slob.

"Another, sir?" There was a slightly derisive tone in Krause's voice.

"Yeah, but put this one on ice with a little water. That's not a bad Scotch, by the way."

Krause poured the drink as Hunter moved toward the bar, one foot finding the brass rail. The drink was placed in front of him.

"If that will be all, sir, please make yourself comfortable. Mr. Villard and Mr. Sommerville will join you shortly."

Hunter was impressed with his surroundings: elegance understated. The tone was rich and warm, with none of the garishness that was often so commonplace on the toys of the nouveau riche. He wandered about the salon looking at the oils on the walls. If he was being watched he wanted to give the impression of casual confidence—a simple business transaction to be consummated.

The soft, whirring noise of a small electric motor caught his attention. A panel behind the bar swung open. Two men emerged. Both were dressed casually in tropical-weight pants and polo shirts. Sommerville looked older than his forty years, his clothes hanging on him like shrouds. His complexion was dull gray, his eyes watery, his breathing labored, emphysemically wet.

The years had been kinder to Owen's brother. Although pale, almost sallow, he seemed fit enough.

Robert Villard spoke first. "I see that the steward has taken care of you. Josh Williams, is it? Shall we drop the charade, Eddie?"

His brother stood behind the bar, with Hunter to his left, facing him. "Whatever name suits you is fine with me," Hunter said. "And since you're back there, brother, how about another drink? That's damned good Scotch." Hunter slurred his words. A knowing grin passed between Robert Villard and Sommerville. "I know a man like you can't be too happy having a brother like me . . . a Merchant seaman . . . an embarrassment. But that's what I've always been, right?" Hunter turned quickly on Sommerville, his voice somewhat surly. "You must have known that sooner or later I'd come back to haunt you. The big shot Canadian cocksman. You probably have a hard time getting it up any more." He chuckled, playing the role of the coarse drunk.

Sommerville coughed and spat phlegm into a badly stained handkerchief. "You weren't brought here so we could listen to your brilliant commentary. You should have been dead years ago."

"You know, Eddie," his brother said smoothly, "I wouldn't have recognized you. Quite an improvement, your new face."

"Then how'd you identify me, Bobbie?"

Villard grinned confidently. "The prints off the shot glass, and your enlistment prints."

"Let's get this over with," Sommerville said. "Why the hell are we standing here wasting our time with some two-bit blackmailing punk? Spell it out, Williams, or Villard, or whatever the hell your name is. What do you want?"

"Jesus, don't you know? A long time ago you and your buddy Regis Bennett raped and murdered a Jewish girl in Toronto. I saw you. I want two hundred thousand dollars to forget it ever happened. Then I'll just disappear like before."

"And you'll disappear just like before," Sommerville mimicked. "And then reappear when you want another two hundred thousand. You stupid son of a bitch."

"That's a very interesting proposition, Eddie," said Robert Villard, "but totally unacceptable." He moved from behind the bar and, turning his head left, pointed to the right side of his face. Hunter could see for the first time the scar that ran from the top of his ear to his shirt collar. He was shocked. He realized what he had always known but had never been able to fully accept: that the third man that night so many years ago was his brother.

"You were with them," he said. "It was you, Bobbie."

"That's right. And no one would have cared. She was just a dumb immigrant girl, and we were three college kids having fun. Drunk. Happens all the time. But you saw it, and you ran away."

"And got away," Sommerville said. "Until now." He nodded at Robert Villard. "Let's get this over with, Bobbie . . ."

Hunter turned white with fury. He almost wished Goldman was not due to arrive at any moment; he would enjoy killing these men himself. If he died making the effort, it wouldn't matter.

He was suddenly struck with a greater realization. The two men before him wouldn't have understood. It was a surprise only to him. Goldman had to know about this . . . MacGregor, too.

The duplicity . . . Jesus Christ. Everybody had known but him. All of a sudden he was alone. Vulnerable, he felt used and desperate, fighting for self-control.

"You're all garbage," he said coldly. "Killers then, killers now. Then it was just one girl—now it's thousands of people, maybe hundreds of thousands. You don't give a damn. You're just garbage, all three of you."

Robert Villard looked quickly at Sommerville, smiling. "I was right," he said. He wheeled again on Hunter. "It seemed a little too pat, your coming out of the woodwork after all these years. I figured you were working with the

Jews. It's your style, Eddie—to choose the losing side. And so we adjusted things accordingly. The coordinates for our rendezvous this evening were slightly incorrect. Not much—just by fifty miles or so. But we let your Israeli friend broadcast them . . . before we had him killed."

At a signal from Sommerville, Plessiers and Giles entered the room. Hunter's arms were pinned tightly to his side.

"Take Mr. Williams below. And this, too," he added, handling the duffel bag gingerly as if it were something untouchable. "Check through his things with a fine tooth comb. If you find anything interesting, bring it to us. When you're through with him . . ." He hesitated, then smiled crookedly. "Weight his body and throw it overboard."

". . . A final drink to your health, brother," Robert Villard said, raising his glass toward Owen in mock salute.

Hunter was shoved heavily from the salon, a gun pressing firmly at his spine.

His time and his options had suddenly become frighteningly limited. He could no longer count on Goldman's force arriving before the Canadians' rendezvous—the position radioed by Goldman's man on board had been sufficiently inaccurate to delay their arrival by at least half an hour. They would be tracking by radar, but by the time they realized that the actual transfer was taking place, they would not be close enough to stop it. Hunter was on his own.

He was shoved roughly to the door leading from the salon to the deck. Terrence Giles led, with Plessiers following. Hunter was in luck. Giles was the dangerous one. He could feel the steady pressure of the gun barrel on his back. His mind was clear again. His training had equipped him well. He assessed his position carefully, silently tabulating the things in his favor.

The deck leading out to the stairs and to the cabins below was narrow enough so that his captors couldn't flank him. His arms were free. The men had been given specific instructions. They were to search him, but they were not to

kill him until after the rendezvous with the Libyans. He had
time, but damn little of it.

Hunter quickly freed the garrote wire which was concealed in his chronometer. The trio had passed all of the
windows in the main salon, and the sudden darkness
provided Hunter with his chance to strike. His eyes adjusted
quickly to the changing shadows, but he feigned confusion.
He stumbled, going to one knee. Counting on Plessiers
becoming momentarily blinded in the darkness, he braced
his foot between the deck and the stanchion of the rail. His
left hand shot up, fingers rigid and extended; with the full
force of his rising body, he stabbed his hand into Plessiers'
neck. Plessiers' head snapped back. As Hunter moved
upward, his right hand went around and under Plessiers' left
shoulder, and his left hip rolled between the man's legs. He
straightened out his legs, lifting and throwing the body high
up over the railing of the ship and out into the darkness.

Wheeling quickly, garrote in hand, with two quick steps
forward he whipped the wire over Terrence Giles' head. He
jerked powerfully, the wire slicing through flesh and
cartilage. If there had been any sounds, the ship's throbbing
engines and the sea's waves breaking hard against the side
of the ship had drowned them out.

Hunter raised the second corpse up over the rail, his nose
momentarily assaulted by the voiding odors from Giles'
body. He pushed the dead man as far out and away from the
boat as he could, trying to avoid telltale blood stains, then
grabbed Giles' revolver from the deck and stuffed it into his
belt. Reaching for his bag, he went straight to the ladder
leading to the cabin below deck.

La Contessa was like his second home. He silently
thanked the Jews for the training they had forced on him.
He was heading for Dietrich. *Click. Slide. Five foot ten;
weight, 180 pounds* . . . the size was about right.

Heinrich Dietrich. If there was anywhere that the intelligence of the Mossad was lacking, it had to do with Dietrich.
No one knew exactly what his mission was, but Hunter
intended to find out. Dietrich was apparently to be trans-

ferred to the Libyan ship to handle some technical aspect of
the material the Canadians had been selling. He was in
Cabin Portside Two, the cabin nearest the entrance to the
engine room.

Hunter moved stealthily down the corridor, pausing just
before he reached an open cabin door, then peered around
its edge. The engineer was opening a locker and the
steward, Krause, his back to the door, was changing
clothes.

Hunter moved silently down the corridor to Dietrich's
cabin. He knocked gently.

"Who's there?"

"Steward, sir. We're making ready for the transfer.
Captain's asked me to make sure that you're ready."

The door opened and Hunter moved quickly, shoving his
entire weight against the door to force his way into the
cabin. He snapped the garrote around Dietrich's neck,
twisting with his left hand and covering the man's mouth
with his right. Dietrich began to shake.

"Don't make a sound," Hunter whispered. He twisted
the wire tighter so that it bit into Dietrich's throat. Hunter
wheeled his captive toward the wall mirror. The sight of his
own blood oozing from his neck caused Dietrich to lose
control. A dark wet spot stained his crotch and spread down
his legs.

"If you do what I tell you," Hunter said, "you have a
chance to live. Nod if you understand."

The man nodded, his eyes rolling. Hunter took his hand
away from Dietrich's mouth and guided him to a chair next
to a small berth. He stuffed a cloth into his mouth and then
pulled Dietrich's arm behind the chair, slipping a length of
wire out of his belt to bind Dietrich's hands. He looped the
last strands of wire snugly around the chair, securing his
prisoner. He finally released the garrote.

Dietrich looked like a condemned man on death row who
had received a last second pardon. His pallor pinked slowly;
he was still alive.

Hunter recovered his bag from the corridor, making sure

that he had not been detected. Moving back to Dietrich, he cocked his gun and spoke calmly. "I'm going to remove the gag. If you make any noise, I'll splatter your brains all over this cabin. Understand?"

The man nodded.

Hunter pulled the gag. "Now, Mr. Dietrich, I want some information and I want it fast."

Dietrich seemed surprised. "You know who I am?"

"I'll ask the questions," Hunter said. "First . . . why are you here?"

"I . . . I'm accompanying some classified material . . . to somewhere in the Middle East for testing."

"What type of material?" Hunter asked.

When Dietrich hesitated, Hunter raised the gun barrel.

"Explosive devices," Dietrich said haltingly, "triggered by special types of fuses. I'm one of the few people in the organization with any experience working with these fuses."

He sensed that Dietrich was holding something back. "That's bullshit!" he exploded.

Then he grew calmer. "Let me tell you what I *do* know. This material is going to the Libyans, probably to be used against Israel. I also know that you're a rabid Jew-hater and that's why you were picked for this job. Now, if you don't want your brains on the ceiling, let's have it. One more time—make it good." Hunter pulled the garrote from his pocket and dangled it in front of Dietrich's face.

The sight of the wire totally unnerved Dietrich. He lost his composure and began to shake and sob. "I don't want to die . . . please . . ."

Hunter looped the wire around his neck, drawing it taut. He fought to control the urge to snap Dietrich's head off. Sensing the danger, Dietrich blurted, "Neutron bombs . . . they're neutron bombs, for God's sake!" The words came in a high-pitched voice.

"Let me have all of it," Hunter said, his calm belying the shock of this revelation. Something else Goldman failed to tell him, he thought. . . . No, that was impossible; he shook off the thought.

Dietrich started slowly. "There are ten neutron warheads aboard. I'm to accompany them to their final destination, check them out and arm them by setting the fusing devises. That's all I know. It's all in that file over there." He waved to a briefcase on a chest of drawers.

"Tell me about the bombs," Hunter said.

"They're small hydrogen devices. They have a small blast area, but they release a high level of radiation. The radiation is lethal within a radius of a mile from the blast site."

The words seemed to hang in the air. Hunter fought to reject this one more dimension of horror . . . killing machines without equal. And Goldman didn't know. He needed time, but he didn't have it. He forced the man's mouth open and stuffed the gag back in, taping it in place. Dietrich's confession had raised the stakes.

Goldman cursed aloud.

The rendezvous between the Canadian ship and the Libyan freighter had been observed by the Mossad, but that observation had unfortunately been limited to radar. Goldman had been radioed a wrong position. The operation, planned to the last detail, had become a shambles, a nightmare. Although the Israeli mother ship was bearing down on the Canadian boat at flank speed, by the time they would be in a position to launch the boarding party the Libyan freighter would be miles away.

It was already eleven p.m. Goldman had hoped not only to gain incriminating evidence against the Canadians, but to have the second team of Mossad commandos board and seize the Libyan ship. He was sure that the evidence to be found there would more than justify his actions, but the only time to board would have been when she was making the transfer, before the sending of an emergency signal. To try to stop them while they were underway would have caused an international incident—hardly an acceptable solution.

And Hunter was in jeopardy, if not already dead.

The Canadian ship was visible now in his binoculars. Two crewmen topside were just finishing winching the launch on board. Nothing was being done to reduce the boat's visibility. She was lighted like a Christmas tree. Goldman judged it was only minutes before she would be underway.

The Israeli boarding party, ten Mossad commandos in two light craft, approached the Canadian yacht. Goldman was in command of one boat, Itzhak Berne the other. At Goldman's signal, Berne's boat proceeded to the starboard side amidships, Goldman's to port. They cut power as they closed in on the ship. Rubber covered the grappling hooks that were swung up and over the boat's rails. Four commandos from each craft boarded quickly and silently. Goldman's group went forward to secure the bridge and salon area; Berne's group worked toward the stern securing the crew's quarters. The crewmen on the deck were removed noiselessly and simultaneously. At the same time, on the bridge of the ship, the captain was given specific instructions by Itzhak Berne. It was all over in minutes. Not a shot fired.

Moments later, Goldman sat quietly facing Robert Villard and Dale Sommerville in the main salon. To Goldman the pair seemed strangely subdued, almost as if they had been expecting him.

"Mr. Villard, Mr. Sommerville, allow me to introduce myself. I'm Samuel Goldman, attached to a branch of the Israeli security service. Excuse me for inconveniencing you, but we have reason to believe that you have been trafficking in strategic materials, illegally, with our friend, Colonel Khaddafi."

"Preposterous!" Villard cried. "You haven't a shred of evidence to support that accusation. You talk about illegal trafficking . . . why, you're armed to the teeth! And you're standing in the salon of a ship owned by the External Affairs Minister of Canada. I suggest that you and your government, not we, are the guilty parties. I would also

suggest that you have your men retire immediately so that
we can avoid an international incident which could be very
embarrassing to the State of Israel.''

"Mr. Villard," Goldman said patiently, "we're aware of
who you are and what you're doing. We also know about
Mr. Hasebe and some material missing from one of your
companies. It has to do with a sub-contract for fuel tanks for
F-15 fighters.''

Goldman sat back, allowing this bit of intelligence to sink
in.

"That surprises you? Let's make ourselves comfortable.
My men are completing a search of the ship.''

Goldman moved behind the bar and poured himself a
cognac. The salon door opened. A scowling Itzhak Berne
stepped in quickly, nodding to Goldman.

"I must see you at once . . . and alone.''

Goldman looked behind him. There was an alcove
leading to a stateroom below. "Over here," he said. It was
what saved them both.

A tremendous explosion ripped through the ship, lifting
the stern high and forcing the bow forward and down.
Shards of glass from the windows cut through the air like
shrapnel. Goldman and Berne were flung to the floor by the
force of the concussion. Even as the ship fought to right
itself, it began to wallow, stern down. Those bastards!
Goldman raged inwardly. He reached down for Berne, who
was brushing shattered glass from his uniform. "Are you
okay? Let's get the hell out of here, Itzhak. I've a feeling
there'll be more.''

Shelving from behind the bar had been blown forward,
momentarily blocking their access back into the salon. A
yellow watertight pouch caught Goldman's eye; it lay
partially exposed inside a steel tube. He recognized the tube
as part of a wall safe which apparently had been dislodged
by the explosion. On an impulse, he reached down and
picked it up, stuffing it into his pants. Shoving the debris
aside, he and Berne staggered into the salon. The roof had
been sheared off and debris littered the floor. Goldman

moved toward Robert Villard, who was lying face down on the floor in a puddle of blood. When he turned him over he could see only the red raw meat that had been Villard's face.

A second blast rocked the boat. Goldman was staggered to his knees by its force. Berne shouted to him, "The other one's still alive! Give me a hand! We haven't got much time, Sam!"

The boat listed dangerously.

Goldman moved swiftly, helping Berne to haul Sommerville from under the upended table. They moved to the deck of the ship where the remaining members of the party were reboarding the assault boats that had been brought alongside. A quick head count showed four missing. None of the yacht's crew had survived. One fully loaded boat was already moving away. Berne and Goldman lowered the unconscious Sommerville into the other.

Behind them, *La Contessa*, her bow rearing high into the air like some mortally wounded sea creature, slid stern first into its Mediterranean grave.

Miles away, a Libyan trawler was making flank speed toward home port. In the half light of the instruments on her bridge, a tall, black-skinned Bedouin stood staring at the horizon to the stern of the ship, then carefully noted the dial of his Rolex.

He looked up, scanning the dark sky above the irridescent rough-hued wake. A light flared briefly in the night and died just as quickly. His expression failed to change as he turned to the other men on the bridge.

"It is done. Captain, you will set course as we discussed. Maximum speed . . . Mr. Dietrich is to be confined to his quarters for the entire journey. See to it that a guard is posted outside his door at all times. Is that understood?"

The captain nodded affirmatively.

21

It had been forty hours since Goldman had last slept. His fatigues were stained with blood, sweat and salt water. His beard hung heavy and blue-black against his pale complexion and dark circles ringed his eyes. He was showing the strain of the last two days, and he knew the worst was yet to come.

Twelve hours after he and his men had escaped the doomed yacht, Goldman had labeled the operation a disaster. They had found Dietrich trussed up, dead, in a closet in his cabin. Hunter was missing. There was no trace of Giles and Plessiers. There were more unanswered questions now than before.

Goldman sat in his office at Mossad HQ, analyzing for what seemed like the hundredth time last night's sequence of events. His confusion grew. He was aware that world newspapers had headlined the disappearance of the Canadian yacht, and a massive air-sea search was underway. Some wreckage of the yacht had already been spotted.

Holding Dale Sommerville incommunicado was a calculated risk; but without Hunter to tie up the details, Goldman faced painful decisions. In order to secure a confession from Sommerville based upon the tape recording found in Hunter's bag, he would have to convince Sommerville that Hunter was still alive. But most importantly, he must warn his own government of the potential danger from Saudi Arabia.

God, he thought, if we'd only gotten there sooner! He cursed silently. With all of Israel's military forces concentrating on Lebanon, he realized the Saudis might be more than they could handle . . .

Since the beginning of the Labanese invasion, the cabinet was meeting on a daily basis. If the Saudis were waiting for the shipment picked up last night, Goldman knew he had forty-eight hours at most. The countdown had already started.

There was a knock at the door.

"Come in!" Goldman barked.

"The lab results, sir. My orders were that you wanted them immediately." Willy Mayerbohm approached his desk.

"Sit down, Willy. Spare me the play-by-play and get to the bottom line . . . and no scientific horseshit, please." Goldman got up and paced as Mayerbohm reviewed his notes.

"Hunter was in Dietrich's room. Fingerprints bear this out. He was also pretty active in the head of Dietrich's room . . ."

"What do you mean, 'pretty active'?"

"Well, you know we didn't have a lot of time, but we found a number of latents on the sink taps, medicine cabinet, and on both sides of the door."

"So what?"

"There were beard residues in the sink," Mayerbohm continued.

"Beard residues?"

"They weren't Dietrich's. They showed great exposure to the sun, with the ends well bleached. It would be more likely that someone with recent, prolonged exposure to the sun last shaved in that sink. Based on what we have, our lab people are sure that it was Hunter. What puzzles us is *why*. Would it make any sense for him to be shaving his beard at a time like that?"

Goldman pondered a moment. "Obviously he wanted to change the way he looked. Anything else?" he asked, turning to Mayer.

"There were bloodstains on Dietrich's shirt that didn't match either his type or Hunter's. Also, the stain pattern would indicate that the blood stain came from a thin object, as if someone wiped something on his shirt to clean it off."

"Could it have been from a wire?" Goldman asked.

"That's possible."

The information was like a shot of adrenaline to Goldman. He suddenly seemed to have lost hours of fatigue. He became animated. "That's all, Willy. Thank you!" He dismissed the lab man.

One look at Itzhak Berne revealed that the strain was taking its toll in him as well, but Goldman could not afford the luxury of feeling sorry for anyone. "Bring Sommerville in," he said. "I think it's time he heard the tape."

"Sam, why don't you rest for a while before you tackle this?"

Goldman looked at him, appreciating the thought. "I wish I could have, Itzhak, but we don't have the time. Let's get on with it."

Sommerville had not fared well on the trip. He had always looked older than his years, but the events of the last twelve hours had been a disaster for him. His clothes hung on him like a scarecrow; his fair skin was blotched and puffy. As soon as he was seated, his manner became abrasive, his tongue bellicose. It was a gambit that lacked confidence.

"I demand to see the Canadian Ambassador. You pirates have gone too far. You know who I am . . ." His voice trailed off.

Goldman eyed him disgustedly.

"Mr. Sommerville, we know who you are, and I suggest that you know very well why you were brought here." The tone of Goldman's voice had become sharp, slashing. "You, Robert Villard and Regis Bennett were involved in private commerce with the Libyans. You've been dealing in some strategic material without the knowledge of your company and your country. Also, a little ancient history . . ." Goldman fingered the file on his desk. "A long time ago you and your life-long friends were involved in a murder. A young Jewish immigrant girl, I believe."

"You can't prove that," Sommerville snapped.

Goldman did not bother to reply. He merely activated the tape machine on his desk. As the conversation of the night before was replayed, Sommerville sagged further into his chair. He waved his hand part way through the tape as if imploring Goldman to stop. He gasped, "Where did you get that tape?"

"From your ship. Last night. It was taped by a man that you and your friends have been trying to execute."

"You mean Williams? He's dead. An accident . . ."

Goldman shook his head. "Wrong again, Mr. Sommerville. He's alive."

"But . . ."

Goldman stopped him. "It's the end of the line for you, Sommerville." He opened a drawer and placed on the desk before him the yellow watertight pouch he had recovered from the yacht's safe the night before. It contained records of all the bank transactions between Hasebe, Khaddafi's former intermediary, and the three Canadians.

"You know what's in there and why. You will arrange to have these funds released to us."

A sigh escaped from Sommerville; his breathing became ragged. "What else do you want from me?" he asked quietly.

Goldman smiled wearily at Berne. "Have a stenographer come in." He looked at the clock. Four p.m. And where the hell was Owen Hunter?

By five o'clock they had Sommerville's confession. It was more than even Goldman had hoped for . . . yet he had the feeling that the Canadian was holding something back. At the end he had been almost too eager to confess. It was damning evidence, and the tape recording from Hunter's bag was corroboration. Hunter had got exactly what they wanted: an admission of guilt. But Goldman wondered: at what price?

They reviewed the tape from Hunter's bag for the last time. As the machine stopped, Berne cleared his throat. "What about Giles and Plessiers? Supposedly they took Hunter down to a cabin in the boat. They were meant to search and question him, but we found that his luggage hadn't been touched. Some things were missing, but the recorder was still there. Hunter must have been the one to get into the bag. It just doesn't add up. . . ."

22

HUNTER HAD BEEN almost totally ignored since he boarded the Libyan trawler. He was on deck for a brief time during the cargo transfer before being confined to a cabin below decks. The time on his own gave him a needed opportunity to study the contents of Dietrich's briefcase; he had quickly inspected the blueprints of the fusing and timing devices in Dietrich's cabin.

The man hadn't lied to him. There was no technical information about the neutron warheads, just some notes about fusing and arming the devices, which were disguised as conventional warheads. They were to be mated to air-to-ground missiles. There had been two deliveries of twenty-five warheads. The current cargo contained fifteen conventional and ten neutron armed warheads. It appeared that the neutron warheads were identified with a color code that differed slightly from the conventional type—the coding done in such a way as to be indiscernible to anyone without access to Dietrich's files. There was one basic difference between the two warhead types: a special altitude fuse had been inserted that would activate the explosive mechanisms in the neutron warheads. The device would then trigger an explosion at a preset altitude of two hundred feet. The radius of the blast would depend upon the terrain and the size of the buildings in the immediate area; but most significantly, the released radiation would be capable of killing anyone within a mile.

Goldman's scenario had been right—as far as it had gone. The planes were being equipped to attack Israel; what he did not know was that these weapons were scheduled to be on board the trawler. If just one of them exploded over a heavily populated area . . . Hunter shuddered, not wanting to think of the results.

Dietrich hadn't guessed that his passage was only a one-way ticket. Hunter had watched without remorse as Dietrich died, as his heart failed. Remorse was an emotion of the past. He had no brother. He had never had a family. He had no past and he had no future.

He set aside the technical material and began to study the maps he had secreted in Dietrich's bag. He had repacked the bag, bringing the most important item from his own. He was trying to estimate a landfall. If the Canadians found Dietrich before Goldman got to him, the game would be over anyway. He didn't fancy his fate at the hands of the Libyans.

Had he been standing up on deck at that very instant, the possibility of his discovery from that quarter would have ceased to concern him. He never saw the brilliant blaze on the horizon that sealed the fate of the Canadian yacht and almost everyone on board.

He applied himself to the task at hand. The contact, he reckoned, had been made about seventy miles south of Cannes and about fifty miles west of Corsica. His experience in the Merchant Marine stood him in good stead—he had become a good judge of a ship's capability. The Libyan boat appeared to be Russian in origin; the smooth throbbing of the large diesels told him that she was very fast. Her cruising speed would be somewhere between 22 and 25 knots. In order to avoid coastal traffic, the most practical route would take them due south. They would maintain a distance of approximately fifty miles off Sardinia and then proceed to the Sicilian Channel off Tunisia. Then he was sure they would turn south into Libyan waters.

With the specific deadly cargo that was aboard, Hunter was also sure that the launch containing the warheads would be used to make the landfall at a small, out-of-the-way port. That suited him—the fewer people in his way, the better the chances for his success. He knew that he would only be alive for as long as they needed him. He needed time alone with those warheads.

He studied the map intently. There was a small town about forty miles from the Tunisian border . . . it was called Zuara. Goldman's map showed a small airstrip just south of the village. If he was right, it was ideal. He estimated that the trip would take from twenty-seven to thirty hours. He was not sure about the time zones. An hour change at the most. The transfer would probably take place before sunrise.

Shoving the maps to one side, he reopened Dietrich's briefcase. In less than thirty hours, he had to become an expert.

Hammering on the cabin door brought Hunter out of a deep sleep. He glanced at his watch. It was eight o'clock in the morning. One of the crew entered with his breakfast. He tried English and French but the man either didn't understand or carefully avoided any conversation.

A brief glimpse outside his cabin convinced him that any attempt to move about the ship would be impossible. Two armed guards were in the corridor. One was directly across from his cabin door, the other down at the end of the hall. They were big and ugly, and they looked professional.

As the day passed, Hunter memorized every detail of the information on the fusing and arming devices. He also studied the important section on the identification. After he finished with each section, he burned it and flushed the ashes down the toilet. He disposed of his maps of North Africa and the Middle East in the same manner.

Following dinner at six o'clock, he repacked his bag and took one of the sedatives Goldman had given him. It was a quick-acting drug designed to induce sleep almost immediately: he would remain asleep for about eight hours and would awaken without any side effects. He judged it would be about four o'clock when he would have to be ready. He wanted to be alert. He needed every edge he could get.

Hunter awakened and sat upright, his senses finely tuned. It was ten minutes to four in the morning. He dressed quickly, bagging his gear, but not before removing his sole weapon, the blue steel garrote which he pulled from his chronometer and secreted in the left arm of his turtleneck sweater.

There was a knock at the door. He feigned sleepiness. "What . . . what's happening? . . . it's the middle of the night . . ." He slurred his voice as if speaking through a thickly cottoned tongue.

A voice said firmly, "Mr. Dietrich, please be prepared to come on deck in ten minutes."

Hunter grunted in acknowledgement. He sat out the ten minutes . . . it gave him time to think. Then the door swung open. An officer was accompanied by the two men he had seen yesterday. They were the guards who had flanked the corridor like jailers.

"You will follow us, Mr. Dietrich," the officer ordered.

Hunter was routed down the corridor and up toward the deck. He slipped on his pea jacket over his sweater. A cutting wind whipped over the sea. His shivering sharpened his senses. His eyes squinted in reaction to the wind as he surveyed the area. On the bridge, a launch was being winched down from its shipside cradle. Hunter became aware of another presence—and Arab dressed in traditional dark Bedouin robes. He was the man in charge, issuing crisp orders that were quickly obeyed.

The boat was ready for launching. Although Hunter could not see the Arab clearly in the dim light of morning, he felt an impending sense of dread. Hunter realized instinctively that if he were to survive, he would have to kill this man.

His thoughts were interrupted by the Arab's smooth

voice. "Mr. Dietrich, you will board the launch, sir. There's a small cabin forward. Please proceed there and remain out of sight until we land."

Hunter nodded; he was now Dietrich, playing the role, subservient and compliant to the hilt. His life depended on it.

They reached landfall within the hour, at nearly seven a.m. The pink-red sun had brightened the eastern horizon by the time the launch was unloaded. Hunter waited at the shore end of a small quay that jutted out into the Mediterranean. The Arab nodded toward Hunter's guard as the last of the cargo was wheeled off the dock. Hunter began walking, and the Arab pointed the barrel of the gun at a jeep parked at the end of the quay, wordlessly directing him to get into the jeep. Hunter slipped into the back seat, his guard following him, clearing an area to make enough room for his large frame and robes.

"May I ask where we're going?" Hunter directed his naive question at the Arab.

"You may, Mr. Dietrich. Let me apologize for our seemingly inhospitable behavior. Time has been an unfavorably crucial factor in our little endeavor, leaving us with little opportunity for the usual social amenities for which my people pride themselves."

The Arab, Ali Djinn, turned fully in his front seat to assess reaction. His face was a treasure map of evil. A scar ran the length of his face, from his forehead down around his left eye, which was tilted awry, and followed to his clefted chin and into his mottled neck. The scar gleamed opaquely against his dark, pockmarked face in the early morning light. The face of the devil, Hunter thought. I've seen it at last.

Ali Djinn continued. "We are proceeding to a private airfield about twenty-five miles from here. Your precious cargo will be loaded aboard a transport aircraft for the final leg of our group's journey. Unfortunately, I am not at liberty to discuss our final destination. I can assure you, however, that by tomorrow at this time, your duties will be finished and your journey will be ended."

Hunter shuddered, choosing to ignore the message.

"How soon will we be taking off?" he inquired.

"Why do you ask?" Ali Djinn was clearly impatient.

"I'll need some time to check the warheads," Hunter replied. "There are very delicate timing devices in each of them. They have been subjected to movement in heavy seas, not to mention loading. And soon, unloading. They should be checked to see that they are safe."

"What do you mean, *safe?* Are you suggesting that we may be in some danger?"

"The chances are remote," Hunter replied, realizing that if the Arab had any knowledge of the type of fusing system involved, his charade would be over. "There are two types of fuses in some of the warheads. One is the standard arming fuse—activated electronically. The second fuse is more delicate—an arming system based upon a preset altimeter. Any shock to the outer casing could damage or alter the presettings in the devices. They could then explode immediately upon arming. The explosion would take place at the point of origin, not at the point of target." Hunter stopped, his diagnosis complete. His hand moved toward his wrist, ready to release the garrote wire in the event the Arab was on to his double talk.

Ali Djinn finally spoke. "You're a thorough man, Mr. Dietrich. Just like a surgeon. How much time do you need?"

Hunter took a deep breath. "About forty-five minutes or so should do it . . ." He hesitated. "It should be completed before they are loaded on a plane."

"You'll have the time. By the way, Mr. Dietrich, there are twenty-five missiles in our truck. They are of two types, if I am not mistaken?"

Hunter nodded in affirmation.

"When we load the plane, two of the warheads of the special type will *not* be loaded. You will first identify these two for me and separate them from the others."

Hunter nodded again affirmatively, but his head throbbed. Another complication! If the plane didn't get through, two neutron warheads would remain in Libyan hands for terrorists to use at any time, anywhere, as instruments for international blackmail.

They arrived at the airstrip just as the sun slipped above the flat horizon. The desert landscape was broken by a loosely patterned group of squat, dull-brown, tin-roofed quonset huts. Next to them, in a fuel depot, sat a rusting ancient hulk of a World War II tanker truck. Two Arabs were filling it. On the runway, its low profile unmistakable, was a U.S.-made Hercules transport plane, fondly nick-named "Hippo" by those who had flown it. He knew a little bit about the model. It was a plane that had been used by the Israelis in their successful midnight raid at Entebbe, and by the U.S. military in Vietnam as a supply workhorse. His mind ran down the workings of the plane . . . *good for desert use . . . short takeoff and landing capabilities . . . extremely quiet operation.*

His thoughts were interrupted as they pulled to a halt in front of one of the quonset huts. Orders were shouted and the unloading began.

The Arab turned to Hunter. "You will work in there, please, sir." He pointed a ruby-ringed forefinger. Hunter noted an amputated stump on the last finger. The mark of a thief's punishment, he realized. "The warheads will be brought in to you for checking, and loaded just as soon as you are finished."

As he entered the hut, Hunter gasped. Gleaming white and blue missiles and warheads were stockpiled from earlier deliveries—enough equipment for an entire squadron. The recipients would accept the additional weaponry without question. Hunter visualized the consequences of this con-spiracy. He had to remind himself to stay cool as he began to work. Personal anger could be counter-productive.

Each group of ten missiles and warheads were set in racks and color coded. The system for identification was simple: a series of color dots in sequences inside the tubular structure

of all the warheads. Each neutron warhead had a reverse
sequence.

By rearranging the sequences, he was able to disguise
them. He marked these with a small, inconspicuous scratch
on the outer casing. He worked quickly through the first
group, changing the sequences. The early morning desert
sun heated the hut quickly. He shed the pea jacket, but wore
the heavy sweater; he couldn't chance someone discovering
the wire.

The last group of warheads was almost finished when Ali
Djinn came into the hut. "Are you finished, Mr. Dietrich?
The plane is ready to go."

"Just one more minute," replied Hunter, making a final
adjustment of one of the two missiles that he had separated
from the others. He screwed the warhead back together,
wiping his hands on a towel after he mopped the sweat from
his brow. He motioned to the Arab with a wave of the damp
towel. "These are the two that you asked for."

Ali Djinn was silent a moment, then frowned and said, "I
understand that you are to be trusted . . . but how am I to
be sure that you have indeed segregated the two missiles
that I requested? They all look the same."

"Let me show you," Hunter said pleasantly, "just in case
something were to happen to me." He unscrewed the warhead that he had just replaced, then motioned to the Arab to
come closer. He pointed out the color code sequence.

"Very simple." The man smiled. "The information is
useful, but I trust that no harm will come to you. Shall we
go?"

A forklift truck raised the last cradle of missiles and
moved off toward the plane. Owen Hunter led; the Arab
followed. Hunter couldn't resist a hidden smile—the warhead he had shown him was conventional; the other did
contain the neutron package, but he had made some fine
adjustments. The next person that touched it would be in for
a surprise, but it would be one that would last only as long
as it took to vaporize flesh.

He was beginning to balance the scale. The killers would

be killed—the hunted had become, in more than adopted name only, the hunter.

He watched carefully as the boarding process was completed. The pilot and co-pilot occupied the flight deck during the pre-flight check. He could see no one else in the cockpit—it was obvious this was a skeleton crew. Probably for reasons of security, the co-pilot doubled as navigator.

Clearly, the two guards that had stayed with him ever since he disembarked from the ship were to remain on the ground. Two well-armed Libyan soldiers were in the process of boarding, when the Arab motioned Hunter toward the rear cargo door. Hunter was pleased; it seemed as if the whole operation had taken on a routine air. No problems expected. He had been accepted as Dietrich, the meek technician, there to perform a function and then due for summary execution. As he approached, Hunter scanned the aircraft quickly. It seemed well-maintained; the crew appeared competent. That would be to his advantage. The last thing he needed was a mechanical failure.

As he stepped onto the rear cargo platform, he was staggered by the sight of military hardware jamming the cargo hold. There was enough equipment to support a major guerrilla action. Three desert camouflaged jeeps equipped with heavy caliber machine guns were chained to the air frame. Hundreds of cases of guns, grenades and ammunition were stacked on wooden skids.

Most of the crates contained cyrillic inscriptions—the Russians, as usual, were exporting terror through Libya. He wondered if it would ever end. The plot that Goldman had uncovered was obviously only a part of a major effort to destroy whatever tenuous political balance existed in the Middle East.

He rechecked his inventory on the crew and was relieved to see that he was correct: the two armed men had made themselves comfortable in the cargo section. Hunter and the Arab made their way forward to occupy a small compartment aft of the flight deck. The whine of the huge engines increased; the plane's frame shook slightly as the pilot held the brakes, building the RPM to obtain maximum thrust. As the brakes were released, the plane shot forward, pinning Hunter to his seat. They were airborne almost immediately.

The plane rose, buffeted severely, as the desert thermals caught the huge wings. The tubulence lasted for about five minutes until they reached cruising altitude. Hunter calculated the likely flight plan, then frowned. He had been right thus far, but he had to make certain. He loosened his seat, moving toward the Arab, his voice raised over the engines' noise.

"Would you mind if I went up to the flight deck and watched? I'm fascinated with flying."

"Be my guest, Mr. Dietrich. But please don't interfere."

Seated in front of the radio, the Arab was strapping on a headset. No doubt, Hunter thought, intending to radio the information on the warhead identification that I've given him. Hunter smiled grimly as he stepped through the cockpit door. They were in for a surprise.

He tapped the Libyan pilot on the shoulder. As the man turned to him, Hunter shouted, "Do you speak English?" The noise level remained high as the engines strained to maintain cruising altitude with a full cargo on board.

The pilot nodded in the affirmative.

"Mind if I look over your shoulder?" Hunter asked, smiling. "I've always been fascinated with planes."

The two men smiled in return, flattered. They were professionals, doing a job under orders—most likely, Hunter decided, unaware of the bizarre scheme in which they were involved.

Hunter filed that away for future reference. Perhaps, if and when the time came, reason might prevail. He sat down quietly in the seat normally reserved for the third member of the crew. He watched the compass heading for a short time, careful not to be observed showing too much attention to any one aspect of their flight.

The direction away from Zuara was almost true southeast. The pilot had a map in his lap, pointing to it, as he and the co-pilot had a brief exchange. They spoke in Arabic—

unfamiliar to Hunter. The pilot engaged the auto-pilot and Hunter could see him tracing the course across the map. It was a little south, but almost paralleled the one he had plotted in the cabin of the ship.

So far, so good.

Hunter continued to observe. "How fast does the plane fly?"

The pilot looked up from his map and pointed to the airspeed indicator, where the needle wavered at 375 knots. "We have a slight headwind, so our ground speed will be about 345 knots," he said.

Hunter stayed in the cockpit for nearly thirty minutes, observing compass headings and radio frequencies. After a few more trivial questions, he excused himself and returned to the compartment behind the cockpit. Ali Djinn had just finished transmitting. He sat down, observing Hunter's return.

"Your curiosity is satisfied, Mr. Dietrich?"

Hunter nodded. "They seem very competent. Thanks for letting me talk to them." As an afterthought, he added, "Planes fascinate me, but they also make me rather sleepy." He nodded toward one of the cots on the bulkhead.

"Make yourself comfortable," said the Arab. "It will be a long flight. You'll want to be well-rested when we arrive." He rose and went forward onto the flight deck. He would be checking on Hunter's behavior and what he had asked about in the cockpit. He was thorough, but Hunter had expected it; in fact, it was a trait that he admired. His experience had taught him to exploit the strengths as well as weaknesses of opponents. The element of surprise could be his most important weapon for survival.

While the Arab was occupied, Hunter went through his bag. He had transferred hypodermic syringes and several vials of strong, fast-acting nerve tranquilizer which had been given to him by Goldman.

An icy, calculating anger had replaced the blood-red fury he had felt initially. With the exception of the Arab, he had determined to kill only if absolutely necessary. The more live bodies, the more evidence to support the conspiracy. He replaced two vials and a hypodermic syringe in the calf of his boot, placed the bag under the bunk, rolled over and feigned sleep.

The Libyans would be flying at high altitude as long as they were in their own air space and until they approached the southern border of Egypt. There, it would be necessary to begin a low altitude flight to avoid detection by Egyptian radar. At low altitude, they would encounter some rough turbulence from desert thermals. It would be then that he would make his move.

He watched the Arab silently. Every thirty minutes he would rise, check the flight deck, then go back into the cargo area. He would remain there for about ten minutes, and return. Hunter observed him three times. Five minutes on the flight deck, ten minutes in the cargo area, fifteen minutes in his seat. That gave him a maximum of twenty minutes to immobilize the two guards.

He wished that this was a nightmare. He wished that he could wake up and find himself back in California, holding Maggie.

23

Four hours into the flight, Hunter could detect a reduction in power, a gradual descent. The turbulence began slowly just as the Arab returned. The intensity of the buffeting increased as Hunter swung his legs over the edge of the cot.

"Are we landing . . . ?" His tongue seemed sleep thickened; he pretended to be confused.

Ali Djinn eyed him warily. "Why do you ask . . . ?"

"Bumping around so much . . . if we're going to be flying through this chop for long, I'd like a chance to check my cargo. The instrumentation is very sensitive. All that bouncing . . ."

At that moment a powerful downdraft buffeted the plane, almost knocking Hunter off his feet as the airframe strained under the pressure, squealing noisily. Perfect, he thought. Right on cue. Keep it up . . .

He lurched, grabbing the bulkhead.

"I'd suggest that we look for some smoother air," he said, "unless you want to see us all blown to kingdom come."

He was not acting—the rough flight constituted a clear danger.

The Arab was convinced. "All right, Mr. Dietrich. Check your cargo immediately. If there are any problems, let me know. While you do that, I'll consult with the captain. Perhaps he'll find us a smoother route."

215

Hunter descended quickly into the vast cargo hold. The jeeps that were chained to the airframe were shaking, but not violently. The crates on skids were held tightly by nylon straps.

He approached the skids where the missiles lay, each in a wooden cradle, five across and two high. Three wide nylon belts secured each of the five skids directly to the ship's frame. He loosened one of the belts just enough to allow a slight twisting motion. Neither of the soldiers paid any attention to him. He moved to the side of the plane where he had earlier noticed a toolbox. He found what he had been looking for: a coil of bailing wire, electrician's tape and an eight-inch spanner wrench. When he returned to the skids, the turbulence had increased and the twisting was more pronounced. Neither of the soldiers appeared able to adjust to the plane's erratic movements. Hunter watched one of them disappear, lurching against the side of some crates. The other approached, moving more quickly . . . and Hunter waved to him, pointing to the loosened nylon strap. The soldier laid his rifle on the floor and bent forward to examine the strap. As he knelt, Hunter drove the spanner wrench into the back of his head. The soldier dropped without a sound.

Hunter tore off a small portion of the soldier's tunic, stuffing it into the man's mouth. He then ran three strips of electric tape around the soldier's jaw and mouth, wired his wrists and ankles and looped the wire tightly around the man's neck. He filled a syringe from a vial and injected the man. Then he rolled the body between two tarpaulin covered skids and resecured the tarp, hiding it completely.

He checked his watch. It had taken five minutes. He had been gone for almost ten. He had only a few minutes left. He had to be ready for the Arab.

He moved stealthily toward the back of the plane, sure that the other soldier had gone there. As soon as he spotted him, he gesticulated wildly toward the front of the plane. The soldier lurched forward—as he did, the steel of the spanner wrench bit into the flesh at the back of his head.

Blood sprayed Hunter's hands and arms. He bent, feeling for a pulse. It was faint, but there.

He worked feverishly, binding and gagging him as he had the other. He had just removed the needle when he sensed imminent danger—the hair on his neck seemed to come alive. It was a sixth sense that had always been with him; it didn't fail him now.

He looked up, turning his head. No more than six feet away, Ali Djinn was moving toward him swiftly, with a long knife drawn and ready.

Neither antagonist would be able to afford the luxury of using a gun. The cargo was too volatile. A wild shot could cause an explosion or pierce the outer skin of the pressurized aircraft. Either situation could be disastrous.

Hunter moved backwards and sideways, crabbing away. Ali Djinn rushed forward, his knife flashing out, grazing the side of Hunter's head. The force of his rush carried him past, so that he stumbled over the soldier who lay inert on the floor. But he scrambled swiftly to his feet before Hunter could press the advantage.

This is a professional, Hunter realized. This man is easily my match.

He moved quickly into the maze of cargo in the plane's hold. He felt no pain, but his hand found the side of his face. Blood was there, warm and sticky. He released the only weapon he had, the wire garrote. He could hear the Arab as he pursued him through the maze. Suddenly it became very quiet. Hunter knew instinctively that he had lost the advantage. Ali Djinn's immediate reaction had been anger; but now he realized that Hunter was not Dietrich, the seemingly harmless technician. He represented an enemy, a danger to be eliminated, someone he needed to hunt with all his natural cunning.

Hunter moved back to where he had left the first soldier. He released the wire from the soldier's neck and ankles and stood the man upright. Sooner or later, the Arab would search this aisle. He waited, sucking in short, noiseless breaths. He sensed that his pursuer was getting closer.

A shuffle of soft slippers on the floor of the cargo hold . . . soft rustling of Bedouin robes. Hunter waited . . . lunged out and pushed the unconscious soldier into the Arab. The surprise of his rush and the weight of the inert body caught Ali Djinn off guard. His knife thrust powerfully upward in an almost instantaneous reaction. The sedated man was disemboweled, but in that moment Hunter moved quickly behind the Arab and snapped the garrote wire around his neck, drawing it tight.

The usual reaction to the garrote was for the victim to attempt to tear it away. Ali Djinn, however, swung his knife backwards at Hunter. It ripped along Hunter's side, tearing flesh and scraping the bone along his rib cage. The knife slashed again, cutting Hunter's right arm at the bicep. He could feel blood flow—then a searing pain.

He knew instinctively that he was badly wounded. His arm was weakening and his grip on the garrote was weakening. He had to protect his side as the Arab thrashed. The Arab's weight and superior strength began to turn the struggle to his advantage. Hunter's grip with his right hand was loosening . . . he could not hold on much longer. He snapped the wire as hard as he could with his left hand, calling upon all the reserves he could muster. He could feel the wire dig into the Arab's neck.

Ali Djinn gasped in pain; his arms flailed, relenting briefly in his struggle.

It was long enough for Hunter to loop the fingers of his left hand around the garrote just as his right arm failed. He twisted his left hand clockwise to secure his hold. He rammed his left knee into the small of the man's back and pushed off backwards as hard as he could. The force of his movement caused both men to topple backwards. Hunter's head struck the floor heavily.

It as one a.m. in Riyadh, Saudi Arabia. Three men worked feverishly, digging in the soft desert earth of a large estate outside of the city. Only one of the men, a Mossad operative, knew what they were after, and only he knew what fate awaited them if they were discovered—beheading for the desecration of holy ground.

A courier had arrived directly from Mossad headquarters. They must have tissue from the corpse to analyze. But why?

He cursed silently as the shovel bit deeper into the earth. In this job you never knew why. Just do what you're told. His shovel struck something hard.

"Hand me the lamp. I think we're there."

The hooded oil lantern was passed down to him. He scraped away the dirt to reveal the concrete vault that held the body of King Saud.

For nearly another hour, they worked at enlarging the excavation. Finally the vault was accessible, but time was growing short. By the dim light he could make out the sealed points on the top of the vault. He quickly placed small explosive charges at each point and packed them tightly. The sound of the muffled explosions could barely be heard at ground level where the other two men stood guard.

His muscles strained as he slid the concrete lid sideways to reveal the coffin. He lifted the lid carefully, exposing the corpse inside. He worked quickly. Clippings of hair, fingernails—all deposited into separate bags. Touching the cold, waxy flesh made him nauseous.

He ripped at the dead man's robes, tearing them open to expose his chest. From a small valise he withdrew a large syringe and a plastic disc which he placed just below the left nipple. The disc had three small holes drilled in the pattern of a triangle. The apex of the triangle was positioned about an inch below the bottom of the nipple. Using a blue marker, he made small circular marks in the chest through the holes. He attached the first of three long hollow steel tubes to the syringe. The end of the tube was carefully placed on the top marker.

Slowly, he applied pressure, plunging the hollow tube its full length into the chest. He carefully pulled the syringe back, allowing flesh and fluid to fill the hollow tube. The tube was removed and placed in a container. He sealed it. The procedure was repeated twice more. He was finished.

• • •

The police had been called as soon as the bodies had been discovered in a deserted warehouse in the outskirts of Riyadh. Children playing there had made the grisly find. Two men, dead, hands tied behind their backs—shot in the head.

The inspector looked at them. Clothes stained with sweat and desert dirt.

Why would anybody want to kill them? And why this way?

At the same time he was examining the bodies, a small brown valise with its odious contents from the coffin was being sped on its way to Israel.

24

CHAIM WEISNER, HEAD of the Mossad, sat beside Sam Goldman. Goldman had just finished briefing the cabinet. Ariel Shamir, Defense Minister, strummed the yellow pad in front of him with a pencil.

The long silence was broken by the Prime Minister. "Let me see if I understand you correctly. You have discovered that Saudi Arabia has secretly been equipping their F-15 squadron with a capability we have argued so long against." He paused, removed his glasses, rubbing his eyes wearily. "The war in Lebanon . . . and now this."

He replaced his glasses and continued slowly. "Our friend Khaddafi is responsible. And the Canadians," he added dourly, "are his suppliers." He turned to his right. "My old friend, we guessed right about Mr. Bennett." Shamir merely nodded.

"So now, Mr. Goldman," the Prime Minister continued, "your man named Hunter has disappeared and you have reason to believe that Israel may face an imminent attack by Saudi Arabia. Why now? Why not two months ago? Why not a year from now? Their King has just died . . . conditions there are unstable."

He was interrupted as the door to the Cabinet room swung open. A soldier in full battle gear stepped in smartly, without invitation, and placed a large sealed manila envelope on the table in front of Sam Goldman. The soldier saluted, spun on the heel of his boot and exited as crisply as he had entered.

Goldman quickly broke the seal on the envelope. He scanned the documents. He looked up, eyes narrowed yet dark and intense.

"Mr. Prime Minister, these papers confirm all the reasons why I feel the attack will come soon. Unfortunately, very soon."

The Prime Minister read slowly.

"King Khalid had open heart surgery twice," Goldman said, filling in the blanks. "His doctors had been prescribing large doses of vitamins by intramuscular injection. The last injection contained enough depressant to stop the heart of a camel. He appeared to have died of a massive coronary . . . but he was, in fact, assassinated."

The Prime Minister had come to the typed report of the chemical analysis on the tissues that had been spirited away from Khalid's desert gravesite.

He nodded glumly.

"Khalid's death," Goldman continued, "has created political instability in the ruling family of Saudi Arabia. The new king is already talking about closer ties to Moscow. It is now possible for a coup to succeed . . . a coup that would bring to power a government that supports an armed attack on Israel . . ."

The Prime Minister had finished reading the report. "Will it never end?" he wondered aloud.

He turned to Weisner and Goldman. "You've done your job well. Thank you," he said, dismissing them.

Goldman and Weisner walked along the empty corridor, away from the Cabinet room, their footsteps echoing hollowly. A lonely sound, somber and disturbing. Goldman felt alone. Their only hope, he knew, was Hunter. He was as capable an operative as Goldman had ever sent out, and Goldman believed he was alive. But if Hunter was going to do something, it had better be quick.

Weisner broke the silence. "Sam, do you know what the

cabinet's facing today? I wouldn't trade places with them for anything in the world. You talk about Catch 22's. No matter what they decide, no matter what action the country takes— the chances are that we'll be destroyed. At best, occupied. Our dream for Israel will be over."

Weisner's hands folded in supplication. The red phone connected directly to the Cabinet room rang shrilly. He reached for it quickly. It was a long conversation, Weisner's part limited to grunts and monosyllabic responses. He replaced the receiver slowly, his complexion taking on a gray pallor.

"The Prime Minister called the Saudis directly. He and Sharon told them of our knowledge of the F-15's, the information on the coup . . . all the details we gave the Prime Minister. Of course, the Saudis rejected our thesis totally. They hinted that they were aware that their F-15's had been modified for attack capability. The Saudi Defense Minister even had the gall to suggest that the modifications were made with the approval of the United States."

"That's bullshit, Chaim, and we all know it." Goldman cut in angrily. "What's the bottom line?"

Weisner hesitated, the lines on his face showing the strain. "The Cabinet has ordered a pre-emptive strike against all military bases in Saudi Arabia."

"My God," Goldman exclaimed. He had been aware of this possibility, but the final decision shocked him.

"When?"

"Our Mirage Squadrons are on full alert. The attack is set for twilight."

Goldman glanced at his watch. They had been back for thirty minutes. He did some quick calculations. It meant that the first wave would take off about five o'clock, leaving Israeli air space no later than 5:20. The final pieces were falling into place, the puzzle almost complete, but the picture had changed from life to death, from peace to war.

"Anything special you want me to do?" Goldman asked his friend.

"Just monitor the radio," Weisner answered wearily. "If you hear anything—anything at all—let me know right away. We'll keep the lines of communication with the Cabinet room open. Just in case."

25

THE SOUR SMELL of blood assaulted Hunter's nostrils. He pushed at the deadweight on top of him, rolling the Arab off him. He gagged, feeling a surge of nausea. The wire had cut halfway through the man's neck, and Ali Djinn had died hard. Hunter rolled to his knees, heaving dryly; the stench of death was all around him. He wondered if it would ever leave him.

He rose slowly, his right arm hanging limp and useless. The bleeding had already soaked his clothing down to his right hip. How long he had laid there, he didn't know. He was losing too much blood . . .

Hunter reached for the Dexedrine capsules he had secreted in his sweater earlier. He chewed quickly, waiting only briefly for the stimulant to begin to take effect. He jammed his last pill under his watchband for easy access. He silently thanked Goldman for the miniature pharmacy that had been included with his supplies.

He checked his watch. By his calculations they must now be approaching the Red Sea. His biggest problem had become how to remain conscious and alert. He stripped Ali Djinn of his robes, tearing a portion off to pack the wound in his own side. He bound his right arm as tightly as he could, staunching the flow of blood. The fingers on his left hand oozed from cuts where the garrote had sliced into flesh.

He hurriedly prepared his last syringe and moved toward the flight deck; in one hand he held a .38 caliber pistol he had taken from the dead guard. He donned Ali Djinn's outer robe and headpiece, hoping that they would provide at least a momentary disguise, giving him time enough to get into the cockpit.

The co-pilot glanced back briefly as Hunter entered. Too late, he saw the gun in Hunter's hand; his cry died in his throat as Hunter snapped the barrel down across his forehead. He slumped forward.

Hunter shoved the gun barrel into the side of the pilot's head. "Now, Captain—follow my instructions."

"What do you want me to do?" The accented English voice was hardly a whisper.

"Take off that headset."

The pilot reached over, killing the radio with a flip of the toggle switch. Hunter motioned to the map. "What's our present position?"

The captain traced a course considerably south of where Hunter estimated them to be. Hunter said angrily, "Captain, you don't seem to realize that I've nothing to lose. Everybody back there is dead. There is no help on the way. Don't try to be a hero. Where are we?" He emphasized his last words by jamming the gun down in the pilot's neck so hard that he cried out.

Trembling fingers moved jerkily to the chart, showing their approach to the Red Sea. "Just south of the Egyptian border . . ." For emphasis, he pointed out of the windscreen of the plane. Blue water could be seen coming up on the horizon.

"Now, sit back and don't touch the yoke." The plane was on auto-pilot. "Put your hands on top of your head."

Hunter moved back just far enough to be out of reach if the pilot tried anything.

Hunter chewed silently on his last dexedrine. His head was clearing . . . but all the drugs were gone. There was nothing left. It was up to him.

He turned to the captain. "Go on manual," he ordered.

The pilot reached for the yoke, disengaging the auto-pilot. They had just crossed the coast and were over the Red Sea. "Now," Hunter continued, "turn north gradually until you've reached the middle of the Sea. Then follow a course directly north . . . and slightly westward . . . equidistant from each shore. I want you to stay on that course until I tell you differently."

The pilot turned. His voice was filled with disbelief and dread. "That means Israel. You're badly wounded . . . you can't fly this plane without me."

Hunter answered evenly. "You don't seem to understand. Whether I live or die right now doesn't matter. I've already accomplished my mission. . . . And I can fly this plane. The only thing I can't do is land it. So you have two choices . . . slim or none. It's up to you."

The pilot was neither a martyr nor a stupid man. He realized that his own survival hinged on his compliance with Hunter's command. He switched off the auto-pilot and began a gradual bank to the north.

Hunter glanced at his watch. It would be almost two hours before he could contact Goldman. He was fighting to remain conscious. The release he had hoped for had come, but it had come as a type of catatonia. He was burned out; all he wanted to do was lie down and die somewhere, quietly, by himself . . . let the sun bleach his bones back into dust.

At 4:45 Chaim Weisner began his third pass in the last thirty minutes through the communications center where Sam Goldman sat hunched in front of a bank of sophisticated radio equipment. Goldman was working on the third pack of filterless Italian cigarettes that he had smoked since early that morning. The mood in the room was somber; everything that they had worked so hard to build was about to come tumbling down.

Goldman glanced up, shaking his head slowly, sadly. "No word. We have no alternative. The jets will be scrambling now." Disappointment was written in the tears in his eyes. "I'm sorry, Chaim . . . truly sorry."

"So am I, Sam." Weisner turned away and left the room.

As the Hercules droned on, eating up miles and minutes, Hunter finished encoding a message for Goldman. Sam had to know it all, he realized. Where I've been, who was involved, how to identify the warheads.

He was losing track of time, fading in and out, but he continued to push himself . . .

At times he mumbled almost deliriously, struggling with his diminished faculties. He checked his watch as he finished his task. It was almost 4:50.

The Hercules rumbled on, hidden in a low cloud cover that obscured the sea. Hunter's glance flicked to the compass heading to make sure the pilot made no course deviations. Noting his look, the pilot pointed to their position on the map. The clouds broke slightly and Hunter was able to catch a glimpse of the Gulf of Aquaba sliding slowly off to the northeast. He indicated a direction change. The pilot banked gently to the right.

"Turn on the radio." Hunter indicated the frequency that Goldman had prearranged. Shifting the gun again, Hunter reached for the headset and snapped it on. The radio came to life. "Hunter calling Sam . . . Come in, Sam . . . Hunter calling Sam . . . Come in, Sam."

Two hundred and fifty miles to go, he decided. Almost over. The thought gave him renewed strength.

On the ground in the Mossad Communications Room, the signal was received. "Hunter calling Sam . . . Come in, Sam . . ."

The sound galvanized Sam Goldman into action. He leaped to his feet, practically pulling the radioman out of his chair. "I'll take it from here," he said. "Get Weisner . . . on the double!"

Goldman glanced at his watch. It was 4:55. He reached for the microphone. Was it too late? Had the jets already taken off for Saudi Arabia? "Sam here . . . Sam to

Hunter. I receive you loud and clear. What is your present position? Over."

After a brief pause the radio blared again. "I just passed the mouth of the Gulf of Aquaba. Heading home, Sam. The package you ordered is aboard. Ten packages, in fact. I could use a little help in getting it to you. Over, Sam."

"It's him," Goldman said to Weisner, in not much more than a whisper. He yelled over his shoulder to an Air Force major who stood nearby. "Scramble a fighter escort! Get me through to the Cabinet Room . . . and hold off all current operations for at least five minutes!" He glanced at Weisner, who nodded confirmation. He turned back to the radio.

"Hunter, this is Sam. Please give me details. Use Code B. Repeat. Give me details in Code B."

In four minutes Hunter had encoded and transmitted his cryptic message. Goldman turned to Weisner.

"Is it good enough for you, Chaim? Will you call off the attack?"

Weisner, nodding, spoke quietly into the black telephone that linked him to the Cabinet Room and the Air Force base in the Negev that, in ten more minutes, would have launched the three waves of fighter-bombers at Riyadh and Mecca.

Goldman sat alone, white and shaken. Neutron warheads, he thought, shaking his head in utter disbelief. The madmen. That's what Sommerville had been holding back . . . God, how close they had come to another Holocaust.

It was well after five p.m. Four Israeli Mirage jets flew in tight formation beside the lumbering Hercules. Hunter sat, drained and hurting.

As the Hercules sat down on the desert runway, Hunter's head snapped from his chest. The pilot was taxiing according to the ground controller's request. Rolling up in front of a hangar, the plane was immediately surrounded by a platoon of battle-geared troops. Hunter unfastened his seat

belt, motioning the pilot to move ahead of him. He still
carried the gun in his left hand; his right arm hung like dead
weight. The cargo door opened. He motioned for the pilot
to precede him, his hands clasped firmly above his head.
Hunter stumbled through the door, waving the gun, mum-
bling incoherently and staggering. The heat of the desert
struck him like a giant hot hand.

A young lieutenant stood silently, his Uzi at the ready as
the Hercules completed its taxi. He was myopic and had
been found physically unfit for combat duty in the Israeli
Army; so he was stuck in the home guard while the real
Army was laying siege to Beirut.

He had been on perimeter duty at the base when he and
several other guards had received an emergency call to take
up positions around the Hercules that had just landed at this
maximum security facility. He was standing about twenty
yards away from the cargo door when he saw a uniformed
pilot step out on the tarmac, hands clasped tightly above his
head. Only a second later the pilot was followed by an Arab
whose robes were soaked with drying blood.

The Arab screamed, "Goldman!"

The lieutenant had been trained well. His mind registered
the fact that the Arab was carrying a gun, and so his Uzi
swung up automatically, firing.

The first burst struck high on the shoulder, spinning the
Arab around. The second burst caught his face and head.

Hunter's scream died in his throat. His head burst into
bright golden and orange flame.

The late afternoon sun was struggling to escape the high
clouds remaining from a long day of Florida rain. The mood
in Paul MacGregor's office at Caldwell-MacGregor was
somber.

Goldman had phoned daily, but Hunter had been missing
for over forty-eight hours. For Hallie Norton and Paul
MacGregor it had become a silent vigil; they had tried
desperately to maintain some semblance of normalcy, but it
was impossible. For the first time in their relationship, they

could give little comfort to each other. They waited, each holding on to personal thoughts pervaded by a growing sense of dread.

Hallie had been tempted to vent her wrath on MacGregor. From the first moment she had discovered what Goldman had in mind for Hunter, she was against it. But she knew no amount of interference on her part would do any good.

Owen Hunter had earned a place in her heart. She considered him the son that she and Mac had never had; and to see his life deliberately placed in jeopardy was more than she could stand. Mac was the creator. Hunter was a product of Mac's past, given the name of Mac's long dead nephew. Hunter had served Mac well, proving to him over and over again that his creation was invincible, performing physical tasks that Mac's advanced age and ill health no longer permitted.

To Hallie it was sad that Mac had not yet allowed himself the pure pleasure of love. If Owen Hunter was his creation, it was a creation of love that Mac did not fully understand. In a sense, each of these men owed the other his life and rejoiced in the other's accomplishments; yet something was lacking.

The phone lit up—the direct line to Mac's office. She quickly opened the door. MacGregor's face was ashen. It was as if he had grown old and brittle instantly. His lips worked noiselessly, imploring words to come. Nothing happened.

Hallie filled a glass of water from the silver pitcher on his desk and handed him a glycerine capsule from the pill box on his credenza. The ritual performed so many times before seemed to bring Mac back from the void to reality.

"Paul, what's wrong?" It was a familiarity used only when they were alone.

"It's Owen . . . he made it back. He did what Goldman wanted him to do. And more. But he's badly hurt." His breath was coming in labored gasps, sweat beading his forehead. "Hallie . . . they don't expect him to live through the night." Mac's body was racked by sobs. "I've killed him . . . my own son!"

He seemed to shrink in front of Hallie, withdrawing into a world of his own. She knew there was no way to help him.

Hours later, after Hallie had finally left Mac's office to keep an appointment with the company accountant, a call came through from the switchboard. Hallie answered mechanically. "Miss Norton, I thought you better know that something is wrong with Mr. MacGregor."

"What do you mean?" Hallie demanded.

"He left here a few minutes ago, in the pouring rain, without an umbrella or coat. He drove off in one of our construction cars. I've never seen him go anywhere except in his limousine . . . Miss Norton, he didn't look well."

Hallie replaced the receiver and hurried into Mac's office. A large, handwritten, sealed envelope lay in the middle of his desk, addressed to Owen Hunter. A short note to Hallie lay beside it. She tore it open.

"Dear Hallie . . . I have written a letter to Owen. In the unlikely event that he ever recovers, I would like you to deliver it to him personally. There is also a file on Owen in my desk. Please transcribe the information on the recorder except the special message for you from me. I've given you damn little throughout these years. Perhaps in some small way this will make up for it."

It was Hallie's turn to finally allow the tears to come.

Rain fell steadily in the dusk at Indian Trace, tracing rivulets in the mud at Paul MacGregor's feet. His suit was soaked, his hair plastered to his head. Indian Trace . . . his lust for the land . . . what had it brought him? And at what cost? His mother, his sister—and now Hunter, all dead.

He reached down, grabbing a handful of mud. The tears that rolled down his face were joined with the rain. The mud and wetness ran through his fingers, as he had let his life slip away from him. He couldn't hold on. Hunter, Hallie, the wife he'd never had, the love he had never enjoyed, the son he always wanted and never could fully embrace. He looked down at his hand. The rain had done its work well. The land was gone and only a few worthless pebbles were left.

A searing pain tore through his chest and he felt a chill in his legs. The pain exploded down his left arm and the mud rushed up to meet his face. He was choking in it, in the earth that he desired so much. Then darkness came swiftly and completely.

26

TEL AVIV—United Press International—June 17th
CANADIAN RESCUED IN MEDITERRANEAN—Israeli officials today reported that Dale R. Sommerville, advisor to Canadian External Affairs Minister Regis Bennett, is resting comfortably in a Tel Aviv hospital. Sommerville was one of the several people reported missing when the Prime Minister's yacht, *La Contessa,* failed to return from an overnight cruise out of Cannes.

The yacht, which left Cannes early in the evening, apparently sank as a result of a massive explosion of unknown origin. Still missing are eight others, including Robert C. Villard, a long-time friend and close advisor to Minister Bennett. An Israeli spokesman explained that Sommerville was able to cling to wreckage until sometime during the early morning hours when he was rescued by an Israeli fishing boat. The spokesman, in explaining the delay in notification, indicated that the crew of the boat encountered difficulties with its radio equipment, so it was not until the boat made landfall that the Sommerville rescue was known. Thus far, he is the only known survivor of the tragedy.

The desert sun beat down on the tarmac, creating a furnace of heat shimmering in small pools on the runway of the Saudi Air Force Base.

Abdullah Al Saud was deeply concerned. Something

major had gone wrong. The plan had been so simple in its own way. King Khalid had been assassinated. The Libyans were to transport weapons and equipment so that he and a small cadre of his loyal officers could support the new king. But they had waited at the little-used installation at Ad Dirah until long after the plane was due.

A long line of F-15's sat on the tarmac like giant birds of prey, their mission against the Israelis aborted. He imagined himself for a moment leading them into attack against the hated Jews.

His reverie was interrupted by a knock on the door of his office. "Come in," he said.

The crossed sword and palm insignia adorned the headband of his first visitor. Behind him were four other men armed with automatic weapons.

He smiled benignly at his visitors. "I did what I did," he said, "because I am an Arab." His tongue rolled back the capsule that he secreted between his gums and teeth. He bit down. The acrid taste of bitter almonds assaulted his senses.

"Death to all Jews," became his contorted cry of death, but no one could understand the words.

Cairo—Reuters—June 25th
DISASTROUS EXPLOSION REPORTED IN LIBYA—
Reports continue to come out of Libya indicating that an explosion of major proportions occurred near Tripoli sometime last week. Dead and wounded are said to number in the thousands, with bodies being buried in unmarked graves. Sources indicated a substantial number of military casualties, suggesting the possibility that military installations may have been involved. Official sources would neither confirm nor deny the rumors, and the Libyan Government has imposed strict censorship of all news emanating from that country.

Washington, D.C.—Associated Press—July 2nd
A Pentagon spokesman today confirmed that an explosion of unusual intensity occurred in Libya last week. The

spokesman added that U.S. intelligence satellites detected an explosion which occurred south of Tripoli at approximately 2:10 p.m. Libyan time on Thursday. Present indications all point to the explosion as having been nuclear in nature. Pentagon experts suggest that the Libyans may have been experimenting with some low yield nuclear device which accidentally triggered the blast. There are also unsubstantiated reports that a military installation was involved.

Tripoli—United Press International—July 5th
The Libyan Chief of State, Kamal Al Hessan, released the following prepared statement to the press today: "An explosion occurred at the combined Libyan Armed Forces military installation south of Tripoli. An investigation has revealed that the initial explosion was triggered by a device planted by agents of Israel who oppose Libya's championing the cause of the Palestinian movement and its continued support of the PLO."

Ottawa—Associated Press—July 15th
GOVERNMENT MINISTER RESIGNS. ILL HEALTH CITED—External Affairs Minister Regis Bennett II submitted his resignation today in a move that surprised even the most seasoned political observers. Mr. Bennett, in a prepared statement, said that ill health and continued depression brought about by the death of Robert Villard contributed to his decision. Mr. Villard, a close friend and advisor, died in a boat accident aboard the Bennett family yacht.

"After much soul searching, I have decided that to discharge the duties of this high office, a man must have the ability to concentrate his entire physical and mental strength on the tasks at hand. Unfortunately, the considerable shock at the loss of one of my most trusted friends and the near loss of another has drained my health to a point where I can no longer, in good conscience, continue to serve this nation."

Mr. Bennett seemed strained after delivering the announcement. He has turned over the operating control of his family's company to an international business consortium located in Geneva, Switzerland. Terms were not disclosed.

EPILOGUE

WHERE THE RUGGED cliffs of the northern coast of California drop abruptly into the sea, free-standing rocks are whitened by the occupancy of sea birds and dotted with families of sea lions. These pinnacles stand like sentinels, vestiges of the old headlands protecting the new, only to be devoured themselves as inevitable victims of the struggle between the sea and the land.

But here there is also peace.

The bungalows among the flowers on the slope overlooking the Pacific had always been a place of tranquility. Only during the winter storms did the sound of the ocean interlude, pounding against the shore. Even then, the water's regular assault had a tranquilizing effect.

It was here they brought Owen Hunter.

By the time the ambulance had arrived, a sophisticated alarm system was in place, monitored twenty-four hours a day by Mossad technicians. Two of the other buildings housed three shifts of guards who patrolled the perimeters of the property day and night. Goldman had seen to everything.

All of the equipment had been brought in by two large campers that were now parked inconspicuously behind the bungalows. To the residents of the nearby town of Point Arena, Mrs. Schmidt had explained that the new owner had been seriously injured in an automobile accident. He'd come to California to recuperate. He had brought along a small staff: a doctor, a nurse and a physical therapist. "After all," she said, "he's a wealthy man." Since the bungalows would not be available for rent for some time, and to eliminate any unnecessary intrusion, the signs had been removed.

In a state close to shock, Hallie Norton and Eva Schmidt had watched Hunter being unloaded from the ambulance. The body on the stretcher resembled nothing that either could relate to Owen Hunter. His cheeks were hollowed; his eyes stared feverishly and unseeing. His color was gray, a deathlike pallor. The hair that showed from the dressing covering his head wounds was totally white.

When each had become aware of the extent of his wounds, their shock changed to disbelief. That he was alive at all was a miracle.

Maggie Mayes sat quietly working on some design sketches at her desk in her San Francisco apartment. The last five months had been empty for her. Owen Hunter seemed a creature of her imagination, a scar on her emotions. She had given herself completely to him and had been cut off almost without a word. She moved through life listlessly. Her friends were attentive, but their good humor only served to depress her more.

Her musings were interrupted by the door chimes. She laid her charcoal pencil aside and went to the door, leaving two chains attached, as she pulled the door slightly ajar.

"Can I help you?"

The woman standing outside her door was conservatively, but stylishly dressed and very attractive. "If you are Maggie Mayes, you can." Her voice was steady and confident.

Maggie nodded.

"Miss Mayes, I'm Hallie Norton. I need to speak with you, about Owen . . ." Her words were cut off as Maggie quickly closed the door, enough to loosen the chains, then pulled it wide open.

"Miss Norton, please come in. I'm sorry if I seemed inhospitable. Let me take your coat . . ."

"I won't be long. I felt you, of all people, deserved an explanation. It won't be much of an explanation because I don't know the whole story. Owen is in Northern California . . . but he isn't the same person that you knew. I've just come from there. I know." The tone of Hallie Norton's voice was somber.

"But why?" Maggie demanded. *"What happened?"*

"He's been very badly injured. At first the doctors didn't expect him to live. He's apparently in some kind of danger . . . placed in seclusion. I know it's not much to go on, but it's all I can tell you." She reached for her purse and extracted a sealed envelope which she handed to Maggie Mayes. "This was to be delivered to you only if he died." Tears welled in Hallie's eyes. Her voice broke. "I've taken it upon myself to deliver it now. Please read it . . . and know that Owen loves you very much."

She tore the envelope open with dread. It was dated in April.

"Dearest Maggie: I am writing this letter with a prayer that it will never be necessary for you to read it. It seems to be the case in my life that I am always being separated from those I love, and by circumstances beyond my control. The commitment I made to you in California is irrevocable. Never in my life have I loved anyone in the way that I love you. Your love represents to me the fulfillment in life that has always, thus far, eluded me. Keep that thought alive. It's real.

"But what is also real is what happened to me when I returned here. I made you aware of my past. You know what grief it has caused me. But something has come up which demands my involvement. At the same time, it will give me the opportunity to confront that past, and possibly erase the fear and shame that has followed me at every turn. There are also other considerations that transcend any personal feelings I may have. I can't be more specific, but believe me: the consequences of my failing to act are so great as to preclude my refusal.

"The possibility exists that I will not return. In this event, I've made certain arrangements for you.

"Hallie Norton, who has been like a mother to me, has been given instructions. She'll handle it with you.

"I'll love you as long as I live. Owen."

When Maggie finished reading, she said, "What have they done to him, Hallie?"

"Maggie, we've all been hurt. Paul . . . you probably know him as Mac . . . is critically ill. The doctors give him only a short time. I've got to go back to be with him. I can't help Owen now."

"But *I* can, Hallie. He needs me."

So she had come, sure in her love for Owen Hunter, but unprepared for what lay in store for her. As days stretched into weeks, she became aware that more of Owen had died than had been kept alive.

Hunter's cranial wounds required the placement of a metal plate in his head, temporarily blinding him. The blindness lasted for several weeks after his arrival. Gradually his sight returned and Maggie and Smitty were able to start on his physical rehabilitation. The muscles of his right side and chest had atrophied during his long ordeal, but they began to respond to therapy.

Most frightening, however, was his lack of mental response. Owen's self-imposed silence remained unchanged.

By November, he had regained most of his lost weight. His arm and side, although cruelly scarred, were strong once again. His hair, now gray, had grown out and covered the scars on his head. A neatly trimmed beard and moustache had changed his appearance. It had been Maggie's idea.

Her reporter's keen perceptions had begun to put things together. It started with her conversation with Hallie, and then a visit with Sam Goldman. She began to realize the enormity of the situation in which Hunter had been involved. She pieced things together from Hunter's letter and from a day spent at the newspaper morgue of the San Francisco *Chronicle*.

All of it strengthened her loyalty to Hunter. Still, he did not speak. Shock, severe physical injuries and extreme mental stress, the doctors had concluded, were the reasons for his silence. They agreed that nothing could be done until something, or someone, broke through the subconscious barriers that had been erected. As one doctor concluded, it was a dam of severe trauma, and what was needed was something to open the floodgates.

The telephone rang shrilly in Maggie's ears. She ran her fingers through her hair lightly, shaking her head, trying to orient herself. Snapping on the light beside her bed, she picked up the phone and mumbled a drowsy, "Hello." It was four o'clock in the morning. The light static on the line told her that the call was long distance.

"Maggie, this is Hallie Norton. I'm sorry to wake you so early . . ." There was a momentary pause. Maggie heard soft sobbing.

"Paul had another heart attack. He died this morning. I was with him until the end."

"Hallie, I'm so sorry . . ."

"There's nothing anyone can do. I just thought you'd want to know."

"I'll tell Owen in the morning," Maggie said.

"Maggie, can I suggest something?" Hallie asked. "Mac asked me to bring some personal things out to Owen. If you don't mind, I'll come out as soon as I can. Don't tell Owen anything. Let me tell him the whole story. Maybe if Owen knew just how much Mac loved him, it might help . . . and maybe . . ."

Maggie thought for a moment. Maybe the trauma of Mac's death *would* break into Hunter's silent world. "Of course I'll do as you ask," she said.

• • •

It was a late November afternoon, and the sun shone warmly on the cliff overlooking the ocean as it began its long afternoon trek toward the horizon. Soft breezes stirred the branches of the pines that stood on the headlands. Owen Hunter sat alone on a small bench overlooking the ocean. His fascination for the sea was almost childlike. He was seemingly oblivious to Hallie, who sat down quietly beside him.

"Hello, Owen. It's been a long time." Hallie did not expect an answer, and continued without waiting for one. "It's so beautiful here . . ." Slowly, his left hand moved toward her face, brushing a tear away, gently. She buried her face in his shoulder and it came out in a rush.

"Owen, Mac is dead . . ." She fought to compose herself. "He loved you like a son. He never got over what happened to you. He blamed himself for everything. He made me promise to give this to you." She handed him a large envelope. "He said it would explain a lot."

Hunter opened the envelope slowly. It was a letter from MacGregor. He began to read silently.

"Dear Owen. You will be reading this letter after my death, which is the way it had to be. A great deal has happened to both of us since we first met in Vietnam. For most of what occurred, I am happy for both of us. You became a business associate for whom I had great respect. As I look back on it now, some of the actions I have taken were selfishly motivated. Still, there's very little I regret about our business association; I suppose what bothers me the most is that I've never taken the time to tell you what you've become to me personally. From the time we met in Vietnam, and since, you've made me proud. You've distinguished yourself in every endeavor. But what I've never taken the time to tell you is that you've become the son that I've always wanted.

"Life is capricious. We always think that we will have plenty of time; as a result, we squander it and fail to show those who are closest to us just how much we really care.

For this omission, I apologize to you—and to myself. I have missed the joys of expression.

"You, more than anyone, have discovered that many times in life we must make a choice between what is most comfortable and easy for us and what is morally right. What you have accomplished for Sam and his beloved State of Israel can never be forgotten. The sad part of it is that you will never receive the recognition you are due. Knowing you, however, that will cause you no concern. Recognition and medals weren't important to you in Vietnam, and you haven't changed.

"But I'm greatly troubled. Hallie has told me of your condition. I've also spoken to the doctors and Sam Goldman. To see you become a victim, especially with all the good you've accomplished, is intolerable. If you feel betrayed by me or Sam, think carefully about what good any of the knowledge we withheld would have done for you; we were just two bumbling old men who needed you. You didn't disappoint us.

"But, Owen, life is for the living. It seems that you've had the good luck to find one rare individual who is right for you. For God's sake, don't make the same mistakes I have. Tell her. Tell her often.

"Please forgive an old man his last ramblings. I had visions of delivering this message to you while we both sat looking out at our joint creations, enjoying a last drink together. Time and distance render that impossible, but I would ask you two things: first, run our business as if you were Hallie's son and mine. Second, look after her.

"I say goodbye with all the love that I have left in my heart for you. Perhaps we will meet again elsewhere, if there is an elsewhere.

"Love,

"Your dear friend,

"Mac."

The sun touched the ocean. Hunter turned to Hallie. It seemed to her that the fire of the setting sun had brought new life into his eyes. Then his lips moved.

"Hallie, it's been too long. So much time wasted in being sorry . . . so much energy wasted on hatred."

Hunter rose and took her hands. They held each other. They had each lost someone dear, but they were survivors.

Hunter looked up at the bungalows as he and Hallie moved slowly up the hill. As Maggie walked down to meet them, the light of the setting sun fell on her face. To him, her radiance was a miracle. God, he thought, it's good to be alive.

Bestselling Thrillers — action-packed for a great read